Praise for In t. T0149979 rmal

"What do we mean when we say 'normal'? In her engaging novel, Cindy Maddox pushes on norms we may assume around inclusion, intergenerational friendships, and the human capacity to grow and change. She builds a small town world the reader hopes to revisit, full of characters across the age range who are relatable in their hopes and struggles with family and faith. When Mish sets out to help a new friend, readers will root for her to fulfill her mission."

—Martha Spong, author of *Denial is My Spiritual Practice (and Other Failures of Faith)*

"'Follow the love,' is the message from the unlikely Jesus discovered in a local diner by a grandmother with a new smartphone. It's the message that changes the lives of several folks in a small church in West Virginia. Unlikely friendships, miracles, doubts, and faith are all a part of this lovely novel by Cindy Maddox. You'll laugh, you'll cry, and you'll cheer! It's a story that reminds us of what we can do and who we can be when we look for and follow love."

—Lynne Hinton, author of *The Beekeeper's Wife*

"Cindy Maddox's *In the Neighborhood of Normal* could rightly come with this warning on the front cover: 'Necessary for your health. This book may cause tears amidst laughter.' Spending the afternoon with Mish, the heart and main character of this folksy, seeking, multi-layered story, is like spending time cocooned in a homespun Afghan blanket, sipping rich hot cocoa with a wise, good-natured friend. According to Mish, 'Sugarcoating is for cereal,' so she says it like it is, no matter if she is talking to Pastor Jeff about his belief in God or sixteen-year-old Juliann about her unplanned pregnancy. The result is salt-of-the-earth wisdom, delivered in 'bacon and eggs gal' style. Eighty-two-year-old Mish has been widowed for one year when she finally buys a smart phone. Upon receiving a mysterious message, Mish meets a woman at the local diner, a woman who Mish thinks is Jesus Christ, and whose message is to 'follow the love.' Mish accepts this missive with brave determination because she'd '...rather die trying to live than live afraid of dying,' all the while making luxury out of ordinary moments. The novel's poignancy surprises, like the sun playing hide and seek with clouds, even during its laugh out loud *SpongeBob SquarePants* dick pic moments. Mish's journey is our journey as she learns how to stand up for herself because she always stands up for others. As she follows the love, she spreads it, making strangers' lives better because 'I think you find what you are.' *In the Neighborhood of Normal* is the exactly right read for this unprecedented post-Trump, knee-deep-in-Covid, uncertain moment. A good dose of Mish's boldness and optimism is what the doctor ordered."

—Alex Poppe, author of *Girl, World, Moxie, Jinwar and Other Tales from The Levant,* and *Duende*

In the Neighborhood of Normal

Cindy Maddox

Regal House Publishing

Published by
Regal House Publishing, LLC
Raleigh, NC 27587

ISBN -13 (paperback): 9781646030736
ISBN -13 (epub): 9781646030989
Library of Congress Control Number: 2020951228

Interior and cover design by Lafayette & Greene
Cover images © by C.B. Royal

Regal House Publishing, LLC
https://regalhousepublishing.com

Printed in the United States of America

For Jackie, my compass and my home

1

Fall, 2017

Mish was pleased as punch with her new phone. The young sales boy told her it was the latest, most popular smartphone on the market, and that's all she needed to hear. Her friend Opal had been bragging about hers for months, and Mish couldn't wait to return the favor.

She plopped down on the sofa and typed in a number she'd known for nigh unto thirty years. "Opal, you'll never guess—oh, blast it, I got her answering machine." She waited for the beep, then started again. "Howdy, Opal. Just wanted you to know I got me a new phone, and it's a really smartphone, and you can call me back on my new phone number. It's…hmm." She tugged a curl behind her ear. "Well, you can call the boy at the phone store and ask him. I'm sure he'll remember me. His name is Brian. Or Ryan. Or something like that. No, wait—it's a cheese. Colby! Oh, never mind. I'll call you back later. Buh-bye."

Well, phooey. Who am I gonna brag to now?

She glanced up at the empty green-plaid chair by the fireplace, where her late husband Floyd had always sat. "I know you don't approve of me spending the money, Floyd. But I got it dirt cheap by signing what they call a multi-year contract. I guess they don't know I'm eighty-two or they wouldn't have taken that bet!" She laughed at her own joke, then sighed when it was the only sound. The silence was heavy in her ears.

I've gotta call somebody who cares. She could try Opal's cell, but she couldn't remember the number. She also thought of calling her son, Bobby, but he wouldn't be excited for her. He'd been telling her for years to get a cell phone. Now it would just seem like she finally listened. Nah, she was going to wait until she saw him, and then act like she'd had it forever. But she could call her granddaughter. Livie would be happy for her. *No, wait! I can send a text message!* It took Mish a few minutes to remember what the sales boy showed her, but she finally figured it out.

> Dear Olivia hi this is Grandma! Can you believe your old grandma is sending you a text message? I got this new phone and I wanted to try it out. So how's school? Are you studying hard? Do you have a boyfriend? He better treat you nice. And if he doesn't, come back to West Virginia because the cute sales boy at the phone store is single. Okay I guess that's it for now. Love you bunches and oodles. Grandma.

She pushed Send. *Whew, that took forever and a Sunday. Why does everybody think sending texts is so much better than talking?*

It was just one of the things about this generation she found confusing. They don't have time to make coffee in the morning but will wait in line for some concoction that takes longer to order than it does to drink. They spend hours on their phones and have to be in constant contact with their friends. Can't they be alone with their own thoughts for more than two minutes? And that son of hers—he never leaves home without his phone, but does he use it to call his mother?

On the other hand, her daughter-in-law called too much. Claudia tried. She really did. She couldn't help that she was just so darn annoying. It must be genetic. Claudia's mother practically invented the trait. Mish had tried to warn Bobby not to marry her. After all, looks fade but irritating lasts forever. He didn't listen, of course, just had to have the pretty cheerleader on his arm. He didn't even seem to like her anymore, and he talked to her like she was a few peas short of a casserole. Mish couldn't remember the last time she'd seen him really happy. She'd even begun to wonder if he had a fling on the side.

She looked again at the empty recliner. "I kept asking you to talk with him," she said. "He probably wouldn't listen, but you could've tried. Or maybe he would have come to church with us again if you'd asked."

The phone in her hand suddenly dinged, and Mish nearly dropped it in surprise. She smiled as she realized Livie had written back.

> Hi Grandma! Great 2 hear from u, congrats on new phone. Schools great, bf treats me just fine. See you at Xmas. Luv u 2!

It took Mish a while to translate the message, but she figured this must be that text-speak people talk about. She studied it to make sure she got it all so she could use it right next time. *I'm gonna be hip*, she thought with a smile. *Hipper than Opal, anyway!*

She looked at the recliner again. "Oh, Floyd, you wouldn't believe how much people are willing to pay for a telephone. Some of 'em cost more than that fancy Limousin bull we bought years ago to breed with our herd. And I saw a woman buying three of them—for her teenagers! Can you imagine trusting a kid with an eight-hundred-dollar phone? Just plain crazy." She paused. "But then look at me, the pot calling the kettle. I'm sittin' here having a conversation with my dead husband. And no offense, but you ain't much of a conversationalist, Floyd. Of course, you never was but that's another matter."

Just then her phone dinged again, and she grabbed it to see if it was another message from Livie. But, no, she didn't recognize the number.

> Hi! I enjoyed talking with you and would love to continue our conversation. Free for breakfast tomorrow?

"Well, that sounds dandy, but who's it from?" Who did she know that would want to meet for breakfast? And why didn't they come out and say who they were? Did they want it to be a surprise? She glanced back at the chair. "Whaddya think, Floyd? A secret admirer?" She knew how Floyd would have responded to that ridiculous idea, but the thought didn't stop her. She'd lived a long life, but it was fairly short on mystery. *I'm not gonna let nobody put a damper on my sunshine!*

Just name the time and place, she typed, grinning. She was going to love having a smartphone.

Mish had a rough, sleepless night. She awoke from a dream in the wee hours of the morning with a sudden realization: she hadn't given her phone number to anyone but Olivia. Nobody she knew could have texted her and invited her to breakfast. It had to be a wrong number. She felt so foolish. It should have been obvious, and she figured a smarter person would have known right away that nobody had her number. She berated herself for an hour or so, and then her mind ran through all kinds of other mistakes she'd made in her life—times Floyd said she'd been too trusting, or downright stupid. She finally drifted back to sleep at four, then was surprised when she awoke at seven. She hadn't slept that late in years.

She lay in bed and stared at the swirling pattern in the textured ceiling as she tried to will herself to get up. It didn't matter if she overslept. No husband was waiting for breakfast. No kids or grandkids needed her. She had friends, sure, but none of them would know—or care—if she slept until noon. If it weren't for salesclerks, she might go days without speaking to another person.

Like that nice boy at the phone store. She caught her breath as she realized...he had her number! She had told him a little about Olivia—maybe he was interested and wanted to hear more about her. Now that Mish knew Livie still had a boyfriend, she obviously couldn't fix them up. But she should at least tell him in person. Besides, maybe there was a nice girl at church she could introduce him to.

As she rushed to get ready, she remembered something else— something that returned her excitement from the night before. The Google. Everybody was always talking about The Google, how they Googled this or Googled that. It sounded like you could find anything or anybody on The Google. Maybe her new cell phone number was already there, so maybe the message had been intended for her after all, and the person had wanted to keep it a surprise.

She grabbed the navy pants she'd worn the day before and put on a fresh flowered blouse. She had blouses in all colors, and today felt like a peach day. She rushed out the door and was al- most to the restaurant when she realized she had forgotten her hearing aid. She couldn't turn around and go get it, or she might miss her breakfast date. But not having it made her feel a little fuzzy-headed.

When she entered the Bluebird Diner, she looked around but didn't see anybody she knew, and nobody seemed to be looking for her. She chose a table near the door, the chair squeaking on the old linoleum floor when she pulled it out and sat down. She pulled the paper ring off the napkin wrapped around the silverware and fiddled with it as she watched the door.

"Good morning, Mish," Jodee, the waitress, said as she poured a cup of coffee. "Are you ready to order?"

Mish smiled. She and Jodee had chatted a few times when business was slow, and Mish liked hearing stories about Jodee's little grandbabies. The woman hardly looked old enough to be a grandma, but it was hard to tell with her bottle-blonde hair. "Thanks, but I'm waiting on somebody," Mish said, then smiled at how good it felt to say that. She was so used to eating alone.

"Ooh, got somebody special joining you?"

"Yes, but I don't know who it is," Mish said.

Jodee frowned. "How can you not know who you're meeting for breakfast?"

Mish tried not to take offense at Jodee's tone. "They sent me a text message and invited me to breakfast, so here I am." Mish craned her neck to see around the coffee pot Jodee held. The woman was sweet and all, but she was blocking the view of the door.

Jodee reached out and touched Mish's arm. "But, hon, you can't go meeting somebody you don't know. It's not safe."

Mish rolled her eyes. People were so fearful these days. Besides, she knew how to take care of herself. "Well, I might know who it is, but I'm not sure. It's a bit of a mystery, you see. And don't you find a little mystery is just what you need to lift your skirt once in a while?"

"Well, don't lift it too high or I'll have to…"

Jodee turned away as she spoke the last few words, and Mish wasn't sure she heard her right. "Call Belize?" she repeated.

Jodee was laughing when she turned around. "Call the police, I said. If you lift your skirt too high, I'll have to call the police."

"It's just an expression," Mish said with a wave of her hand. "I appreciate your good service, but right now I just want to watch for my date."

"Yes, ma'am. I'll be right here if you need me." Jodee shook her head as she walked away, but Mish couldn't be bothered with what Jodee thought. The bell on the door jingled, and she looked up expectantly. It wasn't anybody she knew. *Just a Black lady*, she thought, then clasped a hand over her mouth as if she'd said it out loud. She couldn't believe how racist she sounded! She only meant it wasn't anybody she knew so it couldn't be her date. *Oh, what the lady would think of me if she could hear my thoughts!* She shook her head, as if she could bat her thoughts away like pesky flies.

She looked up to see the woman staring at her. "Are you all right, ma'am?" the lady asked.

"Oh, I'm fine. I'm just…um, expecting someone and thought maybe you was them."

"Oh, how nice," she said pleasantly. "You meeting somebody special?"

"I don't know who it is," Mish replied. It was starting to sound odd, even to her.

The woman tilted her head as she studied Mish. "You don't know who you're meeting for breakfast? Is it a blind date or something?"

Mish laughed at the very idea of having a date at her age. "I'm afraid my courting days are long gone. I'm just meeting somebody who texted me and invited me to breakfast."

The lady cupped her chin in her hand, her pink polish pretty against her skin. "I know it's none of my business, but I'm a little worried about you meeting somebody you don't know. You have to be careful nowadays."

"Oh, I know," Mish replied, a little miffed. Why was everybody worried about her all of a sudden? "I saw a TV show about people taking advantage of the elderly. I'm being careful. See, they wanted to meet in a public place, so I figured it'd be safe."

"Well, that's fine then. I'm glad you're being smart." The woman gave her a reassuring smile. "It does sound like a fun mystery. You don't even know who is wanting to spend time with you."

"Exactly!" It didn't sound weird when the lady put it that way. "Somebody wants the pleasure of my company and said they could use my help. They might even want to pick my brain about something. I've been told that's slim pickings, but I got a bit of wisdom stored up after all these years."

The lady smiled broadly. "Oh, I just know you do!" Her eyes widened. "Or maybe it's somebody who wants to tell you something. Or has a message for you."

"A message? For me?" Mish laughed. "Ooh, I never thought of that!"

"Could be. You know, some people have even entertained angels in disguise."

Something jumped in Mish's heart at the very thought. *An angel? Nah, not for me. I'm not that important. But still, what an idea, even if I am old. Wait! In the Bible do the angels appear to old people or young people?* She started to count the stories she could remember but then realized the lady was staring at her again. "Sorry about that," Mish said with a laugh. "I was just counting angels. Which is weird, because my preacher was just telling us the other day about people arguing over how many angels can fit—"

"On the head of a pin!" the lady finished with a laugh.

"Wait a minute. Do you come to my church?"

The lady shook her head as she tugged on the lapel of her navy jacket. "I don't belong to any one church," she said with a smile. "But you go every Sunday and bring cookies for the coffee hour too, right?"

"Well, yes, but—"

"Just the type of person likely to get a visit from an angel. So keep your eyes open 'cause you just never know." And then she winked.

As the woman turned away, Mish's breath caught in her chest. The lady had given her a "we've got a secret" kind of wink, an "I'm not going to say it, but you know what I mean" kind of wink.

But whatever did she mean by it? Something about the angel? She said Mish was just the type of person to get a visit from an angel, and then she winked. As if Mish would get a visit from an angel someday soon. How could the woman know that? Why, Mish would love to think herself important enough for such a blessing, but clearly that wasn't the case. She was just an old farmer's wife—*widow*, she corrected herself—with nothing meaningful left ahead of her. Then again, the people in the Bible weren't always the cream of the crop either, so maybe it didn't matter.

Mish ran through it again in her head. Keep your eyes open because maybe you'll get a visit from an angel. And then that secret kind of wink.

Like maybe I just did? He heart beat faster at the very thought.

Could this lady possibly be an angel? But how could Mish find out? She couldn't just go and ask the woman, "Excuse me, are you an angel?" She would look ridiculous asking such a thing, and they would think she'd gone and lost her marbles. She had to figure out another way.

The lady had said maybe the person Mish was waiting on had a message for her. An angel would certainly have a message, but it wouldn't be a strange question to ask a regular person. It wouldn't raise suspicions, so Mish decided it was a safe place to start.

The lady had moved a few steps away to the bakery counter and was talking to Jodee, and Mish was having a hard time hearing without her blasted hearing aid. Random words and phrases kept reaching her straining ears.

Twelve...

Increase in followers...

Fishing efforts...

Believe in me...

Some kind of miracle...

Raise the dead...

Raise the dead? Did she hear that right? Mish couldn't wait any longer. She got up and sidled up next to the lady. "Excuse me," she began, "but you said something about a message. Do...do you have a message for me?"

The lady was so pretty when she smiled back. "A message? Why, sure. Follow the love. That will never lead you wrong." She looked away to take the bakery package from Jodee, but Mish couldn't wait any more. She just had to ask.

"Who are you?" Mish whispered.

The woman turned back toward Mish but didn't quite meet

her gaze. Her eyes widened and she whispered urgently, "Jesus Christ!" Then she grabbed her box and was out the door in a flash.

Mish stared at the door in a daze. Had she just heard what she thought she heard? She thought back over the conversation between Jodee and the lady. She hadn't heard everything, but she'd heard enough. Followers and fishing, faith and miracles, and raising the dead? It all fit. And, of course, the message: follow the love. And, finally, there was the woman's own admission. "Who are you?" Mish had asked, and she got her answer.

Well, I'll be a monkey's auntie, Mish thought. *Jesus Christ came back as a Black lady!*

2

So is everybody clear on their assignments?"

The officers of the Women's Society were gathered at the long table in the church library, going over last-minute details for Saturday's bazaar. Mish nodded quickly in response to Opal's question, and so did Ruth and Ethyl. They all knew better than to mess with Opal a few days before the bazaar. The woman sure liked to be in charge. But the closer they got to the day, the more anxious she got; and the more anxious she got, the crankier she got. It was best to agree. You could always do what you wanted later and claim you forgot or didn't understand.

Mish did that a lot. The only problem was she'd been doing it so long everybody thought she was dim-witted.

As if she'd been reading Mish's mind, Opal narrowed her eyes as she zeroed in on her. "You know what you're supposed to do, Mish?"

"I surely do. Absolutely. No problem. I got the bull by the tail and the cat by the horns. I crossed my *I*s and dotted my *T*s and—"

"All right, all right! A simple yes would have sufficed," Opal snapped, but the smile at the edge of her mouth gave her away.

She had a good heart, Opal did. She just got caught up in the details, which is why Mish hadn't yet shared the news she was bursting to share. She had to at least let Opal get through her agenda first.

Opal turned her attention to their special guest for the meeting. "Stephen, thanks for coming. I know you must be busy at work. We sure appreciate your help with the decorations and the Christmas wreaths."

Stephen smiled at the four women around the table. "I'm glad to do it. But if I keep this up, you might just have to make me an honorary member of the Women's Society."

Opal laughed. "That'd be a first! We've never had a pastor's *husband* in the Women's Society before. Then again, I guess you and Pastor Jeff are getting used to shaking things up around here."

"It's not our intention," Stephen said as he leaned back in his chair and stretched. "But it does seem to come with the territory."

"Oh, before I forget," Mish interjected. "Is there any way you can sweet talk Pastor Jeff into making his chocolate cake for the bake sale?"

"For you, Mish, I'm sure he will."

"Are you sure he has time?" Ruth asked. "Is his sermon for this Sunday written yet? The week is half over, you know."

Mish caught Ethyl's glance across the table and rolled her eyes. Ruth Tipton was the busiest busybody she ever did see. And she was always on Pastor Jeff's back about something. Ruth still couldn't believe the church had gone and hired a gay pastor. What she really couldn't believe, Mish thought, was that they hired a pastor without her approval. And she was making them pay for it.

"His sermon is well on its way, Ruth, so don't you worry." Stephen said it with a smile, but Mish thought it looked a bit forced.

"Well, we need the name of the cake to put on the sign," Ruth said.

Stephen hesitated. "Um…let's just call it Pastor Jeff's Chocolate Surprise."

Ruth bristled. "Is it his original recipe? If not, I'll need the official title from the book he used."

"I really think it's best to just call it Pastor Jeff's Chocolate Surprise," Stephen repeated.

Ruth leaned forward and gripped the edge of the table with both hands. "That wouldn't be honest, now would it? And I know our pastor would want to be honest."

Mish and Opal exchanged looks. They were both worried that all Ruth's haranguing would eventually drive Pastor Jeff away. And they both liked him, in spite of his—what was the right term? Sexual orientation, that was it. He was by far the best preacher they'd had in ages, and his cooking wasn't bad either.

Stephen sighed. "Well, if you insist, Ruth. The name of the cake is Better Than Sex Cake. Now, would you like to put that on your sign?"

Everyone started laughing. Everyone except Ruth, of course. "No, I most certainly would not!" she exclaimed, leaning back from the table as if it held a platter of manure.

"I do see the problem," Opal began with a smirk. "We could be accused of false advertising."

Mish leaned forward. "I guess it depends on who you ask. Or who you're married to!"

"And how long it's been!" Opal added.

"I do have some short-term memory loss," Ethyl said slowly. "But I can remember fifty years ago as if it was yesterday." She paused, and everyone waited. As always. "And that cake is rightly named," she finished with a grin.

Mish slapped the table as an idea came to her. "Hey, I bet we could charge more for it if we call it Better Than Sex Cake. We could change the name to all our crafts. Better Than Sex Afghans. Better Than Sex Pot Holders."

"Now, Mish," Opal teased, "have you ever seen a pot holder that was better than sex?"

"No, but maybe if it comes with batteries!"

As they burst out laughing, Ruth raised her voice. "I thought this was a meeting of the Women's Society of the Congregational Church not the Society for the Promotion of Licentious Living!"

Mish and Opal looked at each other, then spoke in unison. "Can't it be both?"

"That does it!" Ruth hollered. "You call me when you decide to act like Christian ladies." And then she stormed out. Or she would've if she could've. It's hard to storm when you use a walker. They all held off, waiting until Ruth had shuffled slowly out the door and down the hall before they gave in to their laughter.

"Oh, ladies, if I'd known your meetings were so much fun, I'd have attended sooner!" Stephen said, wiping tears from his eyes.

"And Lord forgive me," Mish began, "but I do enjoy getting old Ruth going!"

Opal agreed but quickly got them back to business. "Stephen, can you commit to Pastor bringing his chocolate cake, whatever we call it?"

"Yes, ma'am. And if he doesn't have time, I will make it."

Mish patted his hand. "Stephen, you're such a good pastor's wife." She clasped her free hand over her mouth. "I'm so sorry! I mean pastor's spouse! Or husband. Or partner. Or whatever you want to be called. I didn't mean—oh, good Lord, I'm sorry!"

Stephen smiled at her as he squeezed her hand. "Relax, Mish. It's fine. I know you didn't mean anything by it. Besides, I don't think being called a woman is an insult."

Mish breathed a huge sigh of relief. "Oh, thank you. You fellas know I don't have a problem with you two. I got over that," Mish said with a wave of her hand. "I just sometimes get tripped up by the words because I don't want to say the wrong thing and hurt your feelings."

Stephen was still smiling. "Really, it's fine, Mish. I know you would never say anything hurtful on purpose."

She returned his smile at last. "My brain works slower than my tongue sometimes. And I'm an old woman. I'm not always up to date on the latest lingo."

"I do have some short-term memory loss," Ethyl began again. They waited. "And?" Opal prompted her.

"And do y'all remember Pastor Goodpastor? He left here about fifteen years ago."

"Marvin Goodpastor," Stephen began. "He pastored here for fourteen years, preached phenomenal sermons without once making anybody mad, and was always in his office for drop-in visits while simultaneously spending all of his time with the shut-ins. A pastor so good it was even his name."

It seemed to take him a few seconds to realize that Mish, Opal, and Ethyl were all staring at him, speechless. He clapped a hand over his mouth. "Oh, good Lord, I said that out loud! Ladies, I am so sorry. That was incredibly catty."

"No, it wasn't," Opal assured him.

"Well, it kind of was," Mish corrected, "but it was honest. I bet it's not fun for Pastor Jeff to have to walk in those shoes all the time. None of our recent pastors have stayed long, and it wouldn't surprise me a bit if that was the reason. Being compared to Saint Marvin the Good must get mighty old."

"It does," Stephen said with relief. "But I still shouldn't have said it. I am sorry."

"It's all right," Mish assured him. "Now, Ethyl, you was saying…"

"I was saying?" Ethyl looked confused.

"Yes, you asked if we remembered Pastor Goodpastor," Mish reminded her.

"Oh, right! Well, the only thing people didn't like about Pastor Goodpastor was that he wasn't married. Never did get married. Never dated neither. Had this friend from seminary who used to visit pretty regular-like. He wasn't married neither. Nobody ever talked about it, of course, but…" Her words trailed off.

"Are you saying what I think you're saying?" Stephen asked.

Ethyl nodded.

"Pastor Goodpastor was *gay*?" Opal exclaimed.

"Oh, that explains it." Mish smacked her forehead. "I never understood why Floyd didn't like him—which is weird, because I usually knew *exactly* why Floyd didn't like people. But he never would say what he had against Marvin Goodpastor. He would just frown every time Marvin's name came up."

"So your husband wasn't a big fan of 'the gays,'" Stephen replied. Mish shook her head and he returned her sad smile.

"Marvin Goodpastor was gay," Opal repeated, as if saying it again would make it sink in. "Will wonders never cease."

"No, they don't," Mish agreed. Her heart leapt at the opening she'd just been given. It was finally time to share her news. "Like yesterday, at the diner!"

They all looked at each other and then back at Mish. They were confused, she knew. She got this look a lot.

"All right, I'll bite," Opal said at last. "What happened yesterday at the diner, Mish?"

Mish was trembling with excitement. "Yesterday at the Bluebird Diner…" She paused for dramatic effect. "I met Jesus!"

Opal looked at her warily. "You met Jesus."

"I sure did!" Mish declared. "And until then I had no idea Jesus was going to come back as a Black lady!"

Stephen just stared at her. "Jesus came back…?"

"Yes, the second coming. But she came back as a woman, a real pretty Black lady. I met her at the diner."

"Now, Mish," Opal began, "you did not meet Jesus at the diner."

"How do you know?" Mish countered. "You wasn't there."

"I am pretty sure Jesus is not a patron of the Bluebird Diner."

"But I met her!" Mish argued. "And she gave me a message: follow the love. Now, doesn't that sound like the kind of thing Jesus would say?"

"Well, yes, but…" Stephen paused and put a hand on top of Mish's. "Mish, what makes you think this woman was Jesus?"

"She said that was her name. Jesus Christ. Clear as day."

"Wait," Opal interrupted. "A strange woman just came up to you and told you she was Jesus Christ? And you believed her?"

Mish pulled her hand out from under Stephen's. This was not going as she had planned. "No, it wasn't like that." She looked around at their disbelieving faces, and she knew she had to do a better job of explaining. "It started with a text message. Somebody wanted to meet me for breakfast, but I didn't know who it was. So I went to the diner, and I waited. Then she walked in and we got to talking about the Bible and angels and stuff like that. She seemed to know things about me, like we'd met before, but we hadn't." Mish took a breath and Opal started to interrupt, but Mish just talked louder. She wasn't going to let them argue her out of what she felt—what she knew in her heart to be true. "She said she had a message for me. She told me to follow the love. And when I asked her who she was, she told me she was Jesus Christ."

Opal closed her eyes briefly and pinched the bridge of her nose, a sure sign that she was trying not to lose her patience. "But, Mish," she began, "it could've been anybody. It could've been a mentally ill person, thinking she was Jesus. Or a con artist, preying on the vulnerable."

The knot that had been in Mish's throat plummeted to her

belly. Her best friend didn't believe her. Her best friend thought she was vulnerable and foolish to believe she'd met Jesus. She turned to Stephen, praying that at least he would believe her. "You wouldn't think that if you met her," she pleaded. "She was a strong, beautiful woman with a pretty smile and kind eyes, and she saw me—really saw me. And she had a message for me. That's why she sent me the text that brought me to the diner—to give me the message."

"You know, Mish, the text could have been a wrong number," Stephen reasoned.

"Sure, it could have been. But it wasn't, because I got to meet Jesus!" Mish answered. She looked back at Opal, then at Ethyl, who hadn't said a word since she'd started her story. She could see in their eyes that they were worried about her. Well, they didn't need to be. She knew what she'd seen, what she'd felt in the woman's presence. She knew it was real. And she knew what she had to do now. She put on a smile and looked at Opal and Ethyl. "I appreciate your concern, but I have already accepted the mission, and now I'm gonna follow the love." She turned to Stephen. "You got a problem with that, son?"

"No, ma'am."

"I didn't think so. Now if you'll excuse me, I better get going. I need to get home and finish some more pot holders for the bazaar."

She stood and turned toward the door, but she could hear the smile in Stephen's voice as he spoke. "Would those pot holders have any special name, Mish?"

She kept walking. "Follow the love, Stephen."

"Yes, ma'am. Follow the love."

"They didn't believe me, Floyd. None of 'em." Mish paced across her living room as she spoke. "And why should my news be so hard to believe? Don't the Bible say he's gonna come back? And why shouldn't I get a visit?"

She stopped and looked at the green-plaid chair Floyd always sat in and waited for him to answer. She knew he wouldn't, of course, but after being married to the man for nearly sixty years, she figured she knew what he would say anyway. It's not like he'd had an original thought in years.

"I know I ain't nobody special," she agreed. "But shepherds were the first ones to hear on Christmas, and they were kind of like farmers. So why not me? Why wouldn't Jesus come talk to me?"

She fixed herself a cup of instant coffee and dropped down on the old sofa. "Maybe my job on this earth ain't done just because I'm old. Maybe there's more to me than a farmer's wife and mother and grandmother. There's gotta be a reason Jesus would come to me."

Mish looked at the empty chair. "Or maybe I'm just a crazy old woman still talking to her dead husband."

She took a sip of coffee and grimaced at its bitterness. Maybe they were right. It didn't make sense that Jesus would come to her. She was just an old woman with nothing more important to do than make pot holders for the women's bazaar. She was useless. Obsolete. Just like her old landline phone.

But it sure had been nice for a while. It sure had felt good to think there was something meaningful she could do with her remaining years. Opal was probably right. She hadn't met Jesus. And Floyd was definitely right. She wasn't anybody special. It was best to give up this whole idea and get back to what was real.

And what was real was that she was eighty-two years old, had no real purpose in life, and her sole contribution to the universe was crocheting.

Just then her phone dinged with a message from the same number as before.

I don't mean to be pushy, but do you want to try again?

Mish stared at the phone, not sure what to say. Who was this, and why were they writing again? She typed back, *Why,* and then accidentally hit the send button too soon. Before she could finish typing a better response, an answer came back.

Because you're special.

Mish let out a huff. *Not true,* she typed back.
The response came immediately.

How can you say that? Absolutely true. I knew it from the beginning.

Mish tugged on the curl behind her ear. What did that even mean? The beginning of what? Before she could figure out how to respond, her phone dinged again.

I know you. Your beautiful blue eyes are a window to your soul.

Hope began to rise in her heart, just a bit. When they had spoken, she had felt like the woman—the Jesus woman—had really known her. And hadn't she been complimented on her blue eyes her whole life? But she couldn't go all crazy before she knew. She had to come out and ask.

Who are you really and what do you want?

The response was immediate.

You already know who I am. I am who you think I am.

Another text came.

And I want you just as you are.

Suddenly she was grinning again. She'd been right all along. *I am who I am*—that was what God told Moses when he asked for God's name. And she'd been singing "Just as I Am" in church since she was five years old. Her heart knew what was true. The woman was real. The message was real. The mission was real. She just had to follow the love.

Her fingers were shaking so much it was hard to type, but she did it. *When and where?*

Diner at six?

I'll be there!! She paused and then looked back at the recliner. "Is two exclamation points enough? You're right. There should be three. One for the Father and one for the Son and one for the Holy-gosh-darn-Ghost!"

3

Jeff opened the front door and was greeted by the luscious smell of garlic and basil.

"I'm in the kitchen," Stephen called unnecessarily.

Jeff hung his keys on the brass key holder and walked into the kitchen to see Stephen standing at the stove wearing his "Kiss the Chef" apron. He obeyed the instructions, then reached into the fridge for the bottle of wine he'd opened the night before.

"Jeff, we really need to get this burner fixed. It's hard enough to cook a decent meal on this ancient electric stove without one of the large burners being out."

Jeff let out a quiet sigh. After a long day making hospital and nursing home visits, he really didn't want to be greeted by problems the minute he walked in the door. But it was important to Stephen, so he tried not to let his irritation show. "I mentioned it to the trustees at last month's meeting, and they said they'd get to it. I'm sure they're all just really busy."

"Can't we just take care of it ourselves?" Stephen asked. "It's probably a simple matter of replacing the element."

"I know, but it's the church's responsibility to keep up the parsonage. My dad always said it was dangerous to circumvent the trustees. Once you start doing the little repairs, they expect you to do the big ones too. And they expect the next pastor who follows you to do the same. So it's better to let the church leaders handle it all." Jeff filled two glasses of wine and handed one to Stephen.

Stephen took a sip of his wine. "That might have worked for your father, but—"

"I'll ask again at the next meeting," Jeff assured him.

Stephen set down his glass and stirred the pesto pasta. "On second thought, don't bother. During the bazaar on Saturday, I'll just mention the problem to their wives. They'll put pressure on their husbands, and it'll be done within a week."

"Wow. Stereotype much?"

Stephen added the freshly chopped tomatoes to the pan, then looked up at Jeff. "Can you name a single trustee for whom this is inaccurate?"

Jeff went around the conference room table in his mind. "Point taken," he admitted. "Speaking of the bazaar, we need to talk about the Women's Society meeting today." Stephen had given him a quick rundown over the phone, but they hadn't been able to discuss it much.

Stephen looked at him warily. "Which part are you mad about? That I said you'd make a cake for this weekend, or that I told them its real name?"

"Well, both, actually. But I meant baking the cake. I don't have time for that. I haven't even started my sermon."

"I know. Of course, I told Ruth it was almost done. You know how she loves to criticize your sermon preparation."

Jeff frowned. "I bet Pastor Goodpastor never started *his* sermon on Saturday. His was probably written by Tuesday morning at the latest."

Stephen grinned. "Especially if his seminary *friend* was coming to visit."

"Ethyl really believes he was gay?"

"Sure seems to," he answered as he started serving their dishes. "But why is this the first we're hearing of it? Haven't there been gay ministers in your denomination for, like, thirty years?"

"Sure, in California. Not West Virginia."

"Right. I keep forgetting how behind the times you religious types are."

Jeff started to take offense but then saw the twinkle in Stephen's blue eyes. So he put his hand on his heart and returned the joke. "Yes, if only the whole world were as enlightened as those in the theatre, where a homophobe dare not show his face!"

Stephen laughed, as Jeff had known he would. "Well, I still say that the church may have more drama queens than the theatre world does."

"I won't argue with you there," Jeff said and rubbed his neck, trying in vain to ease the headache that had been building all afternoon.

Stephen put the pasta and salad on the table, took his seat, then hurried to take the pressure off. "Seriously, hon, don't worry about the cake. I'll do it. But oh, you should have seen the look on Ruth's face when I told her the proper name!"

"You do love getting the dear old women in my church all riled up."

"Only Ruth, and I know you're not calling *her* a dear."

"No," Jeff choked out, then swallowed. "But I have to admit I'm worried about Mish."

"From what I can tell, Mish has always been…well, Mish. She was odd long before she was old enough to be senile."

"True," he conceded. "But from what you said, she actually thinks she met Jesus and is getting text messages from God."

Stephen's mouth was full, so he just shrugged.

Jeff was surprised at Stephen's apparent lack of concern. "You can't seriously believe her."

Stephen swallowed and began counting on his fingers. "I've heard you preach on God speaking through dreams, visions, a burning bush, and a talking animal. Why not text messages?"

"The stories aren't literal. They're metaphors. You know that. You just love quoting my sermons back to me."

"Everybody needs a hobby," Stephen quipped. "Besides, aren't you glad *somebody's* paying attention?"

Jeff ignored his comment. "She honestly thinks that Jesus is an African American woman she met at the Bluebird Diner."

"The only part I don't understand is the *coming back* thing. I've never heard you preach on the second coming."

"Mish wasn't raised Congregational," Jeff explained. "Primitive Baptist, I think."

"Aren't they all?" Stephen asked with a laugh.

"No, there's a small group of pretty progressive Baptists who—"

"Jeff, I was joking," Stephen interrupted.

"Oh, right. Sorry." Jeff stabbed another piece of pasta. He felt annoyed, and he couldn't quite figure out why.

"Anyway, I find this whole thing fascinating. Racism still runs deep around here, even in a fairly liberal church, and here is Mish seeing Jesus as a woman of color. I think that's pretty cool."

Jeff stopped with his fork in midair. "Cool? Mish is showing signs of mental illness or dementia, and you think it's 'cool'?"

"If this was Opal we were talking about, I would agree," Stephen said with a shrug. "But it's Mish, and the regular rules of sanity do not apply. Maybe she's having some kind of spiritual awakening."

Jeff tossed his napkin on the table in frustration. "It doesn't work that way."

"Why not?" Stephen pressed.

Jeff clenched his teeth and stared at Stephen. "It just doesn't, okay? Mish is not having a spiritual awakening or whatever you want to call it. If she was, I would know."

Stephen looked at Jeff a long time before speaking softly. "Are you sure you'd recognize it?"

Jeff picked up his glass of wine and left the room.

Mish kept watching the door for Jesus, but it had been twenty minutes, so Mish guessed she wasn't coming. She felt disappointed, let down after the excitement of the text exchange earlier, but Jesus was undoubtedly a busy woman. Besides, Mish had already been given her instructions—follow the love—so she turned her attention to those around her. The young man at the next table also seemed to be waiting on someone who hadn't shown up. At first she wondered if he was waiting for Jesus, too, but by the looks of him, he was waiting on a date. He was neatly dressed, had a fresh haircut, and looked as nervous as a turkey in November.

She stopped stealing glances and stared at him until he looked her way. "Well, son, I do believe your lady friend has stood you up."

He frowned at her. "What makes you think I'm waiting for a lady friend?"

"Oh, I'm sorry. I made an assumption. I do believe your *man* friend has stood you up."

The young man looked horrified. "I'm not gay!"

Mish looked him straight in the eyes. "First of all, son, I didn't say you was. You implied it. And number two, being gay ain't nothing to be ashamed of, so don't be acting like I just called you an ax murderer. That's insulting to gay folks, you hear me?"

He ducked his head. "Yes, ma'am. I'm sorry."

Mish nodded her forgiveness. "Now, tell me who you're waiting on and why their absence has your innards in a knot."

He sighed. "I met a girl. A woman. She's beautiful. We had a nice talk and I thought she liked me. But this is the second time she's stood me up."

Mish frowned. "A woman doesn't stand up a man she likes. Not if she can help it. And surely not twice." The young man looked a bit offended, but Mish wasn't sure why.

"You don't sugarcoat much, do you?" he said.

"Sugarcoating is for cereal. I'm a bacon-and-eggs gal."

"Which means…?"

"It means I ain't got time for games. And neither do you. Now what's your name, son?"

"Ethan."

Mish had been told that subtlety wasn't her specialty, so she took a deep breath and tried to speak gently. "Ethan, that beautiful woman you met is playing games with you. Best you move on."

"Move on. Just like that."

"Yep. You gotta follow the love."

"But that's what I'm trying to do!" Ethan argued.

Mish narrowed her eyes. "Where'd you meet your mystery woman?"

Ethan ducked his head, a bit red-faced. "At the bar. Ladies' night."

"And exactly how long was this meaningful conversation you supposedly had?"

He shrugged. "Ten minutes."

"Ten minutes," Mish repeated.

"Maybe twelve," the boy countered.

"And after those ten, maybe twelve, life-changing minutes, you think you're in love?"

Again, he looked offended. "And a text conversation…a really romantic text."

"And then she stood you up," Mish reminded him. "And hasn't called or texted to tell you why." When he looked embarrassed and ducked his head, Mish softened her tone. "Son, here's what you need to know. This thing you're feeling? This ain't love. This is lust. And don't get me wrong—it can be a lot of fun. But don't confuse a rise in your trousers with a hole in your heart. You gotta follow the love."

"Follow the love," Ethan repeated.

"That's the ticket."

"And how, exactly, do I follow the love?"

Mish studied him a moment before answering. "To tell you the truth, I ain't worked that part out yet. But I have a feeling you have to figure it out for yourself."

As Mish drove home from the diner, she tried to think through what had happened. Obviously the first text had been to get her to the diner, where she met Jesus. But the second text, from the same number, didn't lead her to Jesus. Or at least Jesus didn't show up. Instead it led her to Ethan. She didn't know if that was the plan, if he was the one she was supposed to meet, and she didn't know if she had helped him at all. Oh, she did have him laughing before he left, and she did give him Jesus's message. Was it enough? The message seemed so clear at first—just follow the love. But how? Where?

As she neared a line of traffic at the red light, she slowed down to let a waiting vehicle—a white van—enter in front of her. She returned the van driver's wave of thanks, but before she could pull forward again, the car behind that one pulled in front of her too. "Well, that's a bit rude," she said out loud, well aware that the young woman in the sports car could not hear her. "But I'm following the love so I'm not even gonna honk at you."

The little car changed lanes, and Mish pulled up behind the white van. And then she saw it—the message printed on the back of the van. "A shelter dog needs your LOVE today." The *O* in the word "love" was a heart. She was literally following love!

A shelter dog needed her love. Hmm. Well, the shelter would be closed at this hour, which gave her time to figure out whether it was a message or not. Mish *had* always wanted a dog—an inside dog, a dog she could pet and snuggle with on the couch. But Floyd was not a pet kind of man. According to him, the only dogs worth having were the ones who did a job on the farm. Dogs didn't belong in the house any more than cattle did. He hadn't even bent for Bobby when he was a boy, so he sure hadn't bent for Mish.

Over the years, Mish had tried to make friends with the farm dogs, but it never worked. They were Floyd's dogs, and they responded only to him. Not one of them was affectionate with her, and they didn't pay her a bit of attention unless she was feeding them. And even then it seemed like they only tolerated her presence. Maybe she wasn't really good with dogs.

But maybe if she picked out the dog herself—if she was the one who brought it home and fed it and petted it, maybe it would be her dog. Maybe a dog could like her. Maybe there could be someone who would be happy to see her when she walked in the door.

4

It was only eleven o'clock, but Jeff was already exhausted and in pain. It was Saturday, and he'd arrived at church at seven in the morning to help the men set up for the bazaar and had just taken refuge in his office for a few minutes of rest. He had carried five of those old eight-foot tables by himself, and his back was in revolt. Why couldn't they invest in the new lightweight ones instead of those ancient behemoths? But the other men all did it, and he couldn't look like a wimp. Hell, he was half their age! Of course, many of them were still throwing bales of hay around, even at age seventy, while the heaviest thing he had lifted this week was volume seven of his *New Interpreter's Commentary*.

He bent down to pick up his sermon notes, which had fallen on the floor, and he winced with pain. And, of course, Mish chose that exact moment to appear in his doorway, her curly hair a bit wild from the heat of the kitchen.

"You all right there, Pastor?" she asked.

"Of course," he lied. "I'm just fine."

"Yeah, my back's feeling 'just fine' today too." She sighed as she lowered herself gingerly into a chair. "You wanted to see me?"

"Yes, Mish, thanks for making time." He did want to talk with her, to gauge for himself the seriousness of the situation. He had been worrying about her all week.

"I don't have long. The lunch crowd should be starting soon, but I needed a break so thought I'd kill two birds and chat with you for a minute. Then I'll get back to frying okra."

Jeff smiled. "And the Women's Society Harvest Bazaar would not be complete without your fried okra. I promise I won't keep you long." He wasn't sure how to get started and searched around for an opener. Compliments!—that was it. His dad always told him that if you didn't know what to say to a woman, you should compliment her. Of course, that was back when his dad thought Jeff's lack of success with women was because of his shyness.

"That's a lovely blouse you're wearing today," he said with a smile.

She looked down at her blouse, which was already covered in stains from the kitchen. Damn, he should have noticed that.

"Well…um…thank you," she said uncertainly.

"Wait a minute!" He suddenly realized why it had caught his eye. "It's short-sleeved!"

Mish grinned. "Am I showing too much skin for you, Pastor Jeff?"

Jeff laughed. "No, of course not. It's just that—did the doctor change your medication?"

"My medication?"

Jeff wondered if she was getting forgetful too. "You never used to wear short sleeves," he reminded her. "You said your medication caused you to bruise easily, and you didn't like people to see the bruises. Did the doctor change your prescription?"

Her eyes widened. "Oh, that! Yes, of course. New medication. Much less bruising."

"That's great," Jeff replied. "And that blouse does look lovely on you."

"Thank you. But I don't think you called me up here to talk about my clothes." She raised her eyebrows in anticipation.

"No, Mish, I didn't," Jeff admitted. "Stephen tells me that you had an interesting visit at the Bluebird Diner recently. I thought I'd check in with you about that."

Mish narrowed her eyes. "You mean check and see if I fell off my rocker. You heard about me thinking I met Jesus, and you decided to find out if I need a checkup from the neck up."

"Mish, I do love how you get to the point."

"Ethan said something like that the other day too."

"Ethan? Is that your grandson?"

"Nah. Ethan's a young man I met at the diner when I went to meet Jesus the second time," she said dismissively.

"You've met Jesus twice?" Uh-oh. This was progressing quickly.

"No, the first time I went, I wasn't looking for Jesus. I just found her. The second time I thought I would see Jesus, but I met Ethan instead. I gave him Jesus's message. I think that's why she wanted me to go. She is using me to spread the word."

"And what word would that be?" Jeff asked carefully. He knew it was important not to spook Mish if he was going to help her.

"Well, more than one word actually. Three words. *Follow the love.*"

Mish smiled at him. She looked so small and innocent that it was hard to believe she was eighty-some years old. "So you met a woman at the diner who said she was Jesus, she told you to follow the love, and now Jesus is sending you on missions, giving you jobs to do, in order to spread the message?"

"That sums it up quite nicely, Pastor Jeff. Nice chatting with you." She pushed on the armrests and started to rise to her feet.

Jeff held up his hand to stop her. "Not so fast, Mish. We're not finished here."

"Pardon me for saying so, Pastor, but, yes, we are. I'm on a mission from God, and you don't seem to believe in my mission. So we don't have much common ground on this topic. Or were you wanting to talk about something else? Maybe the name of that cake your Stephen made?"

"No, I do not want to talk about that cake," he answered quickly.

"Then if you don't mind, I'm going back to my okra station. I gotta follow the love. And the cornmeal."

Oh, good Lord, she's losing it. "Follow the cornmeal?" he repeated.

Mish looked at him as if he were dumb as dirt. "For the fried okra. You use cornmeal for the fried okra." Then she wagged her finger at him. "Pay attention now, Thomas, or you might miss something."

Jeff inhaled quickly. "Mish," he began as gently as he could. "My name is Jeff."

"I wasn't using it as a name," she replied. "I was using it as a title." On that confusing note, she turned and left, whistling as she went.

A title? Jeff thought. *How is Thomas a title?*

Then he recognized the tune Mish was whistling. An old children's Sunday school song about one of Jesus's disciples. "Don't be a Doubting Thomas…"

Cute, Mish. Real cute.

☙

The bazaar ended at two in the afternoon, and then they had to tear down and clean up, so it was nearly five by the time Mish got home. She heated up some leftover soup Opal had insisted she take, but once she sat down at the kitchen table she just stared at her soup. It felt like the first few months after Floyd died, when she wasn't used to eating alone.

But, no, this was different. This wasn't loneliness, but she didn't have a word for it. It wasn't that she hadn't loved Floyd. She had. And he hadn't been a bad man. He just had a temper to beat the band. He kept it in check most of the time. In the early years it had never been directed at her, and he had loved her in his own gruff way. But over the years he had gotten worse. After Bobby left there was lots of yelling and a few thrown plates, but he had never raised a hand to her. Until the last few years. She had heard somewhere that when people get old, they get less able to keep pretending, so they become more of what they always were. What he always was, was angry and mean. As his body started to fail him, he got angrier—and less able to control it. That's when the hitting started.

She got up and walked into the living room so she could see Floyd's recliner. She didn't know why she did it—only talked to Floyd in his chair. Maybe it was because when she looked at that chair, she could see him clear as day, sitting there reading the paper or watching *Wheel of Fortune*.

She took a deep breath. "Floyd, I did something stupid today. And the words ain't even out of my mouth before I can hear you say 'What's new?' So here's what's new, Floyd. I wore short sleeves out in public. I did it without even thinking about it. I knew it was gonna be hot in the kitchen so I grabbed the first cool thing I put my hands on."

She rushed on before she lost her nerve. "And Pastor Jeff noticed. Remember that time he dropped by for a visit, and he saw those bad bruises on my arm? I told him that they was from some pills the doctor put me on. Today he guessed that the doctor changed my prescription, so I let him believe it. But what if he repeats it? What if one of the ladies starts asking questions? What if they figure it out?"

Mish paused. It was so hard to get these words out. *But they've stayed unspoke for too long,* she thought. *It's time.*

"Oh, Floyd, I protected you. I didn't want the church folks thinking bad of you, especially with you being a trustee and all, so I wore long sleeves. For the last few years, every time I went outside, I wore long sleeves. All summer long, sweating like a whore in church.

"I did it for you, Floyd. To protect you. And, okay, maybe I did it a little for me, because I didn't want to be one of those women that everybody in town pities. But now I don't know what to do. I don't want to keep wearing long sleeves every day just to protect the reputation of a man who's been dead for nearly a year."

Her words were interrupted by the ding of a text message arriving. "Oh, Jesus! What now?" she nearly yelled. She immediately felt guilty and changed her tone. She tried again, more apologetic this time. More sincere. "Oh, Jesus! What now?"

She looked at the phone.

I need help.

Her heart jumped at the thought of Jesus needing her help. But wait—last time she wasn't sure if it was Jesus texting her. Maybe it was just the way Jesus got her to the place she needed to be. She looked again and saw that it was a different number. Still, she had a mission, so she took a deep breath and typed slowly into the phone. *What kind of help?*

The phone dinged two seconds later.

I'm pregnant.

All right, so not Jesus, she thought. Mish stared at the phone while she tried to figure out how to answer. She wanted to say,

"Congratulations," but if the person needed help, they must not be happy about it. But what else *to* say? She compromised by adding a question mark. *Congratulations?*

Seriously?

"Oops, wrong answer." She tried again, this time more professional-like. *I'm sorry. I want to help. Can you tell me about your concern?*

I'm 16.

Sixteen? What kind of girl is making hay at sixteen? When Mish was sixteen, all she knew about the birds and the bees was the cows and the bulls. Come to think of it, she wasn't too sure that was a good way to learn. She figured it did make her unnecessarily nervous on her wedding night. She glanced up at his chair. "No offense, Floyd, but you wasn't nothing compared to my daddy's prize bull!"

Her phone dinged again.

So are u going to help me or not? The website said I could text and then meet with someone confidentially.

Website? God had a website for her? Wow. She had a lot to learn about this mission. *Of course. When would you like to meet?*

Soon. But do I have to come to your office?

Mish laughed at the idea of her den being called an office. She looked again at the number. It was the right area code and the same first three numbers as her cell phone, so the girl must be local. *I can meet you anywhere but west of Charleston would be best.*

Perfect. Mercy Park? At 3:15 tomorrow by the fountain.

That wasn't in town, but it was close. *Sure.*

How will I recognize you?

Mish looked at Floyd's chair before answering, biting her lip. *I'll be wearing a flowered blouse. With long sleeves.*

Mish arrived at the park early the next day. She was a bit nervous about meeting this young gal who'd gotten in trouble. At Mish's age, what did she know about what this child was facing?

She looked up at the sky. *Hate to question your judgment, but you sure about this? Sure you don't have anybody else who'd be more fitting? Somebody who remembers the passion of young love?* She breathed a heavy sigh and pushed open the metal gate that was hanging by one hinge. *Ah well, if I'm the best you got…*

She found the fountain behind the first set of hedges, took a seat on a wood bench, and then tried to enjoy her surroundings while she waited. But Mercy Park wasn't exactly bursting at the seams with good things to look at. Fast food containers and brown paper bags seemed to be hiding under every overgrown bush, and cigarette butts littered the ground at her feet. The words "no mercy" were carved into the bench, making her wonder if maybe Mercy Park was one of those—oh, what were they called? It was a big fancy word that meant the opposite, like jumbo shrimp. Something moron, she thought. *Oh, hush, Floyd.*

Well, whatever the word was, Mercy Park was one of them. She heard about it on the news sometimes, usually something to do with an arrest for drugs or prostitution. She wondered why the girl had picked here to meet.

As soon as she saw the girl, somehow Mish knew it was her. Her shoulders were bent as if she carried the weight of the world on them, and no sixteen-year-old girl should look like that. She had long, straight dark hair and big doe eyes. *A doe on the first day of hunting season*, Mish thought.

She waited until the girl got near her bench and then said as gently as she could, "Howdy, hon. I believe you're looking for me. I'm Mish."

The girl stared at her. Just stared. Like she'd never seen an old woman before. Finally she said, "Seriously?"

"Seriously. Because it's a pretty serious situation you're in, ain't it?"

The girl tucked her hair behind her ear. "I mean, seriously, you're who they sent?"

Mish was confused. "They? As far as I know, Jesus is the only one who sent me."

The girl's eyes widened in obvious fear. "Oh, shit! I called the wrong kind of place!" She turned and clearly was about to run.

"Hold it right there, missy! What would your grandma say about you running out on an old lady after she agreed to meet you?"

The girl turned back to Mish with angry tears in her eyes. "I don't know. She's dead."

"Did she pass recently?" Mish patted the bench beside her. "Come sit down, hon, and tell me all about her."

The girl chewed her thumbnail and nodded, but she didn't sit down. *No, she ain't a doe,* Mish thought. *She's an unbroke colt who ain't yet learned who's safe.*

As she waited for a response, she wondered if she'd said the right thing. She didn't know what made her think of mentioning the girl's grandma—it just popped out. Maybe that's how it was when you're on a mission. The words just come to you. She tried again. "You was close, I can tell. She must've loved you something fierce." And that's when the dam broke. Before Mish knew it, the girl had sunk down on the bench beside her, crying fit to burst. And once she got talking, she couldn't seem to stop. Her grandmother had lived nearby, and they'd always been close. Her parents both worked, and her grandmother was the one who had met her off the school bus when she was younger. They'd spent lots of time together. Then about four months ago she up and died. Just like that, no warning, no nothing. The girl had gone to her house after school and found her body on the floor.

Mish was mostly quiet through it all, just responding with the right kind of sounds to help the girl know she was being heard. When the girl finally seemed to run out of steam, Mish decided it was her turn. "And now you're in trouble, and she's the only person you want to talk to," she began. "And you're mad at her for leaving you, even though you know it weren't her fault. And then you're mad at yourself for being mad at her because what kind of grandchild is mad at her own grandma for dying?" The girl didn't respond. "Am I right?" Mish pressed.

The girl shook her head and swallowed hard. "No. I don't want her to know at all, but people keep telling me she's, like, in heaven watching over me. If that's true, she already knows, and she must be so ashamed."

Mish stroked the girl's hand, just like she used to do for Livie. "She might be disappointed, but the kind of love you described? That's not the kind that gets ashamed. That's the kind that just hurts for you. She might be disappointed in what you done, but she still loves you. Take it from a grandma. I know." The girl nodded and blew her nose. "Listen, hon. I need to call you something other than 'hon.' What's your name?"

"Um…Ann."

Mish hadn't raised a rebellious son without knowing a lie when she heard one, but she knew better than to push it. "Okay, Um-Ann. I'm Mish. Now let's back up a second. I think I'm missing a few pieces to this here puzzle. I need to figure out what you are and are not willing to tell me, all right?" Ann nodded. "Can you tell me who the father is?" Ann shook her head. "Because you don't know or you won't say?"

"I won't say," Ann mumbled.

"All right then. Should I assume he will not be any help with raising this child?" Ann nodded. "Do you know how far along you are?"

"Seven weeks," she mumbled again.

"Are you sure?" Mish asked. "It can be hard to pinpoint these things."

"I'm sure," she said, and she sounded it.

Hmm. Mish had to think about that one. If the girl knew exactly when it happened, she must not have been making hay all over the place. Maybe it was a one-time thing, just one mistake. But that didn't mean she wasn't at risk for other troubles.

"What about DVDs?" Ann looked at her as if she had three heads and one of them was on fire. Was she really that naïve? "Come on, honey. DVDs. The herpes and the syphilis and stuff like that."

Ann started laughing. And she laughed and laughed until tears ran down her face. Mish's feelings were kind of hurt, but she figured the child probably hadn't laughed for a while so she let her get on with it. Finally, Ann choked out, "You mean STDs. Sexually transmitted diseases."

Mish caught onto the joke. "Yes, that's what I meant! Wait. What the heck are DVDs? I know I've heard of them."

"Movies," Ann explained. "They come on discs."

"Oh, right. The ones that replaced the BHS tapes! Now I remember. So when I asked—"

"I thought you were asking if I had a movie of...of...when I got pregnant!" Ann said, still wiping tears off her face.

"Oh, I hope not. You got enough of a souvenir!" Mish chuckled but stopped when she saw the smile fade from the child's face. She patted her hand again. "So about those STDs," she said kindly.

Ann shook her head. "I don't know. I just—don't know."

"We'll see about getting you tested." Mish didn't actually know what that meant, but she'd heard that phrase before, getting tested. She'd figure it out.

Ann nodded. "Listen, can I ask you a personal question?"

"It seems like we're getting pretty personal here, so I'd say so."

"Do they not train you before they send you out? I mean, no offense, seriously. You're really sweet and I like talking to you. But I thought they'd, like, make sure you knew about STDs before they sent you to meet with somebody."

Mish had to figure out how to respond. This was the second time the girl said *they* had sent her. As far as she knew, it was just Jesus who had sent her, but maybe the whole trinity was involved. She wasn't sure how that worked. So she did what she had learned long ago when she didn't know how to answer: answer with another question. "What do you think?"

"Well, I know there've been lots of government cuts. Maybe they can't afford training anymore?"

"Government cuts?" Mish blurted out. "Since when does the government have any say in what Jesus does?" As soon as she saw Ann's eyes widen, she knew she'd made a mistake. "I'm sorry, honey," she hurried on, realizing she better come clean. "I think maybe there's been some kind of misunderstanding." Then a thought occurred to her. "Where did you get my number?"

"From the women's resource center website. Why?" Suddenly she seemed to understand. "Shit, I must have written the number down wrong. I didn't want to look it up on my own phone because I didn't want it to show up on my browser history. So I looked it up at school, and it listed several numbers. I was impressed they had an option for texting, but I was in a hurry, so I must've made a mistake."

Mish didn't know what a browser history was, but she kept quiet.

"If you're not from the women's resource center, then who are you?" The girl's eyes widened even further. "Oh, wow. You're just a nice old lady who got my message and drove down here to help some kid she never met."

Mish didn't know how to explain why she was there. "Well, something like that, I guess. I'm really just trying to follow the love."

Ann started chewing her thumbnail again. "I don't know what that means."

"I don't either," Mish admitted. "All I know is it led me to you. And I'm glad. And I think your grandma would be glad too. If you don't mind me saying so."

Ann gave a watery smile. "I'm glad too. It makes me feel like I'm not completely alone."

"You're not," Mish said as she put her arm around the girl's shoulder. "So, Um-Ann, let's figure out what we're gonna do next."

They sat and talked for a long time, the autumn leaves swirling around their feet. The girl started opening up. Not about the pregnancy so much, but about the rest of her life. Ann was a really good student, but her grades had been slipping the last two months, and she was supposed to be applying for colleges. Then there were her friends. None of them knew.

"You haven't even told your best friend?" Mish asked. Ann shook her head. "But surely she knows about you and your boyfriend, that you're…" She couldn't seem to ask the question and she wasn't sure why. But Ann must've understood because she shook her head again.

Well, that was surprising. Mish thought most girls would've told their friends they were having sex, or even thinking of having sex. What would lead a girl not to tell nobody? If the relationship would be frowned upon, maybe. Like if the boy was a different race or religion. Or if he was too old for her. Or if… Suddenly a thought occurred to her and she blurted it out without thinking. "You wasn't raped, was you?"

Ann's eyes widened and her face went pale. "No! Nothing like that! It was just…it was just a mistake. That's all."

"Oh, good," Mish said with relief. "So…if you're seven weeks along, you'll be due when? April? May? You'll miss some school, of course, but you might still be able to finish the year if you talk to the guidance counselor, get some take-home work, stuff like that. I hear the schools are pretty good about helping girls who get in trouble. Not like in my day, when they married you off right away and then pretended you got pregnant on your honeymoon. Happened to a couple girls in my high school class. Our hospital had never seen so many seven-pound preemies! Don't know who they thought they was kidding. Of course, the girls always dropped out of school, but that's not the case nowadays. Does your school have a daycare? I know some schools do. Is it free?"

It took Mish a minute to realize that Ann had gone even quieter while she was talking. Suddenly she realized why. "You don't want this baby, do you?" she asked at last.

"Of course not!"

"But I mean—you don't want to give birth to this baby." Ann looked down at her feet as they scuffed the ground beneath the bench. She started to say something before finally just shaking her head again. "But you could give the baby up for adoption, let your child grow up in a good home. I'm sure there's a nice couple who would love to have a wee one, if you would just—"

"No!" Ann said, but when she spoke again her tone was softer. "I can't be pregnant. I can't do this. I want it out of my body so I can forget this ever happened." When Mish didn't respond, she went on. "Listen, I know you're probably against abortion. But this is my choice. And if you can't help me, I understand. But you're not going to change my mind. If you can't accept my decision, then…then…thanks anyway." She stood up and tossed her backpack over one shoulder. "It was nice to meet you."

Mish watched, torn, as the girl walked away. Ann was right—Mish didn't like the idea of abortion. But she also didn't believe in turning her back on a girl in trouble. What if it were her Livie? Wouldn't she want someone to walk beside the girl, help her through it? But what about Jesus? Would Jesus approve of her helping a girl get an abortion? She didn't know. But she did know one thing. She was supposed to follow the love. And right now, *the love* was turning the corner and moving out of sight.

If Juliann hadn't stopped at the crosswalk to wait for the light, she probably would have missed her. As it was, the old lady—what was her name?—had to call her twice before she answered, forgetting for a moment that she was just Ann. As she waited for the woman to catch up, she almost laughed at the scene. The little old lady was quite a sight, wearing that ugly flowered blouse and a cardigan sweater, shuffling along in her sensible shoes. But there was something about her—something that was trustworthy. Something that made Juliann smile.

She agreed to meet again in a few days, but only because the old woman—what *was* her name?—had promised not to try to change her mind. That's good because she would be seriously disappointed if she tried.

She refused the offer of a ride. Her grandma's car was just around the corner, though of course she didn't say that. She had her learner's permit but not her license and wasn't supposed to be driving alone.

She didn't know why she felt better. It's not like she had a solution. Nothing was different. *Except I'm not alone*, she thought. *I have a friend. A friend named—that's it!—Mish! I have a friend named Mish.*

5

Mish wished she had somebody to talk to. She wished she could talk to Pastor Jeff about Ann, but since he didn't believe in her mission, there was no point. But she sure would love to know what he would think about her helping a girl get an abortion. Of course, the girl might change her mind. But Mish wouldn't try to talk her out of it. That would just make Ann run away.

She wrote a poem about her feelings, like she always did when her thoughts were swirling. Floyd always told her she was wasting her time, that nobody needed poems about the kind of silly stuff that filled her mind. But it usually helped her so she kept doing it. She read over the one she'd written this morning.

> I call her Ann, but I know that's not her name.
> She was too afraid to tell me so I use it just the same.
> She's too young to be having a baby.
> Being young won't stop it from coming but maybe
> I can help her not feel so alone.
> I'll be her friend in person or on the phone.
> I don't like abortion and I don't know if God does either,
> but I can't speak for God. I'm not Jesus or Solomon, neither.
> She's having a child, but she's a child too,
> and if I can't help both, I have to choose between the two.
> So I'll choose the one who's already here
> because I followed the love and love conquers fear.

She felt better after the poem, felt like she knew what she needed to do. Still, she was in over her head. And she needed some answers before she met with Ann again. But who could she ask? Not her pastor. And not her family, that's for sure. One place immediately came to mind. It had been in the news a lot recently. Bomb threats, she thought it was. But she knew they would help. She got out her phone book and found the number for the women's clinic.

"I would like an appointment, please," she said to the woman who answered the phone.

"Of course. What kind of appointment do you need?"

Mish paused. "Well, I guess the kind where you do more talking than doctoring."

"You want a consultation," the receptionist replied.

"Yes, that sounds right."

"And what type of service would we be talking about? Pregnancy or birth control or—"

"It's a little late for birth control, I'm afraid. I want to talk about an unplanned pregnancy and what the options are."

"No problem. We had a cancellation. By any chance would you be able to come in at three today?"

"Yes, that'd be dandy." Mish gave the clerk her name and address.

"Thank you, and for our records, do you have insurance?"

"Yes, I have Medicare," Mish replied at once.

"You mean Medicaid."

"Isn't Medicaid what the poor folks need? No, I just have Medicare. And a supplement, of course." There was a long pause. "Is that a problem?" she asked at last.

"Um, no, I guess not," the clerk stammered. "It's just unusual, that's all. You're, um, sure about the pregnancy?"

"Yes, ma'am, it's a done deal."

"And this appointment is for you?"

"Of course."

"Okay, then we'll see you at three."

Mish studied the screen and then pushed the red button to end the call. She was a little nervous about the meeting—after all, she'd never done anything like this before. Never even been in such a place. And she didn't really like driving into the city by herself. But it was what she needed to do if she wanted to help Ann. Wait—maybe Ann would want to go with her. Yes, why hadn't she thought of that before? The girl probably had lots of questions too. They could get them answered together. But before she could text the girl, her phone rang.

"Hello, this is George Loveitt from Loveitt Insurance. Is this Marsha?"

"Mish," she corrected him automatically.

"My apologies," the smooth voice continued. "I couldn't quite read the writing on the card I received from one of my reps. I'm told you're interested in talking about life insurance."

"Life insurance?" she repeated blankly. "I'm confused."

"I know. Life insurance can be confusing. And at your age, it may seem premature. But it's never too early to plan for your future."

Mish chuckled. "Well, at my age, the future is gonna take care of itself whatever I do. Sure you don't want to sell me a burial plot instead?"

There was a long silence. "I guess it's my turn to be confused. Didn't you request a life insurance quote at the college fair?"

"College? No, you must be mistaken. I'm a bit old for college."

George cleared his throat. "Well, I was going to tell you about a special program we have for college students. But perhaps you'd be interested in a different kind of policy. Are you in good health?"

"Fit as a fiddle!" Mish said proudly. "But I think I'm doing fine in the insurance department."

"Really? How much life insurance do you have?" he asked.

"Well, um…" The truth was, Mish didn't know. Floyd always handled that stuff, but she was sure she had enough.

"If you don't know right off the top of your head how much coverage you have, then it's probably not enough. We here at Loveitt Insurance would be happy to offer you a quote on some term life insurance. We have many options for people at different stages of life, and our prices are quite competitive. If—"

"Wait—what did you say?" Mish interrupted.

"We have many options" he repeated.

"No, before that. What's the name of your company?"

"Loveitt Insurance. We're a family business, and we've been in the Charleston area for thirty years, helping fine people like you..."

He kept rattling on, but she stopped paying attention. Loveitt Insurance. Follow the love. Did this mean she was supposed to buy life insurance? She couldn't imagine why, but it seemed possible. The man had her number, after all. He had her name—well, sort of. People often confused her name because it was so unusual. But Loveitt—really, it had to be a sign. But how much life insurance did she need? How much would be enough?

"Twenty-five thousand," she concluded.

"Excuse me?"

"Twenty-five thousand," she repeated to the salesman. "I want to buy twenty-five thousand dollars' worth of life insurance, please."

"Oh! Well, okay then. When can you come into the office to complete the application?"

Mish agreed on a day and time, then hung up. Whew. This following the love thing sure was complicated.

Juliann didn't bother wiping the steam off the mirror after she got out of the shower. She didn't really want to see her body. She didn't want to see the changes that were already starting to happen. She could feel them, though. Her boobs were getting bigger, though she wasn't getting any fatter yet, fortunately. All the nausea and vomiting made sure of that. And damn, but she was tired all the time. Was that because she wasn't sleeping well?

She had to be careful—her mom had started to notice how tired she was. Her mom had even let her stay home from school today, thinking she might be coming down with something. If only she could stop the dreams. It was never the same dream. One minute something good would be happening, and then suddenly, the dream would take a dark turn. Or she lost something and couldn't find it. Or her entire school was under water and she had to swim to class. She wished she had somebody to talk to about them, but somehow, she didn't think Mish would be an expert on dream interpretation.

Come to think of it, she wasn't sure Mish was an expert on anything. She sure didn't know about STDs. Or abortion. Or teen pregnancy. Or anything else Juliann was dealing with. But Juliann had to hand it to the old woman—she was all in. She didn't walk away, not even when she found out that Juliann wanted an abortion. And she was clearly a church lady, since she kept talking about Jesus sending her. That was weird, but her grandma had been a church lady, too, so she tried not to freak out about it.

When she heard her phone buzz in the bedroom, she threw on her robe and rushed to get it. *Maybe it's him*, she thought, then chided herself. She had made it clear that she didn't want to hear from him again. It was probably just one of her friends, texting to see why she wasn't in school. But, no, it wasn't Hailey or Emma.

> Hi Ann it's Mish. I got an appointment at the clinic in Charleston at three so I can ask some questions. Want to go with me? I can pick you up.

Juliann's stomach churned, though for once it wasn't morning sickness. She knew she needed to go to the clinic, and the sooner the better, but she wasn't sure if she wanted Mish to go with her. Eventually Mish would want to know the circumstances around her pregnancy, and that was not a story she wanted to tell. It was too humiliating. The national website for the women's center said they wouldn't make a woman say how she got pregnant. But was that true? And what if Mish pushed?

On the other hand, she wondered if Mish might be the solution to her problem. Or one of her problems, anyway. She had dismissed the idea because it just wasn't right, using the kind old lady, taking advantage of her that way. But if Mish was offering to go, how could she refuse? She was running out of options.

She texted back with a place and time to meet.

Juliann had wondered about what she and the old lady would talk about for the thirty-minute drive, but she needn't have worried. Mish kept up a running conversation all by herself. She talked about her granddaughter, a freshman in college in Florida, and about her son who was some kind of businessman, and about living on a farm her whole life. It was helpful, really, not having to make conversation, and Mish didn't seem to mind that she was quiet. Juliann got the feeling that Mish didn't have that many people to talk to so she tried not to let her mind wander. Listening was the least she could do in return for Mish's help.

"My husband has been gone for almost a year now," she was saying. "It's strange, being in the house alone all the time. It's so quiet. He always had the TV on, even if he wasn't in the room. I hated the constant noise, but now sometimes I turn it on, too, just so the house ain't so quiet. The hardest part is there's nobody to listen to my silly stories. Stories need ears to be worth the telling. You know what I mean?"

"I do," Juliann admitted. "That's what my grandmother did for me. She always asked about my day, what I learned, who I sat with at lunch. Sometimes we made up stories together. She would start it, like, 'Once upon a time there was a hippo named …' and I would fill in the blanks. When I got too old for that, she encouraged my creative writing."

"What kind of things do you write? More stories?"

"Sometimes. Mostly I write poetry."

"Really? I write poetry too! Maybe we should trade poems."

Juliann hesitated. "I don't know if you would like mine. I mean, it's a special style that is meant to be performed, not read."

"Like slam poetry? Or spoken word?" Mish asked.

"Wait…you know slam poetry?" She couldn't keep the shock out of her voice.

Mish laughed. "I love surprising people by knowing stuff they don't think I'd know. Yes, I know slam poetry, though I've never tried none of it. I saw a little on one of the daytime shows. I don't have a chance to hear that much of it and don't know how to do it. Mine is more typical old lady stuff, I'm afraid. Rhyming verses like on a greeting card. My husband always said my poems were stupid and worthless and nobody would want to read them." She said this nonchalantly, as if it were a fact and not an opinion. Juliann was starting to dislike Mish's dead husband. "And my grandma always said that only a mundane mind would call art worthless."

Mish was silent for a few seconds, and Juliann was afraid she had gone too far. Then Mish laughed. "Oh, Ann, I wish I'd met you sooner. Or your grandmother. Because I would have loved to see Floyd's face if I'd said *that* in response!" Her smile slipped a little. "Of course, I would have paid for it, but it would've been worth it."

"Paid for it? How—"

"Oh, damn. I'm sorry, hon."

"For what?" Juliann hadn't been paying attention, hadn't realized how close they were to the women's center, but they had arrived at the gate, where half a dozen protestors stood. She should have prepared herself for this, she realized. The protests were on the news enough, plus someone in her social studies class had done a report on abortion last year. So she had seen the signs. She should have been prepared. But she wasn't.

Choose Life. Abortion is Murder. Babies are murdered here. The words were bad enough, but then came the images. A bloody fetus. Tiny arms and legs. Juliann buried her face in her hands.

"You can't hide from the truth!" a woman yelled as they passed. "Abortion is murder!"

And then the yelling came from beside her. "I'm here to get a mammogram," Mish called as she lowered the window. "So, unless you're interested in my floppy old teats, back off!"

Juliann was still laughing when they walked in the building.

❧

Oh, but it was good to see the girl laugh. Mish had gotten worried there for a second, what with those horrible posters and all. And then she just got mad. Those people had no right to judge another person, when they weren't in the other person's shoes. Damn fundamentalists need to mind their own business. So she just blurted out the first thing that came to her mind. She knew she shouldn't have said it—Opal was always telling her that her mouth would get her into trouble. But it made Ann laugh, so it was worth it.

They entered the waiting room, and as soon as the door closed behind them a quiet calm came over Mish. The place was simple but peaceful. Nice music was playing, and the furniture was basic but clean and well cared for. Ann sat down in one of the gray chairs along the wall while Mish walked up to the counter and spoke to the young girl behind the glass window. "I have a three o'clock appointment."

"Write your name on the clipboard," she said without looking up.

Mish wrote her name, but her hand was shaking, and she wasn't sure anybody could read it. "In case you can't read my chicken scratches, it's Mish Atkinson."

The girl's head jerked up and she looked at Mish all peculiar-like.

"It's short for Artemisia," she explained. "That's a plant."

"Yes, ma'am, of course. Please fill out this paperwork. Someone will call for you shortly."

Mish took her seat and then glanced back up at the desk. The young clerk was talking to some other ladies behind the counter, and they were all looking at her. Were they all that interested in her name? Odd.

Before she even got done filling out the papers, a side door opened and a nurse called her name.

"Come on, hon," Mish said as she stretched a hand to Ann. Ann took a deep breath, then accepted her hand. They followed the nurse into an exam room.

"I'm Jennifer," the woman said as they got settled in the two chairs across from her. "And I know that you're Mish."

"Yes, indeed. And this here is—" She turned to Ann. She didn't even know Ann's full name.

"I'm Ann," she said quickly. "I'm her granddaughter."

Mish felt her heart skip a beat. If that didn't beat all! For the girl to be claiming her after so short a time, and after her own grandma meant so much to her? Why, it was one of the biggest compliments she'd ever gotten. She grinned and put her arm around the back of the girl's chair. "That's right," she said with pride.

The nurse smiled. "Well, Ann, I think you have just solved a mystery that has had our office staff in an uproar all day. It started with your phone call, Mish."

"Me? How did I cause an uproar?"

"Well, look at it from our point of view. You called asking for a consultation to talk about an unplanned pregnancy. That's a pretty common thing around here, but not for someone old enough to be on Medicare."

Suddenly she cottoned on. "They thought I was the one who was pregnant? No wonder they was looking at me funny in the waiting room! I bet they was about to call the Guinness World Record folks!"

Ann and the nurse both laughed. "I don't know what the record is, but you did have the place buzzing. You see, usually the appointments are made in the name of the person who is pregnant. Ann, am I correct in assuming that's you?"

Ann tucked her hair behind her ear and nodded.

"Then we'll need to get you to fill out your own paperwork. I'll be right back."

"Wait. Do I…do I have to? Already? I mean, I don't have my insurance card or anything." She paused and nobody spoke, then she ducked her head again. "My parents don't know I'm here."

"I understand," the nurse assured her. "But there are procedures that we have to follow by law. I promise your parents will not be notified at this point."

"At this point?" Ann repeated. "I really don't want them to know. I was hoping I could—you know—get this taken care of without involving them."

"The West Virginia law is pretty strict. You have three options. The easiest way is to get a parent or guardian to give consent for you to have an abortion." Ann started shaking her head. "I know there's nothing easy about telling your parents that you're pregnant," the nurse continued. "But it is the simplest, fastest way. If you were to tell your parents, how do you think they would respond?"

"They'd totally freak," Ann said quickly. She started to say more but then stopped herself. Mish saw a muscle twitch in her jaw.

"Would you be in danger?" the nurse pressed.

Ann shrugged. "Define danger." When nobody did, she took a deep breath and tried again. "My father is a violent man. There would be hell to pay. Telling my parents is not an option."

Mish's heart hurt to hear the news. She knew how it felt to be afraid in your own home, and she hated that this poor child had experienced that too.

The nurse looked at Mish, then back at Ann. "I understand."

Ann's face hardened. "No, you don't," she countered. "Please don't pretend you understand what I'm going through!"

Mish looked closely at the nurse to see if she was mad. But she must be used to this kind of thing. "You're right," she said. "I don't understand what you're going through. I just meant I understood what you were saying. I'm sorry."

Ann's shoulders slumped and her anger seemed to drain away. "No, I'm sorry. It's not your fault. I'm just…"

Her words trailed off, and she looked back at the floor. She seemed to be having a hard time getting her words out. "What about…what about another relative?"

"Another relative?" the nurse echoed.

"I read that in some states, another relative can give permission." She hesitated again. "Like a…like a grandparent."

It took Mish a minute to realize what Ann was saying. That's why she had claimed Mish as her grandma—so that Mish could sign for an abortion. It stung a bit, to realize the girl was willing to use her that way. *This ain't about you, Mish,* she reminded herself. *This is about a desperate girl. So don't get your bloomers in a knot.*

The nurse smiled sadly. "I'm sorry, but in our state, it has to be a parent or legal guardian. And where a grandparent is permitted, usually you have to be living with them. But you do have other options. You could get a judicial waiver—that means you see a lawyer and a judge to get permission."

Ann shook her head. "No. My dad's an attorney. What's the third option?"

"He wouldn't know," the nurse countered. "It's very confidential, and—"

"No." Ann's eyes never left the stained tile floor. "What's the other option?"

"Your primary care physician can sign off that you are mature enough to make this decision on your own. Do you have a family doctor who could speak to your maturity?"

Ann sighed. "I still see a pediatrician. How pathetic is that?"

"Actually, it's not uncommon for girls your age," the nurse said. "What are you, sixteen?" Ann nodded. "And do you know how far along you are?"

"Seven weeks."

"Are you sure? It can be hard to know—"

"She's sure," Mish interjected. The nurse raised an eyebrow at her. "I already asked," she explained.

The nurse nodded. "Do you think your pediatrician would help? Do you feel comfortable talking with him or her?"

Ann sighed again. "She plays golf with my mom."

"Well, if that ain't the baddest luck I heard in a long time," Mish said.

The nurse tried again. "Doctors are bound by confidentiality. Legally, she could not tell your parents if you asked her not to."

"Yeah, well, legality doesn't mean shit apparently." She looked up and saw the looks on their faces, then continued. "Last time I was there, the doctor asked my mom to leave the room so we could have the confidential talk. You know, they all do that now." The nurse nodded. "I asked her what it would take to get a birth control prescription. I didn't want one—I just wanted to know how to get one. You know, when the time came, when I was ready. I thought she was cool. But then my mom came back in, and as we were leaving the doctor said, 'Give me a call about that prescription.' Obviously, my mom knew what she meant. Then I got a big fat lecture. So, no, my doctor is not trustworthy."

"I'm sorry you had that experience," the nurse said. "I can see why you don't want to go that route."

"What about outside of West Virginia?" Ann asked. "I looked it up, and it looks like all the nearby states are just as bad. Are there any states that don't require parental consent?"

"States? Not nearby. But Washington, DC, might be an option. I'm not an expert—you'd have to check with a clinic there to see what the requirements are, and that's pretty far away."

Ann, who had started typing into her phone as soon as the nurse said DC, let out a whoop. "Yes! You're right. But let me check how far that is." Her thumbs flew back and forth, then she swore. "Damn, it's a twelve-hour bus ride. Each way."

"What about by car?" Mish asked.

She typed some more. "It's five and a half hours, but I don't have my license, and—"

"I wasn't talking about you, silly girl."

"But I don't—"

"I didn't kill you getting you here, now did I?"

Ann looked at her, stunned. "You mean, you'd drive me all the way to DC? To get an abortion?"

"Well, of course I will. I'm following the love, remember?"

Ann shook her head. "I still don't know what that means. Besides, I couldn't ask you to do that."

"You didn't ask. I offered. And this is your best option. So be smart and take it."

Ann chewed on her thumbnail for a few seconds while she stared at Mish. She finally seemed to reach a decision. "If you're really sure, then, yes, I accept."

Mish looked back at the nurse, who just shrugged and said they were welcome to call back if they needed anything.

Mish picked up her purse and put her arm through the girl's as they left the office. "It's just you and me, kid. Two West Virginia gals on a road trip. Why, we're gonna be like Thelma and Louise!"

"My mom loves that movie. They don't take shit from anybody. But can we try for a better ending?"

"Good point," Mish said with a nod. "I'm pretty sure that 'follow the love' does not mean drive off a cliff."

As soon as she said it, she wondered if she was doing that very thing.

6

Jeff leaned back in his office chair and stared at the ceiling. He was supposed to be starting his sermon, but he wasn't feeling inspired. He had preached on this Bible passage before, and he just didn't have anything new to say about it. These days it didn't feel like he had anything new to say about anything. Week after week he scoured the commentaries, hoping for something brilliant he could use as a jumping off point for a sermon, because he certainly wasn't coming up with anything good on his own. Everything felt stale. He could hear his father repeating the advice he always gave to young clergy. "If you don't take care of your own spiritual oxygen mask first, you'll never be able to help others with theirs." *Yeah, well, that sounds good in theory, Dad, but what happens when you lose your oxygen mask?*

And then there was this Mish situation, which he couldn't stop thinking about. He knew it wasn't healthy, knew he shouldn't worry about his parishioners this much. But Mish was special. She was just so endearing. He knew that since her husband died, he had become a little too paternalistic toward her, but he just felt himself wanting to protect her.

And now he needed to protect her from some random woman who had convinced Mish that she was Jesus. How can she be so gullible?

No, that wasn't fair. She wasn't gullible, and she wasn't dumb. She had a certain innocence about her, but it was more from being an eternal optimist than from lack of intelligence. She saw the good in people, even when nobody else did. He wouldn't want her in charge of the church's benevolence fund—he had a feeling she would give it all away to the first person who needed it. But because she was so generous, he would certainly want her voice on the committee.

So who was this woman claiming to be Jesus? As far as Jeff

could tell, Mish met the woman at the diner, and shortly after that she encountered this Ethan character. How did that happen? Were the two connected? Was the woman passing Mish's number along to others in her—what? Scam circle? He shook his head and reminded himself that he wasn't going to solve that mystery today, and he had plenty else to worry about.

He scrolled through Facebook—his favorite form of procrastination—but these days his entire feed was filled with political diatribes and talk of collusion with Russia. Nothing much inspirational to be found there. He opened his email and knew instantly he had made a mistake. All down the screen, subject line RE: INCLUSIVE POTLUCKS. With the use of all caps, there was no way this could be good.

Jeff scrolled down to find the first of the thread. It was sent to the whole church email list.

Dear friends,

It has come to my attention that some of our members are not feeling particularly welcome at our monthly all-church potluck dinners. We have an increasing number of vegetarians among us, and it would be so kind if more people would consider bringing vegetarian dishes. Last month there was only one vegetarian entrée, and it was gone before many of us reached the table.

Since a vegetarian lifestyle is a super-positive thing we can do for the environment, I believe that we as a church can do a better job of supporting those who make this commitment. We would prefer that the potlucks be entirely vegetarian so that we didn't have to see the evidence of cruelty at all, and I think we're being very gracious by not demanding vegetarian potlucks. So please think of other people's needs. Or better yet, give up meat and join our healthy lifestyle!

Thank you for anything you can do to help all our members feel welcome at the table.

Yours in Christ's inclusive love,
Sammi

Oh, great. A passive-aggressive email couched in social justice language, wrapped up in Southern hospitality, and tied with a Jesus bow! No wonder his inbox was full. He clicked the arrow to read the next one. It was from Valerie. Jeff's shoulders lowered a bit. Valerie was both level-headed and kind. Her response would be good.

> Dear Sammi,
>
> Thanks so much for bringing this to our attention. Of course we want everyone to feel welcome. I think most people simply provide the kind of food their family prefers. I wonder why this isn't coming out evenly for our vegetarian families. I'll try to be more careful about my selections.
>
> Thanks again,
> Valerie

Good answer, Jeff thought. *So why do I still have seventeen unopened emails?*

> Sammi,
> I personally brought both a green salad and a marshmallow Jello salad last month, and I had leftovers of both. I don't see the problem.
> Carol

Jeff closed his eyes. He took a deep breath, then slowly let it out. Focus on the breath, like he had learned in yoga and meditation. Focus on the breath, he told himself.

It's difficult to focus on the breath when you know the shit is about to hit the fan.

> Dear Carol,
> Thank you for your response. I appreciate your generosity in providing two options at last month's potluck. I'm sure many people enjoyed your iceberg lettuce and radish salad. But I was speaking about entrées. There was an abundance of meat entrées, but for those of us who don't eat animal flesh, only the eggplant parmigiana was a good option, and it went very quickly. I would hate for us to have to put "Vegetarians Only" signs on the food we can eat.

And for the record, vegetarians don't eat gelatin. It is made from boiled animal bones and hooves. I couldn't bear the thought of eating God's creatures!

Peace,
Sammi

Jeff clicked through the emails quickly to get the gist of each one, so he could hurry to assess the damage.

—Why don't they just bring their own entrées?

—Vegetarians shouldn't have to bring entrées every time just so they have something to eat.

—We're cattle farmers. Beef: it's what's for dinner.

—Since the vegetarians tend to be younger, I would think you'd want to do anything to welcome us.

—I'm a vegetarian, too, and I'm very happy with our potlucks.

—Does our church library have vegetarian cookbooks? I wouldn't know where to begin.

Jeff buried his head in his hands. He considered himself a nonviolent man, but he was seriously ready to strangle the person who set up the all-church email list.

"Pastor Jeff?"

Jeff dropped his hands and smiled automatically toward the door. His smile changed to a genuine one when he saw who it was.

"Carl! Come on in!"

Carl ran a hand through his thick gray hair, then rubbed the back of his neck. "Are you sure? I hate to bother you if you're in the middle of prayer or something."

"No, please!" Jeff insisted. He quickly moved around his desk to shake Carl's hand, then motioned for him to have a seat. Jeff took the chair across from him. "It's nice to see you. I missed you last Sunday."

He gave a weak smile. "Thanks. I missed being here."

Carl looked back down and began picking at a loose thread in the side seam of his khakis. *Uh-oh*, Jeff thought. *What have I done now?* Carl was a strong leader—one of Jeff's favorites, if he was being honest—and was widely respected in the congregation. He heard things that Jeff wouldn't hear, and he reported them—not with that destructive "people are saying" gossip thing some people do, but in a helpful way so that Jeff could fix problems before they grew. Carl undoubtedly kept the less helpful criticism to himself.

Usually Carl was pretty direct. If he was this uncomfortable saying what was on his mind, it must be bad news. Was it last week's sermon? He'd been so careful about being non-partisan; could somebody really be upset about his call to feed the hungry? That's a pretty biblical concept, after all, and if anybody was going to give him a hard time about that, well then, he might as well...

"The cancer's back."

The words were so startling, Jeff couldn't do anything but echo what he heard. "The cancer's...back?"

Carl nodded. "I had it about ten years ago, long before you came. The doctors told me it might come back, and they were right."

Jeff leaned back in his chair, feeling stunned. "When—" he cleared his throat. "When did you find out?"

"Friday. I needed a few days to adjust to the news before telling you. But you'll need to find somebody else to lead the budget process this year."

"Of course," Jeff said. "You don't need to worry about church responsibilities. You focus on your treatment and save your energy for beating this thing."

Carl's gaze returned to his lap before he responded. "The doctor wants me to do chemo again—a pretty heavy dose to get aggressive with it. But..." His voice trailed off.

"But?" Jeff said. "What is it, Carl?"

Carl finally looked up, and there were tears in his eyes. "I'm not going to do it, Pastor. I'm done."

"Are you sure? I mean, you're only—what? Seventy-five? Seventy-six?" Surely there were options. Surely Carl had more time. "Carl, don't rush into this decision. You could still have some good years left."

"No, I couldn't," Carl insisted. "They wouldn't be good. I've been down this road before. The doctors told me years ago that if it came back, I wouldn't beat it. If I said yes to their plan now, I'd go through months of being sick from the chemo, only to gain a few more months of being sick with the cancer."

"There's no hope of remission? Or more good quality time?"

"There's a twenty-percent chance. I'm not going through hell for twenty percent. Last time was different. Last time my Joy was by my side. She got me through it. She gave me a reason to get through it. But since she died, I've got no reason."

"No reason to live, you mean?" Jeff asked gently.

"No reason to suffer," Carl corrected.

Jeff took a deep breath. "I understand," he said, trying to smile. "What do you need from me?"

Carl looked him hard in the eye. "I need your blessing. I need to know you don't think poorly of me for my choice."

Jeff swallowed hard against the knot in his throat. To think that this man, so many years his senior, needed his blessing to die, touched him more than he could say. "Carl, you are one of the finest men I know. I could never think less of you for choosing not to suffer needlessly."

Carl gave one affirmative nod, his chin set. "Thank you, Pastor. That's all I needed to hear."

When Carl left his office, Jeff slumped back in his chair. *Not Carl,* he thought. *Please not Carl. Not now.* Carl was more than just a strong leader. Carl had been the chair of the pastoral search committee that had brought him to the church. More importantly, Carl had had Jeff's back since the day he came—probably before, given the power plays that often occur between pastoral leaders. With Carl gone, he would feel less stable. He would feel… What Jeff felt was a knot in the pit of his stomach. Losing Carl would make him feel vulnerable. And Jeff didn't like feeling vulnerable.

Twenty minutes passed, and Jeff finally gave up on his sermon. It was not going to get written today. His heart wasn't in it. He closed the laptop screen with a little too much force and packed up to leave. He needed to get out of his office, out of this building.

The drive from the parsonage to home was five-hundred

yards. It was silly to drive to church when he lived so close, but his most recent predecessor had done it. Jeff wanted people to feel free to drop by if they wanted to talk so he had continued the tradition. Besides, if Jeff's car wasn't in the church parking lot, people assumed he wasn't there. Of course, this also meant that if he left his car in the garage and walked to church, there would be fewer interruptions.

As Jeff got out of the car, the door into the house swung open, and Stephen's head appeared in the gap. "You can't come in here!" Stephen announced breathlessly.

"Stephen, please. I'm tired. I've had a horrible day. And I just want to—"

"You just want to put your feet up and relax. I know. But you'll have to relax on the deck."

"Why can't I come into my own house? Whatever you're doing, honestly, I don't care. I just want to get a drink and—"

"I know," Stephen said. "I will bring you a drink. Just go sit on the deck and I'll be right there with a glass of wine."

"Have you seen the all-church email today?" He heard the tension in his own voice.

"Good point," Stephen acknowledged. "I'll be right there with a glass of scotch. Now go! Sit! Relax!"

Jeff gave a strained smile in return. "You really are cute when you're bossy. Fine, I'll go. Sit. Relax. Happy now?"

Stephen grinned. "Not yet, but I will be!" And with that, he was gone.

Jeff shook his head as he turned and ambled out to the deck. He had no idea what Stephen was up to, but he had learned not to fight it. Loving a drama guy meant lots of surprises, most of them good.

True to his word, Stephen returned within minutes, handed him a glass, and bowed. "A fine glass of scotch for you, sir."

Jeff frowned. "Since when do we have fine scotch?"

"Oh, we don't. This is the same swill we've had for months. But it is a fine glass, don't you agree?"

"Finest lead crystal that Target sells," he replied, then patted the chair next to him. "Sit with me a while?"

"And deny the introvert his quiet time before dinner? Not on your life. I like you much better after you've been alone. Besides, I'm needed inside." After a quick peck on Jeff's forehead, he was gone again.

Stephen was right. Jeff was much easier to live with when he got the downtime he needed. So he tried to relax, to decompress from his stressful day. But his thoughts were swirling. The damn email battle. Carl's horrible news. And then there was the self-recrimination to contend with.

Carl had come to him in pain, and what had been Jeff's immediate reaction? To focus on himself. He didn't even recognize Carl's pain for what it was at first, too busy assuming that he himself was the topic of conversation. Even after he heard the news, his thoughts were all about his own feelings, not his parishioner's. How self-centered could he be? And had he done an adequate job of hiding the fact that he had made someone else's cancer about himself?

How do other pastors do this job? It wasn't the first time he'd had the thought. They make it look so easy, even effortless. His father, for example, was the hardest working man Jeff ever met. Sixty hours a week was standard for him, even with a family, and he never seemed to run dry. He was always the consummate pastor, the perfectionist in the pulpit, the tireless visionary. The great Reverend Cooper. *As opposed to the lesser Reverend Cooper*, as Jeff thought of himself. It was just one of the reasons he went by Pastor Jeff instead of Reverend Cooper.

But the last time Jeff had visited his parents, he thought his dad was finally showing the strain. His father had been a minister for forty-five years, so it was understandable. Jeff had only been doing it for seven, and he wasn't sure he'd make ten.

His thoughts continued down this avenue for a while, and he didn't realize he had drifted off until he awoke to a gentle touch on his arm. "Come, for all things are now ready," Stephen said gently.

Jeff smiled at Stephen's use of the phrase from the communion liturgy. "Are you offering me the bread of life?"

"I didn't have time to make bread," Stephen said over his

shoulder. "Instead I present to you—" He opened the door with a flourish. "An inclusive potluck!"

Jeff stared at their kitchen table, literally covered with dishes of food, then listened for the sounds of a crowd in the other room. "Please tell me you didn't invite people over for a potluck dinner tonight."

"No, of course not! It's an inclusive dinner," Stephen repeated. Jeff stared, still not understanding. "It is inclusive of all your favorite comfort foods," Stephen explained. "See? Meatloaf. But tonight it's called—" He moved his hand like he was envisioning the name on a marquee. "The Meatloaf of Mercy!"

Jeff stifled a grin. "The Meatloaf of Mercy," he repeated.

"That's right. And here are your favorite scalloped potatoes."

"And they're called—?"

"Pentecostal Potatoes. They're so good they'll have you speaking in tongues. And here's your mom's recipe for frozen fruit salad. Only now it's called God's Frozen Chosen Fruit Salad."

"I believe God's Frozen Chosen are the Presbyterians, not the Congregationalists," Jeff corrected dryly.

Stephen nudged him in the ribs. "Hush. You're messing up my presentation."

"Oh, my apologies. Please continue. I can't wait to hear what you're calling the cheese tray."

Stephen waved a dismissive hand. "Oh, that's just Jesus Cheeses."

It was too much. Jeff started laughing, then pulled Stephen into his arms. "What did I ever do to deserve you?"

Stephen smiled broadly, then began to sing in his sweet tenor voice. "Somewhere in your youth—"

"Don't," Jeff warned with a smile.

"Or childhood," he continued.

Jeff put a finger to Stephen's lips, knowing it wouldn't work.

"You must have done…" Stephen paused, looking at him expectantly.

Jeff finally gave in. "Something good."

Their last note was in perfect harmony. As always.

7

Mish was glad for a quiet morning. All this following the love business had made her behind on her chores. Another person had texted her—Emma— thanking her for the chat and offer of help. She knew she hadn't met the girl, but no need to tell her that. Better just to help where she could, which in this case apparently meant helping the girl pick out new shoes. She also met with the insurance man and learned that insurance at her age cost more than her life was worth. So she must've been wrong about that part of the "follow the love" project. *Ah, well, it did inspire me to have some extra cash on hand. Just in case.* She'd gotten her banking done and was now trying to catch up on her housework. Even without Floyd to nag her, she still liked keeping a neat house. Liked it more, actually, now that she wasn't being graded.

"That's one of the few things that improved with your age," she said to the plaid chair as she walked by. "Your bad eyesight made my housekeeping much easier."

She walked into the entryway and dropped her box next to the fountain. She loved the fountain and never got tired of decorating it for the seasons. She had picked it out herself. It started at the top with water coming from a fish's mouth, then the water bounced to two more levels below that. It was her one splurge in the house she secretly called Floyd's Folly. When he had insisted on building this house, she thought he was crazy. What did they need with three big bedrooms and two and a half baths? Not to mention the formal living room they never sat in, the billiards room she used only for extra closet space, and the fancy appliances she didn't need. What in the world did she need with a trash compactor? It did turn out to be a great place to store the potato chips, but beyond that, it was useless. But there was no sense in trying to change Floyd's mind once it was made up. He had wanted to show all the professional upstarts in the valley that an old farmer could make good, even without an education.

It wasn't a fancy house—not by the new standards in the valley. People built all those—oh, what did Opal call them? McMansions, that was it. Their house was no McMansion. It was just a big ranch with pillars on the porch, but it sat on a hill above the pasture they still owned. Mish would've been happy staying in the farmhouse they'd raised their son in, but Floyd had insisted on the bigger house. So Mish had insisted on the fountain. She'd always loved the sound of running water, like the creek behind her house growing up. Besides, she'd heard that nice houses often have a water feature.

She also thought that nice houses should have a dog. It just completed the picture—the house on the hill, the pasture below, and a dog on the hearth. The idea was definitely growing on her. She wished she knew more about dogs, so she'd know what kind to get. She'd always liked those Lassie dogs, but somehow that didn't feel right. She wanted a snuggler, maybe a little white dog that nobody would mistake for a working dog.

She gathered up the plastic daisies, sunflowers, and daylilies from around the edges of the fountain and put them in the box at her feet. She was just finishing putting the autumn leaves in their place when her phone buzzed in her pocket. She carried it with her all the time now, just like the teenagers.

> I got an appointment in DC for early Monday afternoon. We'd have to leave pretty early in the morning but we'd be back by bedtime. Will that work?

Mish's heart sank. There and back in one day? That was eleven or twelve hours on the road, and she didn't think her old body would put up with riding in a car that long. *Driving* a car, she corrected herself. That was even harder. But how could she tell the girl? She couldn't let her down, not after they'd come so far. Maybe they could drive up the day before. That could work.

> Guess you've changed your mind, ok, no worries.

Mish was horrified. Her delay had sent the wrong message. *No!* she immediately texted back. *I was just thinking.* She pushed Send and then kept typing. *And I'm not very fast on this thing. Can we just talk?*

Five seconds later the phone rang.

"Sorry about that. I forget you don't text all the time like I do."

"No, I'm the one who's sorry," Mish said quickly. "I was just thinking and forgot how that would feel on your end. The thing is…" Her voice trailed off.

"If you've changed your mind, I'll understand."

"Have you changed your mind?" Mish asked.

"No."

"Then I haven't either," Mish assured her. "It's just that—well—I'm old!"

Ann laughed. "And that's relevant how?"

Mish let out a sigh, somehow embarrassed to admit her limitations. "I can't drive twelve hours in one day."

"Oh."

Mish waited for more, but nothing else came. She took a deep breath. "So I was thinking—could we maybe drive up on Sunday? Break the trip into two days? I'll pay for the hotel. Don't worry about that part. But with my arthritis, I think one day is just too much. Whaddya think?"

"Hmm. Since that's a Sunday, that could work. I just need to text a friend and see if she'll cover for me. Hold on."

"You can do that? Text somebody while you're using the phone? I know how to use the phone, and I know how to use the text machine, but I thought you had to hang up the phone to get to the text machine. How does it know which one you want to do? I guess these smartphones are smarter than me."

"Okay, that'll work."

"What'll work?"

"Leaving on Sunday. My friend will cover for me."

"You already texted her? That's amazing! You're gonna have to show me these tricks of yours."

Ann chuckled. "We'll have plenty of time in the car and the hotel. You'll be an expert by the time we get back."

They chatted for a few more minutes about the details. Ann was taking care of everything at the clinic, so Mish didn't have to worry about that part. "I'll find us a hotel too," she said. "But I don't have a credit card. Can I give you the phone number and you make the reservation? I'll pay you back, I swear."

"You will not," Mish shot back. "I told you on the way home from the clinic that I'd pay for this thing, and I will."

"But the...the procedure...is really expensive," Ann argued. "I don't want you paying for that and the hotel too. I have a savings account, and I think I can take some without my parents noticing."

"It's my fault we need a hotel. Besides, I want to stay someplace decent. I don't go away that often and when I do, I don't want to worry about bringing home souvenirs of the bed bug variety. So find me one of them hotels that comes with free breakfast. And make sure there's a waffle maker. I like me a waffle in the morning."

"Yes, ma'am," Ann said. Mish heard the smile in her voice, and it made her heart glad.

After getting Ann's assurance that she didn't need to go to AAA and get maps, Mish hung up the phone. She returned her box of flowers to the garage, then plopped down on the sofa. She was trying to figure out how she felt, and she couldn't quite put her finger on it. She was a little excited about the trip—going out of town and staying in a hotel was still a bit of a treat, even at her age. But she also was sad. Sad for Ann, that she was in such a difficult spot. Sad that a girl so young had such heavy burdens. Sad about her home life.

But that wasn't all. What was that other nagging feeling? Guilt? Maybe a little. She still wasn't sure about this whole abortion issue, and she felt like she was getting in deeper with every step. But it wasn't her choice, and she just knew she was doing the right thing to support Ann. If she had to stand in for the girl's family, she would do it, even across state lines.

Wait. *Across state lines.* That phrase triggered something in the back of her mind. Taking a minor across state lines. Was that illegal? If so, would she be breaking the law to take the girl without her parents' permission? That was a mighty big risk to take.

Ah, well, in for a penny, in for a dollar, as they say. What they gonna do? Throw me in jail? She laughed at the very thought of what the church ladies would say about that.

Her only worry was that something might happen to her while they were gone. She was in good health—no real reason to be concerned—but if something did happen, or they had an accident, there'd be nobody to explain. She didn't want the girl to get in trouble. She'd leave a note, that's what she'd do. Just in case.

∝

"Do you have a title yet, Pastor Jeff? I'm ready to print the programs."

Jeff looked up from his computer to see the secretary standing at his door. "Bulletins," he automatically corrected. Rachel had worked for the school system before coming to work for the church, and she still thought of the Sunday bulletin like a school concert program.

She cocked her head to the side as she looked at him. "Right, bulletins. Order of worship. Whatever you want to call them. But the people in the cheap seats call them programs. You know that, right?"

He chuckled. "Yeah, I know."

"So, do you?"

"Do I what?"

She rolled her eyes. "Do you have a sermon title? I know you don't like for me to print them without your sermon title."

Actually, Jeff didn't care a bit about having a sermon title, but Ruth always got mad if he didn't have one. She'd come down the aisle pushing her walker with one hand and shaking her finger at him with the other. She considered it a sign that he wasn't doing adequate sermon preparation.

He'd been working with this week's scripture all morning, but he still couldn't figure out what to do with it. He usually preached from the lectionary—the three-year cycle of Bible readings used in many Protestant churches—because it was easier than trying to figure out what to preach on each week. But this week the Old Testament reading was a snippet of a longer story that didn't make sense out of context, and the Thessalonians passage featured the Apostle Paul being a bit melodramatic. That left the Gospel reading, but it was one he found rather annoying and irrelevant, an argument in semantics.

He sighed. "How much time can you give me?"

Rachel looked at her watch. "I have to start printing them in fifteen minutes, whether inspiration has struck or not."

Jeff agreed and clicked on the link for an article that sounded promising. He was wrong. He X-ed out of it and was looking for another when his phone buzzed with a text message. One glance told him it was from his mother.

Please call when you can.

Jeff waited. Usually she followed such requests with two words: nothing urgent. She'd spent enough years as a pastor's wife to know that he couldn't always call back right away. But this time the words didn't come.

Is it urgent? he asked.

There was a pause. Then came:

Not urgent but important.

She answered on the first ring. He could tell immediately that she was in her car. "Hi, son. Thanks for calling me back."

He got an ominous feeling at the word "son." She only called him that when she felt he needed to be reminded of his role. He tried to release the tense muscles in his shoulders as he answered. "Sure, Mom. What's up?"

There was a slight hesitation. "I thought you should know I'm going to stay with your sister for a while."

"Is she okay?" Jeff knew his mom sometimes helped out with her grandchildren. The three young boys were a handful, and with Jessie's husband frequently away on business, Jessie sometimes got overwhelmed. This was nothing new, and he glanced back at the list of articles he hadn't yet read in his sermon preparation.

"She's fine."

He clicked on another article: "Jesus, the Pharisees, and Fairness."

"I'm leaving your father."

"Leaving him where?" Jeff asked vaguely as he scanned the article.

"I'm leaving him," she repeated. "I'm filing for divorce."

Jeff heard the words but couldn't make sense of them. Divorce? That word had never once occurred to him in relation to his parents. He had never even imagined such a possibility. They had been married what—? Forty-three, forty-four years? His parents would never get divorced. Divorce was for lesser mortals, not for the Rev. and Mrs. Gordon Cooper.

The silence stretched between them. "You can't be serious," he said at last.

"Oh, I'm serious," she said hotly. "Because apparently he's pretty serious about his girlfriend."

He almost laughed out loud. "Girlfriend? What is this, an early April Fool's Day joke or something?"

"If it is, the joke's on me," his mother said, her voice cracking.

It was the crack that convinced him. He dropped his head in his hands. "Oh, dear God, you're serious. Dad has a—Dad had an affair?" He immediately thought of his father's new secretary. An attractive woman in her forties, she was hired last year after the previous secretary finally retired at the age of seventy-seven. Jeff had met her on his last visit. "Please tell me it wasn't his secretary," he retorted, his voice rising. "Of all the tired, worn out stereotypes…"

"No. Actually, the secretary is the one who reported him to the board. His affair was with a church member."

"He screwed a church member? Are you friggin' kidding me?" he yelled. "How stupid can he be? Every minister right out of seminary knows you don't f—" He stopped himself, suddenly remembering he was in the church and yelling profanities was frowned upon. "Oh, dear God," he said again. He leaned back in his chair and closed his eyes. This was unbelievable. An affair with a parishioner? Because of the power differential between clergy and laity, even single ministers couldn't date church members. It was a clear breach of clergy ethics—something his father had always taken very seriously. Or so Jeff had thought.

"I found out about a month ago, and we've been trying to deal with it in counseling. But he refuses to give her up, even though it definitely means he'll lose his church. They're talking about filing charges on an ethics violation."

"I can't believe this," Jeff said again. "I mean, I know what you're saying, and I believe you. But it's so far removed from my image of Dad that I can't..." His voice trailed off. He couldn't find the words.

"Cognitive dissonance." His mother, always the psychologist, provided the correct term. "It's the mental stress or discomfort caused when a person is confronted with new information that conflicts with existing beliefs, ideas, or values."

"I'm familiar with the concept, Mom," Jeff reminded her.

"I know. I just have to keep naming it. I've been feeling it for a month and it's not getting any easier. I still can't believe your father would do this to me. To the church. To his entire career and legacy."

The pain in her voice twisted like a knife in his gut. "Mom, I don't—I don't know what to say to you. I'm so sorry. This has to be..." His voice trailed off, but his mother picked up the thought.

"The most painful thing I've ever experienced," she said without hesitation.

"Mom, I'm so sorry. Really. How are you coping with this?"

"Counseling and chocolate. Not necessarily in that order."

Jeff tried to smile in response, but he couldn't manage it. He did, however, marvel at his mother's ability to joke when her world was falling apart. And it made him even angrier at his father. "What was he thinking?" he said, fully aware that his father's brain most likely was not the part of his body that was in charge.

"There's only one thing that would cause a man like your father to turn so far away from his values. And that's what hurts the most." She fell silent.

"Meaning?" Jeff prompted her.

"Love," his mother choked out. "He could only do this for love."

☙

Juliann had a plan. A good plan. A perfect plan for a good student to tell an unsuspecting parent. She had already told her mom that she and Hailey were working on a project and presentation together. She planted that seed yesterday, and they were leaving tomorrow, so it was time for the rest of the plan.

She ambled into the kitchen, trying to act casual. Her mom sat at the island, reading through a cooking magazine. "Hey, Mom, you know that presentation I told you about? The one I'm doing with Hailey?"

"Mm-hm," her mother mumbled, not looking up.

"We're going to work on it tomorrow afternoon and evening."

"That's fine," she said as she turned the page.

Juliann knew that the good part about never lying to your mom is that she has no reason not to trust you. The bad part about never lying to your mom is that you have no experience in doing it. Juliann was accustomed to lying to other people because of her dad—making excuses why her friends couldn't come over, stuff like that. Somehow lying to her mother felt different. She opened the fridge and stuck her head in as she called, "We might be working late so Hailey asked if I could spend the night. Then I'll catch the bus to school with her Monday morning."

Her mom finally looked at her. "Spend the night?"

"Right. To work on our project."

"Oh yes, fine." Her gaze went back to her magazine, but Juliann had the feeling she wasn't really seeing it.

"It really is important, you know," Juliann said, as much to remind herself as to remind her mom.

Her mom nodded curtly. "Of course. Your grades are important. I understand. I just had hoped we'd have a family dinner together tomorrow night. We haven't eaten together in a while."

"What about tonight? Could we do it tonight?"

"No. Your father has a meeting."

Juliann let out an exasperated sigh. *Another Saturday night meeting? Yeah, lawyers have tons of those.* She should check the latest pool of clerks in his legal office for thin blondes. She knew, of course, what her mother was really concerned about. Her dad went golfing every Sunday afternoon and often drank too much on the course. If he lost, he came home in a horrible mood. Around their house, drunk and pissed was a bad combination.

But it wasn't her fault. She was doing what had to be done. "Who's he golfing with tomorrow?"

"Arthur Kendrix."

Juliann breathed a sigh of relief. "That's good, right? Doesn't Dad usually beat Arthur?"

Her mom gave an odd smile. "Yes, he does."

"Then he should be in an okay mood when he comes home," she pressed. "Right? You'll be fine if I leave you."

Her mom climbed down from the stool and picked up a towel—one of the microfiber ones she used all the time to keep the fingerprints off the countertops. "Yes, honey, I'll be fine. You don't have to stay home all the time for my sake. You deserve to have a life beyond these walls."

Juliann tried to catch her mom's eye, but her mom wouldn't look at her. "You do too, Mom."

"I do have a life," she insisted as she stepped away. "I worked all week. I had brunch at the club with friends this morning and played golf this afternoon."

Juliann couldn't keep the bitterness out of her voice. "Of course you did. All Dad-approved activities. You have to keep up appearances, after all."

"Juliann!" her mother scolded.

She knew she was crossing the line, but the anger boiling up within her demanded release. "Did he schedule lunch for you, or were you allowed to make the plans yourself? Did he tell you what to wear?" She slapped her hand to her forehead. "Oh, right. He doesn't need to. He inspects all your purchases when you bring them home. That way he doesn't have to worry about you embarrassing him. You know, it's amazing he even lets you work!"

"Juliann!" her mother repeated. "Stop that!"

But something had broken open and the words were pouring out of Juliann as if she'd been saving them up her whole life. "Why? He's not here. He's probably off screwing his latest clerk."

"That's enough! Show some respect for your father."

Juliann put her hands on her hips and spat out a single word. "No."

Her mother looked confused, like she didn't even understand the meaning of the word. "No?"

"No!" Juliann repeated. "He doesn't deserve respect. And besides, he's not my father."

Her mother took a step back as her hand went to her heart. "What? Of course he's your father. How could you think—"

"He's not my father. He's a sperm donor. He is an arrogant, abusive prick who doesn't deserve the title of father. What I don't get—what I don't understand—is why you put up with it. Why do you even stay? For this?" She waved an arm around the kitchen. "For stainless steel appliances and marble countertops? For the country club membership?"

Her mother turned around and began wiping the counter. "I don't expect you to understand. I have obligations. Besides, I made my bed and now…" Her voice trailed off as her hand moved rhythmically over the same spot.

Juliann stared at her mother's shoulders—stiff yet bent. "Now you have to lie in it," she said, finishing the familiar quote. "The problem is, you're not the only one."

She barely made it to her bathroom before she vomited.

8

Mish was fidgety. She was never good at sitting still, but this morning her legs seemed to have a mind of their own. They kept bouncing, her toes tapping an uneven rhythm on the wood floor under the pew. Opal looked at her funny once or twice, and she tried to smile like she was just full of energy and happy to be alive. That seemed to make Opal look more concerned.

Nerves is what it was. She and Ann would be leaving in a couple of hours, and she had a case of the nerves that wouldn't quit. The choir sang a somber number that didn't help her mood any. Why did this choir director insist on singing them highfalutin' songs? This was West Virginia, for God's sake. What ever happened to "Unclouded Day" and "May the Circle Be Unbroken"? Something you could tap your toe to without being looked at funny. What in the world was—she looked at the bulletin again. "Kyrie Eleison"? She listened to the choir, trying to figure it out. All they sang was "Kyrie Eleison" and "Lord, have mercy." Hmm, maybe that's what it meant.

Well, that was okay then. Maybe she did need the Lord to have some mercy on her. She was terrified by what she was about to do. She was taking a teenage girl out of state to get an abortion—and was even paying for it. It had seemed like the right thing to do when she offered, but now that the time had come, she wasn't sure. Was it even legal? And by paying for it, did that make her a—what was the word? Like the person who drove the getaway car. An accomplice! *Am I an accomplice in ending a baby's life before it even begins?*

Mish tried to pull herself out of her own thoughts long enough to listen to at least some of Pastor Jeff's sermon. He seemed off, distracted, but Mish had enough worries of her own to consider. He was talking about Jesus getting in trouble with some of the religious leaders of the day. They had strict rules about what was and wasn't right, and Jesus kept breaking those rules by doing things like healing on the Sabbath.

"Religion is not supposed to be a heavy burden upon the people, weighing them down rather than lifting them up," Pastor Jeff explained. "They said the wounded person should come back the next day to be healed, but Jesus knew what they did not: that there is no 'wrong day' to bring healing. Our faith should drive us to end suffering wherever and whenever we encounter it."

No wrong day to bring healing. Her heart began to buzz. She felt like she always did when she heard truth—like a tuning fork had been struck and her heart reverberated with the sound. There was no wrong day to bring healing. No wrong time. No wrong way. Our faith should drive us to end suffering. And that meant driving to DC. Follow the love. Jesus said it—way back then, and even now.

The song they sang after the sermon was the icing on the cake of the message Jesus had for her. They sang "In the Bulb There Is a Flower." It was the song they'd sung at Floyd's funeral. Just the thought of that service brought a smile to Mish's face.

She had lied to Pastor Jeff when they met to plan it. Floyd had told her several times over the years what songs he wanted for his funeral, but Mish hated his choices. "The Old Rugged Cross" with its "emblem of suffering and shame"? No thanks. So she picked the songs herself and told Pastor Jeff they were Floyd's choices. She needed what that new hymn had to offer. *In our end is our beginning, at the last a victory.*

When he died suddenly, of course she was sad. But she also felt like she had a chance for a fresh start. A new beginning before her end. Today she sang the song with gusto.

She was still glowing with the sunshine of it all during fellowship time after worship. On Sundays she always got as many hugs as she could—she stored them up since she wouldn't get more until the next Sunday. But this week she also made a point of telling each person something she liked or admired about them. It just felt important for folks to be reminded of the best that was in them.

Just as she was fixing to leave, she noticed that Pastor Jeff seemed to be cornered by Ruth and her neighbor Tom. Ruth and Tom both looked mad, and Jeff looked downright miserable. So she decided to make a little trouble. She walked right up to the group and grabbed Jeff's arm. Smiling at Ruth and Tom, she said, "Excuse me, folks, but I need a chat with this dear man about his wonderful sermon this morning. It really laid a conviction on my heart, and I need him to say a prayer with me. Y'all don't mind, do you? I just know you wouldn't stand in the way of prayer."

And with that she led him out of the room.

When they got out to the hall, Pastor Jeff said, "Mish, what's wrong? You need prayer?"

"Oh, good Lord, no!" she said with a laugh. "Well, I probably do, but I just said that to get you away from the hen-pecking!"

He laughed and put an arm around her shoulder as they walked. "Thank you, Mish! Your timing is impeccable, and your kindness knows no bounds."

Mish stopped and looked up at him. "I also wanted to say something to you. I know we don't always see eye to eye. But I want you to know that I think you're a wonderful preacher and I hope you stay here a good long while. This church needs what you have to give." And with that she pulled his lapels until he bent toward her, and she kissed him on the cheek.

When she pulled away, she noticed that his eyes were misty, so she gave him a wink. "By the way, those hens back there giving you a hard time. You might want to give them a laxative."

"A laxative?" Jeff repeated.

She leaned in and whispered, "That's what I do when *my* hens are full of shit."

Two hours later she pulled into the parking lot where she and Juliann had agreed to meet. The car was barely in park when the door opened, and Ann slid in. She was wearing a ball cap and sunglasses, and after tossing her backpack into the back, she buckled her seatbelt and then slouched down in the seat.

"So," Mish began. "Are you going *in cognito* the whole trip or just until we leave Micky D's?"

Ann looked at Mish over her sunglasses. "That obvious?"

Mish chuckled. "Pretty obvious, but I understand. So let's blow this joint. Or is it blow this lemonade stand? What's the phrase you kids use?"

Ann laughed. "I think the phrase you're looking for is 'blow this popsicle stand,' but that's more my parents' generation than mine."

"Ah, well, I never was good with the lingo." She pulled out of the parking lot and headed toward the interstate. "You're my navigator, right? Where are your maps?"

"Actually, you have them. On your phone." Ann pointed to Mish's phone in the console. "May I? I had to leave mine with my friend."

"Sure, but I didn't think kids your age went anywhere without their phones—especially out of town."

"Well, I didn't do it by choice. My parents use an app that tracks my phone. So it has to be wherever I'm supposed to be, which right now is at my friend Hailey's house. I gave her your number so she can contact me if there are any problems. Hope you don't mind."

"Of course not. In fact, you can be in charge of my phone the whole trip. Just put it down once in a while to keep me company. When my son comes to visit, he hardly looks up from his. I know the top of his head very well."

"Actually, I was looking for something to play for you. You mentioned that you are interested in spoken word poetry. Want to hear some more?"

"Ooh, I'd love to," Mish said.

They spent the next half hour listening to some poets Ann had chosen for her. Mish especially liked Taylor somebody's poem about teachers and Katie somebody's poem about being pretty. But when she asked Ann if these were her favorites, the girl admitted that they weren't. She liked the younger poets—people in high school and college who used poetry to talk about the really hard stuff in their lives.

"Do you use poetry that way?" Mish asked.

Ann shrugged. "Sometimes. About the big stuff in society, like racism and sexism and stuff."

"But not the personal stuff?"

"Not recently. I haven't wanted to…" Ann's voice trailed off.

Mish understood. "Sometimes it's hard enough just having the bad stuff in your head. Seeing it with your eyes, too, just makes it realer."

The girl nodded and then stared out the window. They were silent for a few minutes until Mish's phone dinged again with a text message. "Somebody sent you a picture. No, two pictures. And she wants to know which you like."

"Oh, that's Emma," Mish explained. "She writes to me for advice."

"Fashion advice?"

Mish laughed at the surprise in Ann's voice. "Sometimes life advice, sometimes relationships, but mostly clothes. She seems to have trouble trusting her own opinions. So I help sometimes."

"Interesting," Ann said. "And how do you know her?"

"I don't really. I just know her on the text machine. But I try to help anyways. What did she send, pictures of clothes?"

Ann looked at the phone again. "Yeah, in one she's wearing leggings and a long blue shirt, and in the other—"

"I don't need to know," Mish interrupted. "Just ask her which one she likes best, and—assuming it's not horrible—then tell her you like that one too."

Ann looked sideways at her. "Seriously?"

"Seriously." Mish chuckled. "She needs to learn to trust herself. So compliment her. Give her a little pep talk."

Ann shrugged and took a deep breath. "I'll do my best."

Mish watched as she typed on the phone, got replies, typed back. A few minutes later Ann said, "All right, I did what you said. She liked the same one I did, so that was easy. I told her she looked really cute—which she did—and she wrote back with a bunch of emojis."

"Are those the little smiley faces and hearts and stuff?"

"Yeah, some kids use a lot of those. I think more in high school than in college, and she seemed college age. Is that right?"

"I think so. She mentioned a party at a sorority one time. I'm not sure where she goes."

"And how did you say you met her?" Ann asked.

Mish knew she was fishing, but she didn't mind. "I haven't met her. I don't even know how she got my number. But she said she was so glad to have it and it meant so much and now she writes me for advice. She's really insecure so I just go with it, try to help her out."

Ann just stared at her, then shook her head. "Wow, that is really nice—to just help people you've never even met."

Mish almost laughed at the irony. "I guess. I just never thought you needed to know somebody in order to want to help them."

Ann faced the window, and Mish decided to leave her alone with her thoughts. They drove quite a way in silence before the girl finally spoke again. "My name's Juliann."

"Okay," Mish said simply.

Juliann pushed her hair back from her face. "I just thought you should know. Since you're driving me to DC and all, I figured we should be on a first name basis."

"Seems fair," Mish agreed. "Anything else you want to tell me?"

"Yes."

Mish glanced sideways. Was the girl finally ready to open up to her? To tell her story? To talk about when it happened and who the father is and how she feels about the abortion and why she's afraid of her dad? There was so much she didn't know and wanted to know but wouldn't ask.

"I forgot to pee before we left."

"Oh, goodie!" Mish said with a laugh. "I thought I'd be the first one to make us stop! So find us a fast food place to stop at. I hate them gas station toilets."

They took an exit a few miles down the road. As soon as they turned, Mish heard a voice say, "Return to the route."

"Who was *that*?"

"That's the map app. It knows we got off the interstate. It's trying to tell us to get back on."

"Doesn't it have a hold-on-we-have-to-go-to-the-bathroom button?"

Juliann tapped on the phone. "I don't think so. I haven't used this app much since I'm just learning to drive. I think it's just going to keep telling us that until we get back on the interstate."

Mish pulled into the closest parking lot.

"Return to the route."

Mish leaned toward the phone. "We have to go potty," she said.

"I'm pretty sure it doesn't work that way," Juliann told her.

Mish tried again. "We have to go potty!" she yelled. That's when she noticed the young couple in the convertible next to them, both staring at her. Juliann slouched in her seat again, but this time she was laughing.

"Fine," Mish said. "I'll go potty by myself. You just stay here and be embarrassed."

"No, I'm coming with you!" Juliann said as she jumped out of the car. She turned and looked at the couple in the convertible. "I have to go potty too," she explained. Then she put her arm through Mish's as they scurried into the restaurant, laughing as they went.

☙

They got back in the car ten minutes later with chocolate shakes and french fries. Mish leaned toward the phone. "All right, boss lady, we're ready to 'return to the route.' Happy now?"

"Wouldn't you just freak out if she answered?" Juliann asked.

"Not as much as I would if Floyd answered, and I still talk to him every day!" Mish guided the car back onto the interstate. "I know he can't hear me, but I was never sure he was listening anyway. So no big difference, I guess."

Juliann tucked her hair behind her ear as she looked out the window. She'd been wondering about Mish and her husband and what their relationship had been like. It sounded like he was pretty cruel, the way he put Mish down. She wondered if he was physically abusive, too, and hated the thought of that. She couldn't imagine Mish putting up with what her mother put up with. Mish wasn't weak, like Juliann's mom. She was…Juliann searched for the right word. Salty? Fiery? Spunky. It's not a word she remembered using before, but somehow it fit this old woman who had become her best friend.

Woah, where did that thought come from? Juliann asked herself. How could an eighty-two-year-old woman be her best friend? They had nothing—absolutely nothing—in common. But somehow, she felt more comfortable talking to Mish than she did to any of her friends. She could even say things to Mish she never could have said to her own grandmother. Why? She knew her grandma loved her. Adored her, even. Thought she was perfect and the best and...

That was it. Her grandma thought she was perfect. Being perfect is a helluva lot of pressure.

"Mish? Can we talk about something serious for a minute?"

"Of course. Do I need to pull over?"

"No!" Juliann said quickly. "I mean, it's fine to keep driving. I just—I just need to tell you something."

"You can tell me anything, hon."

"I know, that's just it. I can say anything to you, and that's so weird."

Mish tilted her head to one side. "Maybe because I'm weird?"

"You're not weird," Juliann rushed to assure her.

"Really, it's all right," Mish said. "I am strange. I know this about myself. An odd duck, my mama used to call me. I used to try to fit in but I was no good at it. Then I realized that because I'm just me, odd as I am, sometimes other folks can just be themselves with me—like they don't have to pretend or nothing. They tell me things they wouldn't say to nobody else." She shrugged. "I'm not normal, but I don't mind. I'm at least in the neighborhood."

"I think I know what you're saying. I do find myself being sillier with you than I do with anybody else. But that's not what I mean."

"Okay, then why is it weird that you can talk to me?"

"It's not weird—it's great. It's just that..." Juliann sighed. For someone who considered herself a poet, she sure was having a hard time finding the words. She tried again. "I don't have any pressure not to disappoint you. You don't 'expect great things from me' like my teachers do, or expect me to make you proud like my parents do. You already know the worst thing about me. So I don't have to worry about you finding out more. You know the worst, and you still want to help me, seem to care about me, even. I have no idea why, but you do. And that makes me feel bad because I tried to use you." She rushed through her words because she was afraid she wouldn't get them out otherwise. "When we went to the clinic and I said you were my grandma, I said it because I thought maybe they'd let you give permission for the abortion. Then your face lit up, and I felt so bad and…"

Mish put her hand on Juliann's leg. "Oh, hon, did you think I didn't know that? I mean, sure, at first I thought you meant it, but then as soon as you said you thought another relative might be able to sign for you, I knew what you was doing."

"But didn't that hurt your feelings?"

"I know your grandma was special to you. I know you don't feel about me the way you did about her. But this ain't the 4-H."

"What does—"

"I mean this ain't a contest, with a blue ribbon going to who you love the most." Mish patted Juliann's leg, then put her hand back on the steering wheel. "And if it was, I'd be happy to have an honorable mention."

Juliann smiled. "Okay, you definitely get at least an honorable mention. But I think I need a name for you."

Mish grinned. "Mish isn't good enough for you, Um-Ann?"

"Mish is just fine. I should've said I need a new *title* for you. You're like a cross between a grandma and a best friend. Maybe you're my friend-ma. Or my best-grand."

"Ooh, I like that one! I'm best AND grand! But I think I'm gonna need me a tiara to go with it. Or at least a beauty pageant sash."

Juliann grinned. "I'll see what I can do." She picked up Mish's phone to check the time and saw that somebody had texted her a photo. She clicked on it and—"Holy shit!" she yelled.

Mish swerved and almost drove off the road. "Don't do that to an old woman!" she yelled back.

"I'm sorry! But you just got a dick pic."

"A what?"

"A picture. Of—of somebody's penis."

"Well, that didn't come from Jesus!" Mish exclaimed.

Juliann didn't know why Mish would say such a thing, but she was too freaked out to ask.

"Why would somebody send me that?" Mish persisted.

"I'm sure it's a wrong number. I've gotten wrong number texts before. Not like this one, though!"

"I've heard on the news about men doing that. One of the politicians got in trouble for it a while back. But I don't understand why anybody thinks that's a good idea. Are they so in love with their own parts they just have to share 'em with the world?"

"I don't know, but this guy obviously is sending it to someone he doesn't know well enough to even have them in his contacts list. Probably hitting on some girl in a bar who gave him a fake number."

"Can you delete it for me?"

"Sure, but can I have some fun first?"

Mish looked over at her skeptically. "What do you have in mind?"

"I saw something that someone else did one time. Let me get into your photo editing app."

"My what?"

"Hold on." Two minutes later the guy's dick bore a striking resemblance to the little one-eyed green guy on SpongeBob SquarePants.

"Lemme see! Lemme see!" Mish said it with such enthusiasm that Juliann couldn't help but comply. And the resulting fit of giggles made Mish seem about twelve years old.

When the siren sounded, the laughter died in Juliann's throat. Then the police car came up right behind them with its lights flashing, and Juliann knew they were in trouble. Had her parents found out? How? Hailey hadn't texted to say anything was wrong. But if they knew, "shit storm" was not a strong enough way to describe what was about to go down.

Mish pulled over, then patted Juliann's knee again. "You all right with being my granddaughter again? For five minutes?" Juliann nodded. "Then calm down. It's gonna be fine. Just get my registration out of the glove box for me."

Juliann shook her head. "My driver's ed teacher said you're not supposed to go rummaging around when a cop stops you. They might think you're going for a gun. Just sit still with your hands in plain sight."

"Good thinking." Mish put her hands on the steering wheel and looked in the rearview mirror. "What's taking him so long?"

"He's checking your plates, making sure the car isn't wanted for outstanding tickets or accidents."

"Well, aren't you just a fountain of information!" Mish smiled at her, but Juliann was too nervous to smile back. She chewed on her thumbnail while she tried to peer into the rearview mirror. Pretty soon the police officer or trooper or whatever he was got out of his car and approached the driver's side door.

"Driver's license and registration," he said sternly. Juliann noticed that the man's hand was not resting on his gun. She took that as a good sign.

"I'd be happy to," Mish replied, "but my purse is in the back seat and my registration is in the glove box, and my granddaughter tells me I'm not supposed to go reaching for them until you know what I'm doing. Is it all right with you if I get those?" When he nodded, Juliann rummaged in the glove compartment for any official-looking papers while Mish reached for her purse and got out her wallet.

The trooper looked over both documents but didn't give them back. "Mrs. Atkinson," he began.

"Please, call me Mish. Everybody does," Mish said with a smile.

"Mrs. Atkinson, do you know why I pulled you over?"

"No, I'm afraid I don't. I don't think I was speeding, and I don't think it was for my good looks."

Juliann saw a muscle twitch beside the officer's mouth. "No, you were not speeding. In fact, you were going five miles under the speed limit. But you were swerving a bit back there. Slow, erratic driving is often a sign of someone driving under the influence."

Mish laughed. "Oh, that's right, I did swerve a little back there. It was because of the dick pic."

The officer's eyes widened. "Excuse me?"

"Some young man thought it was a good idea to send a photo of his lil' chubby. So my granddaughter here just made some improvements to the picture and I had to see it before she sent it back." Mish took the phone from Juliann's hand and showed the officer the picture. "Now can't you see why I swerved just a bit?"

The officer took one look at Mish's phone and burst out laughing. Mish turned to Juliann and winked, and Juliann gave a weak smile in return.

"Ladies, I have to say I admire your spunk! Now, on a serious note." He ducked his head to see Juliann better. "Miss, are you under eighteen? Because if an adult sent this to you, I can take this phone and charge him with sending pornography to a minor."

"I'm afraid you can't do that," Mish said. "It's my phone."

He looked at her blankly. "Yours?" He shook his head. "Sorry. I assumed the latest model iPhone belonged to the teenager."

Mish sat up straighter. "I wanted the smartest smartphone I could get, and the sales boy said this was it. I bought it so I can be hip!"

The officer laughed again. "Yes, ma'am, I can testify to the fact that you are hip." He returned Mish's license and registration, then tipped his hat and told them to drive safely. He was still shaking his head when he climbed back in his car.

Juliann laid her head back against the seat and closed her eyes, willing her stomach to stop churning. They didn't know. She wasn't in trouble. It was going to be okay. *She* was going to be okay.

And by this time tomorrow it would all be over.

Juliann lay in the dark, staring at the ceiling and wondering if sleep would ever come. It was still early by her standards, but Mish said it was past her bedtime, so, of course, Juliann had gotten ready and turned off the lights. She stayed on Mish's phone for a little while, but she didn't want to risk using all Mish's data plan.

She ran her hand over her belly, something she intentionally hadn't done very often. She didn't want to risk bonding with this *intruder*, as she thought of it. But now that their brief relationship was almost over, it seemed safe. She thought her belly felt a little rounder. She wasn't sure why—the embryo was only half an inch long. She had looked it up. It wasn't even a fetus yet and didn't even look human. No matter what the pro-lifers said, it wasn't a baby. Not yet. She wasn't ending a life. She was preventing one. She could live with that. She would have to because she didn't have a choice.

She wished she had a choice about these pillows, though. They were all too poofy. She pulled one out from behind her head and put it with the others, then lay back without one. She already had enough of a headache without her neck being at the wrong angle. But at least the pain in her head took her attention away from the constant queasiness.

The nausea was another thing she'd looked up. Of course, she'd looked it all up. Learning was her way of dealing with the world. If she could understand it, she could cope. She had learned that morning sickness doesn't happen only in the mornings. And different people react in different ways. She hadn't actually thrown up that much, though she read that some people did. Still, she felt like she was constantly just a little bit nauseated, like she had motion sickness or something. Crackers seemed to help. So did coffee. But other strong smells were horrible. She couldn't stand the smell of garlic or bananas.

Of course, it could all be in her head. Or it could be nerves. Maybe if she'd been happy about the pregnancy, if she had welcomed this little parasite inside her, she wouldn't have felt nauseated all the time. The thought alone was enough to make her queasy. She let out a heavy sigh, then turned on her side and retrieved the pillow to try again.

"Can't sleep?"

Juliann hadn't realized Mish was still awake. "I'm sorry—am I bothering you?"

"No," Mish assured her. "I often have trouble sleeping,

especially in a new place. And these pillows are horrible. They're all too poofy! Four pillows on the bed, and they couldn't give us one skinny one?"

Juliann chuckled. "I thought the exact same thing."

Mish paused for a moment, then said, "But it's not the pillows keeping you awake, is it?"

Juliann shook her head, then remembered Mish couldn't see her in the darkened room. "No," she said.

"Nervous about tomorrow?"

"A little bit. I read all the info on their website. There are a couple different options, and I chose the one that sounded best. So I know what to expect…" Her voice trailed away.

"You know what to expect for your body. You don't know what the rest of you will be feeling."

They were silent for a few moments, while Juliann tried to figure out what she was feeling. She didn't speak again until she had a full list. "Nervous, a little bit scared, embarrassed, eager, and soon-to-be-relieved. Oh, and stupid."

"Why stupid?"

"For getting myself pregnant in the first place."

"Well, I don't think you did—get *yourself* pregnant, I mean. It's been a while, but I'm pretty sure somebody else was involved."

"Well, of course, but it's not his fault."

"And it's yours? That doesn't make sense."

"Yes. I mean no." Juliann rolled back over to stare at the ceiling again. "I mean I should have known better. He's not to blame."

"I'm sorry, hon, but I gotta disagree with you. It takes two to tango, and it's not fair for one to take the blame. Unless one forced the other, and that's a whole 'nother thing entirely."

"This is different," Juliann insisted. "There are things I should've known. Things everybody knows. But I didn't know and that was stupid. So, yes, it's my fault."

"I don't—"

"I know you don't understand, okay?" Juliann said, her voice rising. "You couldn't possibly understand—nobody does—because nobody knows."

"And is that the way you want it?"

"I—" Juliann stopped herself, not sure how to answer. It was a good question. Did she really want to keep this story secret? Would it do any good to tell anybody? She'd have to say it out loud. It would be hard to find the right words and even harder to hear them. On the other hand, keeping it to herself wasn't doing her much good anyway. Maybe it would loosen the band around her chest that she'd felt ever since that night. And if she could tell anyone, it was Mish.

"No. It's not what I want," she finally admitted, then took a deep, fortifying breath. "It happened at a party…"

9

Juliann had been excited to be invited to the party. She considered herself socially awkward—had felt that way since she skipped third grade. She had friends, of course, but not a tight circle of them. Her friends came from scattered interactions—the French club, her AP classes, and, of course, the dance studio where she had taken lessons for years. But none of them hung out together. She was more on the fringe, and she often found out about parties after they had already happened—or even while they were happening—via social media. Naturally, it hurt her feelings not to be invited, but she understood. She wasn't in the A group. She was in the B group or "backup" group of friends. And backup friends rarely get invited to parties.

But this one was different. She was friends with Shelby from French club, and she knew Shelby's older brother Sean from her AP classes the previous year. So when Shelby and Sean threw a party together while their parents were away, her name made the cut. She had been depressed ever since her grandma died, and a party sounded like a perfect antidote. She had chosen her outfit carefully, aiming for the casual cool that seemed so natural for other girls.

Sean had brought a couple of his college friends home with him, plus some other guys that graduated with him the previous year. A couple of the guys had a beer or two, but there wasn't a lot of drinking, and Juliann was glad. She'd seen enough alcohol-fueled bad behavior at home.

She gravitated to the dance floor—which, of course, was just the living room with the furniture pushed to the edges, but the hardwood floors and large expanse of their open-concept house created a great place to dance. She was comfortable dancing, and she was good at it. Plus, it meant she didn't have to make small talk, which she wasn't good at, so it was a win-win, as her grandma would have said. Somehow—she wasn't sure how it happened—she found herself dancing with Aiden. She knew him, of course, or at least knew of him. Everybody did. He had been one of the stars at their high school the previous year. He was athletic and smart—and still not a jerk, which was pretty miraculous. Juliann was shocked that he was dancing with her, of all people.

When a song came on that neither of them liked, he led her to the couch, then went to get her a drink. As soon as he was gone, Shelby appeared. "I can't believe you're dancing with Aiden!"

"I know, right?" Juliann responded, grinning. "But now we've stopped dancing, and I don't know what to say to him. Quick—give me a conversation topic!"

"If he's like most guys, just ask him one question about football, and you'll never have to say anything but 'wow' for the rest of the night!"

Juliann laughed, then shooed Shelby away as she saw Aiden winding his way back to her through the crowd. "So, what college do you go to?" she asked when he handed her a can of pop.

"WVU," he said with a shrug. "I know it's not exciting to go so close to home, but they have a good program in engineering, and money was a factor. In-state tuition is really low, plus they offered me good scholarships. I don't want to graduate with a ton of student loan debt, and since my parents aren't in a position to help much, it was an easy decision."

Juliann was surprised. Most people in their school didn't admit if their family didn't have money. It didn't really matter to Juliann who was rich and who wasn't, but to some of the kids—especially the popular kids—what kind of car you drove was a pretty big issue. She gave Aiden extra points for his honesty.

"What about you? Where do you want to go?" he asked as he opened the bottle of beer he'd been holding.

"I'm not sure yet," she admitted. "I want to go away. I know that much. I don't want to consider anything within four hours."

He tilted his head and frowned. "You don't think you'll get homesick?"

She let out a cynical laugh. "For my home? Not likely."

"Well, that sucks," he replied.

"What does?"

He reached out and tucked a strand of hair behind her ear. "That you don't have a home you'll miss," he said simply. "It probably sounds stupid, but I really miss my family when I'm at school. What's so bad about your home that you want to get away?"

Suddenly Juliann was sorry she had chosen school as the topic of conversation. The talk was turning more personal than she'd anticipated. She tried to laugh it off. "Oh, you know, the usual. Demanding parents, too many rules."

Aiden chuckled softly. "Oh, you're a big rule-breaker, are you?"

"Juliann? A rule breaker? You can't be serious!"

Juliann looked up to see Kirstin standing above them, one hand on her hip and the other playing with her large hoop earring. Kirstin was one of the most popular girls in their school, and Aiden seemed to be the only guy Kirstin wanted that she hadn't gotten.

Kirstin leaned down between them, putting her boobs right at Aiden's eye level, then flicked her hair so that Juliann had to lean back to keep from getting whacked in the face. "Juliann has probably never broken a rule in her life. She might break into hives at the very thought."

Aiden leaned around Kirstin so that he could see Juliann better. "Hives, huh? Are they anywhere interesting?" And with a wink, he took her hand and led her back to the dance floor.

The rest of the evening they spent dancing or talking or both. Juliann was amazed at how much they had in common. They both enjoyed science and math, though he didn't love English the way Juliann did. They both were fans of *Hamilton,* the musical, even though neither one really loved hip-hop. He laughed at her jokes and looked at her as if she was the only one in the room. And she was equally unaware of their surroundings. When he suggested they go somewhere quieter, and took her hand and led her upstairs, she didn't even consider saying no. It felt so natural, so right, and she felt alive for the first time in—well, as long as she could remember.

She was eager for his kiss, but he took his time. He drew her close, then bent his mouth to her ear. "No pressure," he whispered. "We'll only do as much as you want, okay?" Then he pulled back and looked into her eyes until she nodded.

When his lips touched hers, she stopped thinking, stopped feeling anything but his mouth against hers, his tongue, his hands. She had kissed boys before, but not like this. This was new. This was different. She needed more. She pulled his shirttail out of his pants but when she fumbled with the buttons, he stilled her shaking hands with his, then deftly removed his shirt and hers.

Skin. When she felt his skin against hers, it literally took her breath away. How could skin feel that amazing? She wanted to feel, to smell, to taste. He lowered her to the bed. She lost track of time, lost track of anything and everything but him and her and how amazing he made her feel. She was barely aware of him removing the rest of her clothes, but she obviously chose it. She wanted it. At one point he stopped and leaned over the side of the bed, and when she heard the rustling of his clothes, she was afraid he was leaving. She clutched at his arm, but he was back in an instant, something in his hand. A few seconds later he had transferred it to her hand, and she looked down long enough to realize it was a condom. But in the moment, she didn't know why he'd given it to her and didn't want to stop to ask. She let it drop on the bed and pulled his mouth back to hers.

Her body was hot and cold, aching and comforted, alive in ways she had never known or imagined. When he pulled away a second time, asking her if she wanted to stop, she tried to pull him back to her again, but he resisted. "Stop and think," he said. "Be sure."

She forced herself to do what she always did. She thought through the reasons, the pros and cons, but none of them made sense. Her mother had warned her against sex because it had consequences. Her father had warned her against sex because no daughter of his would be a slut. Even her grandmother had warned her against sex because it was a sin. But nobody had told her how it felt. Nobody had told her that it would feel so damn good that she wouldn't want to stop.

Everybody had told her it was wrong. Nobody had told her it was good. And it was so good and real, and she was alive and aching and the ache was the center of her universe. And so she said she didn't want to stop. She spoke truth. And it was hers to speak.

She didn't tell Mish all the details, of course. But there, in the dark, in a hotel room in Washington, DC, she finally admitted to someone the worst part of it all. She hadn't known it would feel like that. She hadn't realized that a body could come alive—especially a body still grieving death.

Mish had been silent throughout the story, but when Juliann ran out of words, she finally spoke. "So that's what you're embarrassed about? That you didn't know it felt good?"

"It's stupid!" Juliann exclaimed. "Everybody knows sex feels good—that's kind of the whole point and why people want to do it. So how did I not know that?"

"Oh, hon, it wasn't that you didn't know sex could feel good. It's that you didn't know *you* could feel that good. Because nobody ever made you feel it before. And I'm guessing you haven't seen a whole lot of good expressions of love in your own house. Of course you was surprised. Plus, you were still grieving the loss of your grandma. You were still missing her arm around your shoulder or her fingers in your hair or whatever it was that she did to show you she loved you. There's only one thing that surprises me in your story, and it ain't that."

"Then what—?"

"I'm just surprised a young man his age was so good at it! I mean, most young bucks don't think about what feels good to the girl, just themselves. At least that's my experience."

"Well, that sucks!" Juliann said, smiling as she realized she was repeating what Aiden had said to her about her family.

"That it did," Mish admitted. "It took me a while to convince Floyd that I'd be a more eager participant if he made it worth my time. So what happened to this fella of yours? Are you dating now? Is he okay with your decision?"

"No, we're not dating. Not anymore."

"But why?" Mish asked. "He sounds wonderful."

"He was," Juliann admitted. "He is. But once I realized I was pregnant, I had no choice."

"No choice? Of course you had a choice."

"No, I didn't," Juliann argued. "He might think he was supposed to marry me or something stupid like that. I was not going to be the girl who made him come home from college and give up his dreams."

Mish was quiet for a minute. Finally, she whispered, "I don't think that's the only reason. It's just not big enough to explain breaking up with someone you care about."

Juliann waited a minute before responding. She was glad it was still dark in the room. "I couldn't take the chance that he would try to make me keep it," she whispered back. "That was not an option."

"Not an option," Mish repeated. "Because of your dad?"

Juliann wiped tears from her eyes. "Everything is always because of my dad," she sniffed. "But we're almost done. Everything will be fine in a few hours."

"I hope so, hon," Mish whispered. "I truly do."

Mish woke up at her usual hour, even though she'd gotten to sleep late. When she'd laid down last night, she kept her hearing aid in just in case Juliann wanted to talk, and she was glad she had. She wondered how the girl would feel this morning after sharing her secrets. Mish decided to just act like nothing had happened.

But first she needed breakfast, and she knew Juliann wouldn't be up for a while. So she got dressed in the dark and snuck downstairs to eat. The girl had been true to her word—the hotel she had picked had a waffle maker and everything. Mish had so much fun making waffles that she made them for everybody else who wanted one. But she'd been back in her room for an hour and Juliann was still asleep. She wasn't sure if she should wake the girl. Juliann must be exhausted, but she needed a good breakfast too. Besides, Mish had some things in mind she wanted to do in Washington before their appointment.

Maybe if she made a little noise. She pushed the desk chair against the desk with a little more force than was necessary, then looked back at the bed to see if the noise had any effect. Nothing. She walked to the bathroom and turned on the light and fan. Still nothing. She cleared her throat. No movement. She plopped back down on her bed and harrumphed.

Then a muffled moan came from somewhere under the pile of pillows.

"You awake?" Mish asked eagerly.

"No," came the response.

Mish giggled. "Well, if you keep sleeping, you're going to miss breakfast. And you won't want to miss breakfast because it's really good. They have a waffle maker and eggs and sausage patties and bacon—it's floppy, but it'll do—plus yogurt and fruit and four kinds of cereal and three kinds of juice and there's a really nice young man who cleans up—his name is Miguel, and he's in college—and the lady in charge is Maria and she told me all about her kids—two girls and a boy—and they're all doing well except the oldest girl who is getting awful thin and might have that skinny sickness—you know, the one where they think they're fat and they stop eating. What's that called?" Juliann was sitting on the edge of the bed, just staring at her. "You all right, hon?"

Juliann wiped both hands down her face as she yawned. "How long you been up?" she mumbled.

"Since the wee hours. That's why I'm so chatty. But I can tell you're not a morning person. That's fine. I understand. You don't have to talk. I can talk for both of us." She looked again at the girl's face. "Or I can shut up and let you wake up before I talk your head off. Sorry about that." Mish picked up a restaurant guide that was lying on the nightstand and pretended to read. Juliann stood up slowly, shuffled over to her backpack, and then drug it by one strap into the bathroom and closed the door.

Mish eyed the back of the door warily. She sure hoped Juliann wasn't mad at her. She hadn't looked mad, just kind of overwhelmed. Mish knew that she could be overwhelming sometimes. Floyd used to get so mad at her for rattling her trap, as he called it.

A few minutes later the door opened and Juliann came out,

fully clothed and looking slightly more alert. She held up a finger and said, "Coffee."

"Got it!" Mish hopped off the bed and silently led the way to the breakfast buffet. She watched as Juliann poured herself a cup of coffee, added cream and sugar, and then sat down. After half the cup was gone, Mish whispered, "Can I get you breakfast now?" The girl smiled slightly and nodded, which sent Mish hurrying back to the buffet tables. She filled a cup with waffle batter to exactly the right line, then poured it carefully into the waffle maker. She closed the lid and flipped it, just like the sign said. While it cooked, she gathered another plate of goodies—bacon and sausage, but no eggs because the smell always made her queasy when *she* was pregnant, and a small cup of yogurt—peach, not strawberry-banana, because bananas bring out strong feelings in folks.

The waffle maker beeped, but Mish knew that if she took it out now, the waffle would be just a little soggy. Another twenty seconds and it would be perfect. So she picked up the big plastic fork to remove it, but waited until it was time.

"Your waffle's done," a man said. He was wearing a suit and holding a plastic cup of waffle batter that was way too full.

She smiled politely. "No, it's not."

"That's what the beeping means." He looked at her impatiently. "It means your waffle is done."

"No, it's not," she insisted as the beeping continued.

"Oh God, just move out of the way!" He grabbed her arm and started to push her to the side, but Mish was ready for him. She took the big plastic fork she was holding and poked him hard in the hand.

He jerked his hand away and rubbed it. "What the hell?"

"My waffle will be ready when I say it's ready, which is in another five-four-three-two-one." She opened the waffle maker to a beautiful, perfect golden-brown waffle.

He crossed his arms and glared at her as she removed it and put it on a plate. Then she returned his glare. "Son, let me give you two pieces of advice. Number one: never stand between a woman and her waffle." She took a deep breath. "And number two: never *ever* lay a finger on a woman without her permission."

If her words hadn't pushed him over the edge, the applause that broke out around them surely finished the job. Mish didn't know who started it, but Juliann, Maria, and two other women in the breakfast area were giving her a standing ovation. The man threw his cup of batter onto the floor and stormed out, yelling about the "crazy old bitch" as he went.

Juliann threw her arms around Mish. "That was so awesome!" she declared as she pulled away. "I can't believe you stood up to him like that!"

"I can't either," Mish said with a shaky laugh. And suddenly, she wasn't sure if she could stand at all. She heard a buzzing in her ears and it seemed like the whole room had tilted. She tried to grab Juliann's hand but the girl had already turned away and she grabbed at thin air, setting her off balance. She lurched forward and took a few stumbling steps, trying to find her feet. "Help!" she said, but before Juliann could offer any assistance, Mish felt a strong arm reach around her waist. Miguel, the busboy, was at her side. She let herself lean into his strength.

Before Mish knew it, she was sitting in a chair, being offered a glass of juice, and trying to catch her breath.

A woman in a hotel uniform rushed in. "Are you okay? Should we call 911?"

"No, no, I'm fine. I just got a little light-headed is all." She took a sip of juice and wiped her clammy forehead.

"Are you sure you don't want an ambulance to come take a look at you?" the hotel lady asked.

"Lord no," Mish replied. "I just got overexcited from telling off that rude young man, and it made me lose my balance for a second." She looked at the circle of people who had gathered around her. "Y'all need to quit looking at me like a heifer just gave birth to a pig. I'm fine, I tell you!"

They all chuckled and the other customers wandered back to their seats. "I'm terribly sorry about this incident," the manager said.

"I hope that's a sympathy sorry and not an apology sorry because it sure weren't your fault," Mish said to the manager.

"Nevertheless, we would like to comp your hotel stay."

Mish wasn't sure what that meant, but she didn't want to admit it in front of Juliann so she chose to ignore it. "Well, I'm afraid I owe *you* an apology because if I get down on the floor to clean up that mess, I won't be able to get back up."

The manager looked horrified. "Oh no, ma'am. We would never ask you to clean up your own mess, let alone somebody else's. We'll take care of that. I just want to take care of your bill because I want your experience at our hotel to be a positive memory."

Oh, so that's what comp means. "That's not necessary," Mish argued. "We have enjoyed our stay and I don't want to cheat your company out of a night's fare."

But the manager would not be swayed. After a few more assurances, she finally left them alone. Mish looked at Juliann, who still looked worried. "I really am fine. But I gotta ask you one question." She grinned. "Are you proud of me?"

Juliann laughed. "So proud! Seriously. You were quite impressive."

"I'm pretty impressed with me too!" said Mish. "I've never done anything like that before. But the way he grabbed me, on the arm—well, it just set me off. I thought, what would I do if he grabbed my granddaughter that way—or Juliann! I wouldn't stand for it, that's for sure. And I suddenly realized that if I would stand up to a bully for somebody else, maybe I could stand up to one for myself. You know what I mean?"

Juliann smiled at her weakly and nodded.

Mish looked down at her hands clasped in her lap. "I just wish I could've done it with Floyd."

10

On Monday morning Stephen and Jeff were raking leaves in the front yard as they caught up on the Sunday news.

"Anything new on Mish and this mystery mission of hers?"

Jeff paused and adjusted his glove before he answered. "You mean the whole 'follow the love' business? I don't think so. Our last conversation was not particularly productive so I haven't wanted to ask. But I'm not hearing anything about her seeing Jesus again so I'm hoping that issue has resolved itself."

Stephen raked his pile of leaves onto the blue tarp. "And how's the great potluck controversy coming along?"

"I think it's quieted down, but honestly, who knows with Sammi."

Stephen nodded. "She is definitely a pot-stirrer."

"Yeah, and it's always couched in this pseudo-liberal justice language that sets my teeth on edge. It's so manipulative. One of these days I'm going to have to talk to her about it, but that will be one ugly conversation."

"Speaking of ugly conversations, are you ready to talk about your dad?"

"What's to talk about? My dad is apparently a lying, cheating hypocrite who can't keep his pants zipped."

Stephen furrowed his brow. "That's a bit harsh, don't you think?"

Jeff stopped raking the leaves. "Was any of that untrue?"

"I'm not arguing with your facts, just your perspective." Before Jeff could respond, he put up both hands. "I'm not defending him. I'm just saying that we both know it can happen."

"What can happen? Adultery? Betrayal? Clergy misconduct?"

"Falling in love. We both know people can't always control

who they fall in love with. Do I need to remind you that you were with someone else when we met?"

Jeff attacked the pile of leaves with renewed fervor. "Seeing. Dating. Not married for forty-two years."

"You had been dating for a few months, as I recall."

Jeff looked at his partner in exasperation. This really was not the time to argue about his past relationships, especially one that was, in his counselor's words, not his most shining moment. "That's irrelevant. My parents have always had a solid relationship. They led marriage enrichment workshops. When I was growing up, Dad was even careful about having lunch with a woman alone, just to avoid the 'appearance of evil.' This is just unfathomable."

Stephen just shrugged. "You should talk to him."

"No."

"See what he has to say for himself."

"No."

"Have you even answered his texts?"

"No."

"If you won't talk to him, at least talk to me about how you're feeling."

Jeff frowned. "That's what I'm doing."

"No, you're just ranting about your dad. You're not talking about your feelings at all."

A car drove by and gave a little honk. Jeff waved without looking. "My feelings? Fine. I'm angry."

Stephen put his hand on his hip. "Really? I'm so surprised!" He gave a smile to soften his sarcasm. "What else?"

"Pissed."

"And?"

"Furious."

"I'm serious, Jeff. What else are you feeling?"

"Fine. I'm also enraged, livid, and incensed."

Stephen rolled his eyes. "Obviously I don't need to buy you a thesaurus for Christmas. Are you feeling anything that's not a synonym for mad?"

"No." Jeff attacked the leaves with the rake. "Anger is all I've got." When Stephen didn't respond, Jeff looked up.

"I find that hard to believe," Stephen said, staring at him.

Jeff shrugged and kept raking. "Sorry to disappoint you with my lack of emotional depth," he said.

"Oh, please!" Stephen muttered as he began raking leaves onto the tarp again.

"What?" Jeff demanded. "I don't have a right to be angry that my father has been screwing around?"

"Of course you do," Stephen countered, "but that can't be all you're feeling. Your dad was your mentor, your guide, your… your…shining example of everything a pastor is supposed to be. His fall from grace has to stir up more than just anger."

Jeff felt his irritation rising. He knew he shouldn't respond, but he couldn't seem to stop himself. "Gee, thanks for naming the situation so clearly. I feel so much better."

"I'm not trying to make you feel better," Stephen said. His hard swipes with the rake were sending as many leaves under the tarp as on top of it.

"Good, because if so, you're failing miserably."

"Damn it, Jeff, I just want you to talk about it, tell me what you're feeling." He sent another pile of leaves flying.

Jeff gritted his teeth. "I'm not ready to talk about it."

"It's been three days," Stephen pressed. "You need to talk about it."

"Damn it, Stephen, you are like a dog with a bone. Would you just give me a break?" He looked at the leaves Stephen was sending everywhere. "And will you *please* stop raking leaves under the tarp!"

Stephen stopped and glared at him. "Why? You seem to like sweeping things under the rug."

"Oh, please," Jeff said as he rolled his eyes. "Save the dramatics for the stage."

Jeff knew instantly he'd gone too far. Stephen dropped the rake and stormed into the house.

"Stephen, wait—" Jeff called after him. The slam of the door was the only response.

Jeff fumed for a few minutes as he fished the leaves out from under the tarp, then hauled the whole load around back and dumped them in the woods behind the house. He stopped to rest, and as he breathed in the scent of damp earth and old leaves, he was taken back to other woods and the many hikes he had shared with his father growing up. They had spent countless hours hiking together, exploring nearby trails. Sometimes they walked in comfortable silence, and other times they talked about deep things, important things. It was on a hike that he first came out to his dad. His dad had not been terribly surprised, but he had been surprisingly supportive. He told Jeff he loved him. Jeff had cried. He talked to Jeff about the importance of sexual ethics, regardless of sexual orientation—that the best sex was not with strangers but within the context of a relationship. In college, Jeff had not always followed his father's advice; but as an adult, he had treasured it. It told him he could have what he really wanted—not just sex but love. A partner, hopefully for life. Where did that man go? What had happened to that man who'd lectured him on ethics? Could Jeff's mother be right? Could this really be about love?

Back at the house, as he sat on the front porch, his anger toward his partner waned, and he admitted to himself that he was being unfair. Stephen was only pushing because he cared. Jeff knew there was something more there than anger. Anger was most often a cover emotion, with the true emotion hiding underneath. But he was too afraid of what was hiding to go exploring.

The door behind him opened, and Stephen took a seat beside him. They sat in silence for a few minutes before Jeff finally broke it. "I'm sorry I'm so stubborn."

"And I'm sorry I'm so pushy." Stephen took his hand. "But remember, that's how I finally convinced you to marry me—because I was charmingly persistent. Or persistently charming. I'm never sure which."

"More like gum on the bottom of my shoe," Jeff teased. This old joke between them never seemed to get stale. In fact, even though they repeated it almost word for word, it always brought them back—back to the playfulness, back to the clarity of who they were together.

"Well, either way you're stuck with me. I am your annoyingly tenacious husband. But I'll try to be more patient."

Jeff leaned sideways and bumped his shoulder against Stephen's. "Okay, and I'll try to…" His voice trailed off as he reached in his pocket for his buzzing cell phone. "It's the office."

"It's your day off," Stephen reminded him. "A day you desperately need, I might add."

"And Rachel doesn't call unless it's important." He punched the button on the phone. "Hello?"

"Hi, Pastor Jeff, I'm sorry to bother you, but Opal says it's urgent that she speak with you. She's right here."

Jeff let out an exasperated sigh. "Fine, put her on."

"Hi, Pastor Jeff, this is Opal."

"Yes, Opal, I know. What can I do for you?"

"Well, it's about Mish," she began. "She didn't come to the Women's Society meeting this morning."

"Okaaaay." Jeff wasn't sure why his day off was being interrupted by an attendance report.

"She has never missed a Women's Society meeting—well, except the week Floyd died, and even then she called to say she wasn't coming. We called her house and there was no answer."

"What about her cell phone?"

"She never gave any of us the number."

"So you think she might be ill," he surmised. "Does she have one of those emergency contact buttons some people wear?"

"No, her son wanted her to wear one but she refused. But, Pastor Jeff, that's not the strangest part. We got to talking about how she acted at church yesterday. She was very nervous at first, jumpy even. But by the end of the service, she was very happy, like she'd come to a decision or something. And as we were talking about it, we realized that she had come to each one of us separately and complimented us or told us how much she appreciated us."

"Yes, she did the same to me," Jeff said. "But I don't see—"

"Think about it, Pastor Jeff," Opal said nervously. "It was almost like she was…" Her voice trailed off, and immediately Jeff knew why.

"Like she was saying goodbye."

He heard a sigh from the other end of the line. "That's what we thought too."

He looked into Stephen's face and saw that he was hearing the conversation. "I'll drive over there right now and check on her."

"Thank you so much. I'd go myself but I'm—well—"

"It's all right, Opal. I understand. I'll call back to the church as soon as I know anything. Stay where you are, okay?"

"Oh, I will!" she said quickly.

As Jeff ended the call, Stephen opened the front door and retrieved his keys from the hook. "Come on. I'm driving."

Jeff started to say Stephen didn't need to come along, but stopped himself. He knew Stephen cared about Mish too. And besides, depending on what he found, he might really appreciate the support.

He told Stephen where Mish lived, and they drove there in silence. He found himself looking in ditches as they passed, making sure she hadn't run off the road. He didn't want to voice what was racing through his mind. *We're overreacting.* There are dozens of good reasons why she might not have come to the Women's Society meeting. *But she didn't call.* She forgot. She got a flat tire. She got a last-minute doctor's appointment. *But what about her saying goodbye to everyone?* He took a deep breath and reminded himself that they didn't know that's what she had been doing. Maybe she had just been trying to spread some sunshine or—or—follow the love! That was it. Mish had not been depressed. They were not going to find her dead body.

Jeff was relieved when Stephen's voice pulled him away from the images in his mind. "Is that the house? At the top of the hill?"

"That's the one."

"It's bigger than I thought it would be. I guess I was expecting a farmhouse."

"I thought the same thing first time I was here. There's a story there, but I don't know what it is." Jeff tried to remember the last time he was here. He didn't think he'd been here since the week after Floyd died. *Damn, I need to do a better job at home visitation.*

As soon as the car stopped in the drive, Jeff hopped out

and hurried to the front door. He rang the bell. No answer. He knocked on the door. Still no answer. He pressed his ear to the door but heard no cries for help. He turned the knob, but it was locked.

"Let's check the other doors," Stephen called from the driveway.

The door by the garage was locked and the white curtains on the door window kept them from seeing inside. They hurried around the back and found the door to the three-season porch unlocked. In three long strides, Jeff was at the sliding glass door, which moved soundlessly on its well-oiled track. He breathed a sigh of relief as he stepped through and into the kitchen.

"Mish?" he called softly, then louder. "Mish?"

He looked back at Stephen, who gave him a resolute nod. Room by room they went, each time expecting to see Mish passed out—or worse. Nothing. Every room was clear.

"Garage!" Jeff called as he raced back through the house. The garage was empty. Her blue sedan was gone.

He walked back into the house, not sure if he should feel relieved that they didn't find her. He was still worried and was no closer to knowing where she had gone.

"Jeff."

Something in Stephen's tone of voice made Jeff's heart quicken again. He returned to the kitchen to find Stephen holding a piece of paper. He looked up at Jeff, and the worry was evident on his face.

Without a word he took the note, noticing as he did so that his hand was shaking. He sat in the chair Stephen offered without question.

> If you are reading this, I am gone. I'm sorry if I worried anyone or caused any problems. It was my choice to go. I had to follow the love, and sometimes that means doing things you never thought you'd do.
>
> I left one piece of business undone. This money is for a young lady named Ann. That's probably not her real name, but by this time you'll know who she is. Don't blame her.

None of this was her fault.

All my papers are in my box at Valley Bank.

I love you all.

Mish

Jeff read the note twice, trying to make sense of it. He finally looked up and saw that Stephen held an inch-high stack of bills, his jaw slack. Stephen fanned them out. They were all hundred-dollar bills.

They stared at each other for a long time without speaking, then suddenly Jeff shifted into gear. "Put everything back where you found it and step away. Don't touch anything else. The police will want to investigate, and we've already touched too many things." He vaguely noted that Stephen was following his orders without question. "Call the church. Tell Rachel that Mish isn't here, but we need Opal's help. Ask her to come right away."

"Why—"

"I don't know how to reach Mish's family. Opal will. Just get her out here. I'm calling the police."

Jeff and Stephen were standing in the driveway when Opal arrived. Jeff asked Stephen to take her into the house and fill her in on what they had discovered, while he waited outside for the police. He sat down on a large rock, closed his eyes, and took a few deep breaths. He wanted to be calm and rational when the police arrived. After four or five breaths, he opened his eyes again and rubbed his hands on his thighs. For the first time he noticed how dirty his clothes were. Even his usually immaculate fingernails had dirt under them. Not the professional image he typically tried to portray. But Mish was more important than his image.

Apparently, she was a priority for the police as well, because they pulled into the driveway just a couple minutes later. As two officers emerged from the car, Jeff automatically moved to the driver's side and extended his hand. "I'm Pastor Jeff Cooper. Thank you for coming so quickly."

"Officer Duvall," the young man said. "And this is Lieutenant Samson."

Too late Jeff realized his mistake in greeting the driver first. The lieutenant was clearly the more seasoned officer. His crew cut had more gray than brown, and he had the look of a former athlete. Jeff shook the lieutenant's hand—making sure to give a very firm handshake—and directed his next statement to him. "So where do we start? What do you want to know?"

"Let's start from the top. Name of the individual, her age, and when you first discovered she might be missing."

"Mish Atkinson…around eighty years old, I think. No one has seen her since noon yesterday." He noticed that the lieutenant was not taking notes, but the younger officer was. "She didn't show up for a meeting at church this morning, which she always faithfully attends."

"And what caused you to think she might be missing, rather than simply absent?"

"She was acting odd at church yesterday, talking to people like it might be the last time she saw them. It made some of her friends wonder if…if…"

"If she was suicidal," the officer supplied.

"Yes," Jeff admitted. "It probably sounds like we were jumping to conclusions, but we wanted to err on the side of caution. Besides, Mish has been acting strange recently."

"Strange how?"

"Well, she met a woman at a diner who she thinks is Jesus, and now she thinks Jesus is sending her on missions via text messages."

"That is pretty strange," Lieutenant Samson agreed. "Any diagnosis of dementia?"

"Not to my knowledge. So I came to check on her and instead found the note she left. I'm sorry to say that I touched it—and several other things in the house—before I realized I shouldn't have."

"No problem. I doubt we're dealing with a crime scene."

"That's what I thought until I saw the cash. An envelope full of hundred-dollar bills." Jeff glanced at the younger officer and saw his eyes widen and his jaw drop. Lieutenant Samson was less easy to read. "Come on in. It will make more sense when you read the note." Jeff led them around back and into the kitchen, pointing out the note and money before stepping back to let the police do their work. He heard voices in the other room and peeked into the dining room to see Opal on the phone.

"She reached Mish's daughter-in-law," Stephen whispered, taking Jeff's hand. "They don't live far. She and Mish's son should be able to come right away."

Jeff squeezed Stephen's hand and quickly dropped it. He wasn't sure why, but he was uncomfortable holding hands in front of the police officers. Stephen didn't seem to notice.

He returned to see the young officer reading the note, which had been placed inside an evidence bag, while the older one leaned against the counter. "Tell me what you know," Lieutenant Samson said to the younger man.

His Adam's apple bobbed as he swallowed hard. "Well, this is a note written by an old woman who might be crazy."

"Not crazy," the lieutenant corrected. "Possible undiagnosed dementia. That's different."

"Right, sorry," he responded. "Yes, a note written by an old woman who might have dementia."

"And how do you know she wrote it herself?" he asked. Before his officer could answer, he looked at Jeff. "Officer Duvall is new to the force—a recent graduate of the academy. His partner is out sick today, so I decided to go on patrol with him. It's a good teaching opportunity." He returned his attention to the young officer. "How do you know?" he repeated.

The young man was ready with his answer. "We don't know for sure, but the writing is a little shaky and appears to be consistent with how an old woman would write."

"Good," Samson responded, and the officer gave a weak smile. "And how would you characterize this note?"

"Characterize it?" He looked at his boss, clearly not knowing what he was being asked.

"Define it. Give it a title. What is it?"

"Well, it's a—a—suicide note," he began.

"You sure about that?"

He studied the note again. "I thought so, but I guess it's not clear. She just says she's gone. But she's left money for somebody whose name she doesn't even know, so it can't be a relative. There could be some foul play, or maybe coercion. Could be cause for murder."

Jeff was studying the older man's face and noticed a slight twitch to his mouth, almost like he thought this was funny. But what could be funny about suicide or murder? His dismay must have shown on his face because the lieutenant's next words were addressed to him.

"New recruits always go for the worst," he said with a smile. "So eager to solve a murder that they see them everywhere."

"So this isn't a murder case?" the officer asked.

"Nope. I'm not even sure that's a suicide note."

"Then how do you explain—" Jeff began.

Samson took the evidence bag and note from the recruit's hands. "Look at this here. 'If you're reading this, I am gone.' She doesn't name it. That's not completely unusual—sometimes even people taking their own life can't put it into words. But there's not a lot of emotion. There's no talk of depression or 'I just couldn't take it anymore.' Instead she wrote, 'I'm sorry if I worried anyone or caused any problems.' That doesn't sound like suicide."

"Then what is it?" Jeff asked, not at all convinced.

"I think it's what I call a 'worst case scenario letter.' Just in case there's a car accident, or in case the person gets sick while away. I've seen older folks do this before. But I don't know what this 'follow the love' business means."

"That's the phrase she uses with these missions she thinks Jesus is sending her on—that she has to follow the love."

"That makes sense—well, not really, but you know what I mean. Still, I don't get the feeling that she is in danger."

Jeff took a deep breath—it felt like his first since Opal's call. "What about the money and this person whose name she doesn't know?"

"That is a mystery," Samson admitted. "Why would she want to leave money for someone who she believes has given her a fake name? Is she the kind of person who could be taken in by a scam? Before her recent behavior, I mean."

"I think so," Jeff said. "She is compassionate and generous, and she wants to believe in the best in people. And, of course, she firmly believes some lady she met in a diner was Jesus, who wants her to 'follow the love.' So yeah, she could be taken in."

The officer nodded grimly. "I see it a lot in older people."

"So, what do we do now?" Jeff asked. "Just hope for the best and wait for her to come home?"

"No. First I want to speak with the family. See if they've noticed the behavioral changes you mentioned. Find out if there has been a history of depression, that sort of thing—just to be sure. I also want to find out if they know this Ann person. Do you know how to reach them? Or should I call the office?"

"They're on their way," Stephen answered from the doorway.

"Good," Samson said. "Officer Duvall, take a look through the house and see if you find any clues to Mrs. Atkinson's whereabouts." The young man nodded and left the room, and Samson turned his attention back to Jeff, Stephen, and Opal. "I will need her full name, date of birth, and a recent picture. Do I need to wait for the family or can you help with those?"

While Opal wrote down Mish's full name and birth date, Jeff took out his phone and pulled up the app that came with their recent church directory. Mish's picture was good. She obviously hadn't paid the extra money for the "light touch-up" the company offered. Several of the ladies, and one or two of the men, looked ten years younger in the directory than they did in real life. But Mish's picture was pure Mish, even down to the slightly mischievous smile and twinkle in her eyes. He cleared his throat before handing his phone to the lieutenant and walking into the living room for a moment of privacy.

He surveyed the odd collection of furnishings—furniture that would seem more natural in a farmhouse than in this big place. When he had sat in this room with Mish after Floyd died, Mish had stared at the ugly green-plaid chair and told Jeff what happened. Floyd had been ill for quite some time with a variety of ailments, so his death wasn't a shock, but it was a surprise. She hadn't realized he was that bad.

"Maybe his heart just gave out," Jeff offered.

"It did that a long time ago," Mish had responded. Before he could ask her to explain, she changed the subject, started talking about funeral plans, the songs Floyd had wanted. Jeff remembered being surprised by his choices. He expected more traditional songs, but then, he hadn't known Floyd all that well.

Mish, though, he thought he knew. She had changed since Floyd died. That's typical, of course. Grief changes people, ages them. He had seen many older people never fully recover from a spouse's death. But this was different. Mish had been quiet for a while after Floyd's death, more serious, but she pulled out of it fairly quickly. Now she laughed more frequently and cracked more jokes. She had even started playing pranks on some of the other ladies, like the time she had taken big swigs from a bourbon bottle all throughout a Women's Society meeting. It was only when they confronted her about her drinking problem that she confessed she had filled the bottle with sweet tea. The memory made him smile despite the current circumstances.

He had wondered at first if it was an act, if she was pretending to be lighthearted so her friends would stop worrying about her. But it seemed so genuine, so real, so *Mish*, that he finally determined it had to be authentic. On the other hand, this left him with a more serious question. Had her grief *not* been authentic? Had she only pretended to mourn her husband's passing? For a woman who lived her life pretty straightforward, she sure was surrounded by mystery.

But her new obsession was the biggest mystery. Meeting some woman who claimed to be Jesus, believing Jesus was sending Mish on missions? This was beyond normal even for Mish. He had been looking for other signs of dementia but hadn't seen any. She was always on time, never arrived a day early or late for an activity, knew everybody's names, seemed fully aware of her surroundings. It was just this one area where she seemed deluded.

And now she was off to who knows where, doing God knows what, ready to give thousands of dollars to someone she barely knows. Her family would have to get involved now, take a more active role in her daily life, maybe even take over her finances. Mish would hate that, but it probably needed to be done.

The young officer came striding through the living room on his way to the kitchen, and Jeff followed.

"What did you find?" Lieutenant Samson asked the younger officer.

"There's no toothbrush, and only unopened toothpaste and deodorant."

"So she definitely planned on going away. Any idea how long?"

"Yes, sir. There is a set of suitcases in the closet. The large and medium are both there, and a small over-the-shoulder bag is there. But the smallest rolling suitcase is missing. There are a few empty hangers but also some dirty laundry, so without knowing what's missing, I would guess she was planning to be away no more than a few days. Plus, according to the calendar on her wall, she has a hair appointment on Thursday. If she's anything like my granny, she will do everything she can to be back by then."

The lieutenant smiled. "Thank you, Duvall. That's solid, helpful information."

The young man smiled back. "Yes, sir. Want me to call in her info, see if we get any hits on her license and plates?"

"I've already called them in, but I told dispatch to contact you with the results. You should hear shortly."

As if on cue, the back door opened, and a middle-aged couple came rushing into the kitchen. Jeff remembered them from Floyd's funeral. The son was Bob, but he couldn't remember the daughter-in-law's name. He mostly remembered her annoying laugh and the way she fluttered her hands like a bird. A large, annoying bird.

"Where's my mother?" the man demanded. "Is she okay?"

"That's what we're trying to find out," Lieutenant Samson said. He put out his hand and introduced himself.

"Bob Atkinson," the man responded, shaking hands perfunctorily, then returned to his questioning. "What do we know? When did she go missing?"

Jeff started to answer and then remembered that he wasn't in charge. Fortunately, nobody saw him open his mouth to speak because all eyes were on the lieutenant.

"She was at church yesterday but did not show up at a meeting this morning, so she could be missing as long as twenty-four hours, though probably shorter. Her car is gone, and she took a small suitcase and some toiletries. After we finish talking, we will ask you to look around for other things that might be missing. We think she may have simply gone away for a day or two without telling anyone."

"Oh, she wouldn't do that," the woman interjected. "She tells us everything."

"I'm sorry—I didn't catch your name," Samson said. Jeff thought that was a polite way of saying that her husband hadn't bothered to introduce her.

"Claudia Atkinson," she replied. "I'm Mish's daughter-in-law. We speak at least once or twice a week, and she would never go away without telling me. We're very close."

Unless things had changed since Floyd's funeral, Jeff was pretty sure Mish would not have described their relationship with those words.

"Great. If you can call her on her cell phone, perhaps we could solve this whole mystery."

"She doesn't have a cell phone," Claudia replied. "We've tried to get her to buy one, tried to tell her how it would give us peace of mind, but she refused."

"Actually," Opal said rather quietly, "she's had one for a week or so. But none of us have the number."

"If she bought one, why didn't she tell us?" Claudia asked. Her hands started fluttering at her sides.

When nobody answered, the lieutenant continued. "Then perhaps you can tell us more about this young woman that Mish left money for. Her note said she might or might not be named Ann."

"What note?" Claudia asked.

"What money?" asked Bob.

The officer handed the evidence bag to Bob. Claudia stepped closer to read it too. Everyone waited in silence while they processed the info.

"Where's the money?"

Jeff's heart sank when it was this, of all questions, that seemed to interest Bob. He looked to the lieutenant for a response, but his face was unreadable. "We will need to keep it in police custody until we can return it to your mother, but you can look at the bag." He nodded to the young officer, who handed over the bag of cash. "There's twenty-five grand." He returned his attention to Claudia. "Do you know who this young woman might be, and why Mrs. Atkinson would be giving her so much money?"

Claudia's fluttering hands raised a few inches. "No, I've never heard of her! It must be somebody she just met."

"What about signs of dementia?"

"My mother does not have dementia," Bob answered. Claudia nodded vigorously in agreement.

"Then what do you know about the woman she met who claims to be Jesus? And about these missions she's been on?"

"What?" Claudia's fluttering hands had reached waist level.

"I have no idea what you're talking about," Bob said rather defensively.

There was a moment of silence before Jeff realized that the lieutenant was looking to him to share that part of the story. He told Bob and Claudia what he knew, with Opal and Stephen filling in the details. By the time he was finished, Claudia's hands looked like two birds trying to break free.

Opal stepped forward, clasped Claudia's hands in her own, and led her to a chair at the kitchen table. She kept hold of the younger woman's hands, patting them occasionally. Jeff wasn't sure if Opal found her fluttering as annoying as he did, or if she was just that caring. Probably the latter.

"Okay, we can get her cell phone number. It will just take a little while. In the meantime—"

"Sir!" Officer Duvall interrupted. "We got a hit on her license. She got stopped yesterday in Maryland, but no ticket was issued."

"See if you can talk to the officer who stopped her," Samson said.

"I'm on it. It's his day off, but they're trying to reach him."

Jeff sincerely hoped the guy hadn't gone hunting without his cell phone.

11

Juliann was still a little worried about Mish. Mish had only lost her balance for a few seconds, but she was still awfully pale. But she insisted on sightseeing, so Juliann stopped arguing. Thirty minutes later they were checked out of the hotel, had stored their belongings in the car, and were now debating the best way to get around town. Mish had decided a taxi was easiest, and when Juliann had expressed concern about the cost, Mish had told her to shush. "You start telling me how to spend my money, and I'm gonna start calling you 'Floyd.' And that ain't no compliment," she said with a wink. "Besides, Mr. Waffle Man got us a free night's stay!"

"Then at least let me call a Lyft driver instead of a taxi," Juliann replied. Before leaving home she had downloaded the app and signed up with a visa debit card she had gotten for her birthday. She typed in where they were and where they wanted to go, and by the time she finished explaining to Mish how it worked and why people who aren't taxi drivers would want to just drive people all over the city, their ride had arrived.

"Good morning. I am Ziena," the man announced after lowering the window of his silver sedan. He had an accent that sounded Middle Eastern, and Juliann thought maybe he was Muslim, based on his short, round hat. "I am here to take you to the Lincoln Memorial, yes?"

Juliann simply nodded, but clearly that was not enough for Mish. "Oh yes, please," Mish gushed. "I've always wanted to see it, and I've never gotten the chance. And would it be possible to get a glimpse of the White House too? Not a tour or anything—I just want to see it."

"Yes, ma'am. I can do that. Would you like to ride up front with me, so you get a better view?"

Mish nodded eagerly, literally bouncing on the balls of her

feet. *She's so cute,* Juliann found herself thinking—which was odd, given their ages. Maybe it was because Mish hadn't left the farm much, but she got so excited about the little things. Sometimes Juliann felt like she was the older one of the duo. Or maybe she was just the more jaded, which she admitted to herself was pretty sad.

Mish chatted with the driver and soon knew where he was from, how long he'd been in the U.S., and what he'd done for a living before he came here. Juliann had expected the driver to resist what many would describe as nosiness, especially in today's anti-immigrant environment, but somehow people always responded openly to Mish. There was just something about her that made people feel safe about opening up.

As they drove through the city, Juliann was glad for the distractions of sightseeing. She had dreaded the idea of sitting in the hotel room until it was time for her appointment, and she wondered how much of the morning's itinerary was because Mish really wanted to sightsee and how much was just to keep Juliann's mind occupied. "And you, miss?" Juliann looked up to see the driver looking at her from his rearview mirror. "What has surprised you about our city?"

She looked out the window and took in the surroundings. "Well, I guess it's greener than I expected. The only big city I've been to is New York, and you don't see much green there except in Central Park."

The man nodded knowingly. "Yes, I have been to the New York City, and it has steel instead of trees. I could not live there. In Washington I miss my home country, but in the New York City I think I would forget how to remember her at all."

Juliann wasn't sure she understood what that meant, but Mish seemed to understand. Mish and the driver continued an animated conversation about memories and the smells of home, and Juliann let the conversation fade away again until Mish's excitement caught her attention.

"There it is!" Mish pointed through the front windshield, and Juliann looked up to see the White House in the distance, impressive against the bright blue sky. "Can you get us any closer?" Mish asked.

"Only a little," the driver replied. "Foot traffic only on the streets by the White House. But if you want, I can go around the corner and let you out, then wait for you to come back."

"No, I just wanted to see it with my own eyes. Look there, Juliann. Thirty good men have guided our country from that building."

"Mish, we're on president number forty-five now," Juliann corrected her.

"Yeah, well, all of them wasn't good," she replied. "So now let's go see one of the best."

"Next stop, Abraham Lincoln," the driver agreed.

When they arrived at the National Mall, he hurried around to the passenger side and opened the door for Mish. She slipped him some cash, and Juliann realized Mish might not know she'd handled the tip through the app.

"Are you sure you don't want me to wait for you?" he asked.

"That would be lovely, but we're gonna be here a little while so you'd better go on and get another rider."

"I will park nearby to wait for my next call. When you are done, and if I am available, I will come and get you. Okay?"

Mish thanked him, said goodbye, and slipped her arm through Juliann's again as they walked away. "Have you ever noticed that there are nice people everywhere you go?"

Juliann thought for a minute. "Well, actually, I don't think I've ever thought about it. But then again, my dad is much more likely to say there are assholes everywhere you go."

Mish shrugged. "No offense to your father, but I think you find what you are."

"No doubt," Juliann agreed. "My dad is—" But she didn't finish her sentence, because Mish's phone buzzed. Juliann saw that it was a text from Hailey.

> Your mom just texted, school called her to ask if you were sick

Shit. She'd forgotten that the office calls your parents if you're absent. *Did you answer?* she typed.

No didn't know what to say

Juliann needed a moment to think. "Mish, I need to take care of something here. Can you go on without me?"

"Sure, hon. I'll start climbing the steps to see Lincoln. It'll take me a while anyway. Catch up when you can."

Juliann sat down on the nearest bench and tried to come up with a lie. She was starting to believe her honest nature was a serious handicap. Hmm. What would her dad do? Of course! He would blame somebody else!

Send her this. Office lady is clueless. Missed homeroom because I went to nurse's office with bad cramps, heading to math now.

Juliann chewed on her fingernail while she waited for Hailey's response.

She sent a heart, do I heart back?

No just send a 2.

Why?

It's our way of saying I love you too. Just do it!

Done, chill! BTW r u ever going to tell me where u r?

Told you, just needed to get away

Right, whatever. Don't forget you owe me

I won't, I promise

Juliann closed her eyes and sighed in relief. She would be really glad when this day was over. For so many reasons.

She climbed the steps to the Lincoln Memorial and found Mish standing at the feet of the giant statue. Other people were milling around her, but Mish just stood there, staring up. When Juliann reached her, Mish didn't turn to greet her, so Juliann stood silently at her side, staring up at the monument. After a few minutes she glanced over to see if Mish might be ready to move on, only to see tears streaming down her face. Juliann didn't say anything, just took Mish's hand and squeezed it. Mish squeezed back.

A few more minutes passed before Mish gave another squeeze and let go, reaching into her purse for a tissue. "I probably seem like a silly old woman to you," she said after blowing her nose, "crying at the statue of a man long gone, a man I didn't even know."

Juliann wasn't sure what she was supposed to say so she said nothing.

"It's my heritage, you see. One of my cousins did some genealogy work a while back, found some things I'd just as soon not know about my people. About myself. I knew my mama's daddy was a moonshiner, of course, and my daddy's papa was a bootlegger. Those stories was told around the campfire and seemed kind of reckless and fun when I was a kid. My daddy joked that he married Mama because between the two families, they covered manufacturing and distributing." Mish gave a grim smile, then continued. "But that cousin of mine dug up some dirt from before then. From my great grandfather on my mama's side."

She stopped again. They were still standing at the feet of Lincoln, but Mish was no longer staring up at him. Now she stared at her feet, and it looked like every word was causing her pain.

"People," she said at last. "My great grandfather owned... people. Slaves. I found out a few months ago and I still can't believe the man my grandmother rattled on and on about—how wonderful he was, how smart and funny he was—he was a slave owner. And she never told me. I get nauseous just thinking about it—that my kin did such a thing. Now I'm ashamed to carry their blood."

She finally looked up at Juliann. "I guess I shouldn't have been surprised. My people was from Virginia, and I know that was a slave state. But I never thought it was in my family." She let out a long sigh, then looked back up at the statue. "So I wanted to come here to President Lincoln and thank him for doing the right thing, for signing that proclamation that set all them people free. Especially the ones who picked tobacco for a Eugene McAllister of Lynchburg, Virginia."

Mish turned and started walking slowly down the steps. Juliann gave one last look at Lincoln, then hurried to catch up. She hadn't forgotten how unsteady Mish had been that morning and wanted to be there in case Mish needed help. She slid her hand into Mish's, noticing as she did so how comfortable that had become.

"It's not your fault. You know that, right?" she asked.

"Of course I know. In here." She tapped her own head. "But here?" She rubbed her chest as if it ached. "I feel dirty, like there's something spoilt inside me. I know it don't make sense. I know it's not logical. But that's how I feel. And you can't think your way out of feelings. You just gotta feel 'em until you don't no more."

They walked in silence down the steps, then stopped at the reflecting pool, the Washington Monument in the distance. Juliann was glad the place wasn't crowded. She saw two women in bright-colored saris making their way toward the monument, a young couple on a blanket on the grass beside the water, and a dark-skinned woman running barefoot on the path.

Mish suddenly turned her back on the Washington Monument. "I've had enough of the big dick, haven't you?"

"The big—?"

"Big dick, yes," Mish repeated. "The Washington Monument is a—a—oh, what's the fancy word for it?"

"Phallic symbol?" Juliann said.

Mish nodded. "A fancy word for big dick. Only men would build such a thing. Can you imagine a woman ever wanting her monument to look like that?"

Mish had a point. Juliann would never hear about the Washington Monument without remembering this conversation. She smiled at the thought of calling the Washington Monument the "Big Dick" on her AP American History exam.

"She stopped running." Mish pointed to the runner she had noticed a minute ago.

The woman had stopped, and she had one hand against a tree as she leaned forward, catching her breath.

"I guess lots of people probably run along here. Seems like a good place if it's not too crowded," Juliann said.

"She wasn't running for exercise," Mish said. "Look at the way she's dressed."

Mish was right. It wasn't just that she was barefoot. She wasn't wearing workout clothes, either. And there was something about her that said she was troubled. Juliann looked in the direction from which the woman had run. "I don't see anybody following her. Do you think she's in danger?"

"Not like you think," Mish said quietly as she walked slowly toward the woman. "Only demons or ghosts make a body run like that."

Juliann wasn't sure which she found weirder—that Mish believed in ghosts or in demons. Well, to be fair, probably lots of people believed in ghosts. But demons? Like the devil kind of demons? "What do you—"

Mish cut her off with a wave of her hand. "You're too young to understand. You haven't faced your demons yet. But this woman has. More than her share."

Juliann suddenly realized what Mish meant. Metaphorical demons, not real ones. She was relieved. With everything on her agenda for the day, she was pretty sure she did not need to add an exorcism. She looked back at the runner, who was now standing straighter but with her forehead against the tree and her hands on either side of its trunk. "How can you tell?" Juliann asked.

"I don't know," Mish admitted. "Sometimes I just get a feeling and I know I'm right. This here woman is running away from heartache."

Mish stopped about ten yards from the woman, and Juliann stopped behind Mish. "Ma'am?" Mish said gently.

It always surprised Juliann when Mish called younger people "ma'am" or "sir." Southern rules insist you call your elders by the honorary titles, but Mish used them for people younger than her, like their Lyft driver, and now this woman. Juliann made the connection. They were both people of color. Mish used "sir" and "ma'am" as a way to show respect to people who might have reason to doubt how an old white lady would treat them.

"Ma'am?" Mish repeated, and the woman looked up, surprised that she was being addressed. "I'm sorry to bother you. I wanted to check on you but I can see you're better now."

The woman studied Mish for a moment, then her face relaxed a little. "Yes, thank you."

"You've decided to stop running?"

Mish was stating the obvious, but the woman seemed to be considering it as a question. She looked over her shoulder, then back at Mish. "I'm tired of running."

"Being tired of something still don't mean you're ready to stop."

Juliann got the odd feeling that she was missing something in this conversation—like the two women were communicating on a level that was beyond her reach.

"You already know what you gotta do," Mish said softly. "You gotta follow the love."

The woman stared at Mish again before speaking. "It's not that simple," she said at last.

"Love never is. You don't follow love because it's simple. You follow it because that's all there is." She gave the woman one last smile, then turned toward the parking lot, Juliann once again following at her heels.

☙

Jeff, Stephen, and Opal were seated at the kitchen table with Claudia, while Bob paced the kitchen floor. The trooper from Virginia had finally called back, and the lieutenant was outside talking to him. Bob had tried to follow, but the lieutenant made it clear that he would not be putting the conversation on speaker phone. When the door opened, they all looked up expectantly.

"Good news," Lieutenant Samson announced to the room. "The trooper remembers Mish very well. She was traveling east on I-68 in Maryland. He had pulled her over for slow, erratic driving. Turns out she had just gotten distracted by something her granddaughter showed her, and she was fine."

"What? Olivia's with her?" Bob interjected. "She's supposed to be in school. In Florida."

"If she were leaving school, she would have told us," Claudia insisted.

The lieutenant seemed to be measuring his words carefully.

"Well, there seem to be lots of things going on in your family that you're not aware of. I suggest you take some time to calm down, then contact your daughter. But since there is clearly no crime, this appears to be a private family matter now. I'll write this up as a simple well-being check, though I will need to keep the things I've already put in evidence bags until your mother returns." Bob opened his mouth as if to argue, but the lieutenant was faster. "I'm sorry. Department policy." Bob's face hardened but he nodded.

Lieutenant Samson and Officer Duvall collected their things and left a business card in case the family needed them. Opal was quick to follow the officers out the door. Jeff stood to leave also, but Bob stopped him with a raised hand.

"You owe me an apology. Or at least an explanation."

"Excuse me?" Jeff replied.

"If you knew my mother was showing signs of dementia, why didn't you tell me?" he demanded.

Jeff was so surprised it took him a few seconds to respond. "Well, I only met you the one time, and besides, anything Mish said to me was said in confidence, and—"

"You're not a priest," Bob interrupted. "There's no seal of the confessional, or whatever it's called, because as far as I know, there's no confessional in the Congregational church."

"No, of course not," Jeff agreed, "but I wouldn't want to betray her trust."

Bob gave a snort of a laugh. "Oh, that's rich. It's all about trust, is it?"

Bob was clearly angry with him, but Jeff had no idea why. "I'm sorry. I don't understand."

"Did you even think about calling me, her only son, to tell me about your concerns? I'm willing to bet it never even crossed your mind."

A ripple of guilt ran through him. "Well, no, I guess I didn't. Like I said, we only met the one time and—"

"And people like you don't care much about family values, do you?" He looked from Jeff to Stephen and back again, disdain written all over his face. "I still can't believe the church I grew up in let someone like *you* have the pastor's job."

Jeff wasn't usually surprised by anti-gay rhetoric, nor was he particularly bothered by it anymore. But after the drama of the last few hours, it sent him reeling. He couldn't think of a single word to say in response.

Apparently, Stephen did not have the same problem. "Someone like *him?*" he repeated as he stepped forward. "This particular *someone* dropped everything, on his day off, to come to your mother's house. He walked in not knowing if he might find her passed out or dead. He searched the house, called the police, and stayed here until we knew she was safe. He has done all of this not because he has 'the pastor's job' but because he has a pastor's heart. And if he knows your mother better than you do, *he's* not the one to blame!"

Bob's hands clenched at his sides, which was all the warning Jeff needed. He took Stephen's hand and pulled him out the door before he could say anything else. Jeff looked back one last time to see Claudia's hands taking flight.

12

Juliann looked around at the waiting room, trying to take it all in. The room itself was plain—just simple cushioned chairs with wooden arms grouped in small rectangles around the room. But it wasn't the furniture that caught her attention.

Sitting across from them was a girl who looked like she was around twenty. Her boyfriend kept trying to hold her hand, but she seemed too nervous to let him do so for long. Nearby a woman was frantically trying to keep her toddler from eating the magazines. In the next group of chairs sat another girl who looked to be in her twenties, but she was sitting alone. Her thumbs were typing on her phone at a furious rate, interrupted only by her repeated glances at the door.

But the people she kept staring at were at the far end. It was a girl, around her age, maybe a little older, and sitting beside her was a woman who was clearly her mom. They were both thin and kind of elegant, with the same strawberry-blonde hair. While others in the room looked nervous, this girl was incredibly sad. She kept pulling a tissue out of the pocket of her hoodie and wiping her eyes. Her mother looked like she was in pain, too, but not for herself. Even from across the room, it was clear this mother was hurting for her child.

Just watching brought tears to Juliann's eyes. She tried to imagine how it would feel, having her mother beside her instead of an old woman she'd only known for a week. She tried to imagine having a mother who would hurt so badly for her. She tried to imagine that arm around her, protecting her instead of the other way around. Looking back, she couldn't even remember when it had happened—when she had become her mother's protector. She guessed it was sometime around second grade when she realized that if she could make her dad proud of her, if she could distract him with her grade on a test, or could tell a story that made him laugh, he was less likely to yell at her mom. Then she discovered that if she broke a glass or spilled something, he would just give an exasperated sigh. But if her mother did it, he came unglued. Pretty soon she was claiming every accident as her own. Her mother confronted her about it one time, told her she didn't need to do that. But they both knew better. Juliann was the only one who could keep the peace. So she kept it. And she never told anyone how much it cost her.

She looked back down at the paperwork she was supposed to be completing. Name, age, date of birth. It looked like every other form she'd ever filled out but somehow it felt different. She almost laughed when the form listed "Sex." She wanted to write "Obviously" but wasn't sure the abortion clinic was the place to make a joke. But then it asked for date of most recent period and she wasn't sure. She had never been good about keeping track of the date. She knew the exact date of conception, of course, but they didn't ask for that. She knew the time and the place and the way it had made her feel. She knew the smell of Aiden and the taste of his mouth. She knew she was making the right choice. Then again, it was her only option, so did that make it a choice? Did it count as a choice if it was the only thing she could do?

She shook her head and returned to the form. Type of service requested. She checked the boxes for a surgical abortion with local anesthesia. She would have preferred general anesthesia, so she would be asleep for the whole thing, but that cost two hundred dollars more. Mish was already doing so much for her, she couldn't ask for that luxury. She could stand a few minutes of pain.

She looked back at the mother and daughter. The mother had an arm around her daughter and was whispering to her as she stroked her hair. The daughter looked up, gave a soft smile and a nod, and then leaned into her mother's protective embrace. Juliann felt tears start to form.

"Juliann?"

She looked up to see a nurse at the door, waiting for her. She nodded, taking a deep breath as she picked up her backpack and stood. She was surprised when she felt Mish standing at her side. Of course. Mish was here. Mish wasn't even family, but Mish was here. It wasn't her mom, but it was something. Someone.

But this someone had done quite enough. She gave Mish a quick hug, then stepped back. "Thank you, Mish, but I can take it from here."

Mish looked confused. "But I thought—I thought you'd want me—"

"I need to do this on my own."

"But—"

She took Mish's hand and squeezed. "Just wait for me, okay?" Mish bit her lip and nodded.

๛

Mish watched Juliann disappear through the door and had to fight the urge to run after her. *What kind of kid would want to do this alone?* She must have done something wrong—something pretty bad if Juliann would rather be alone than have a friend by her side.

Maybe Juliann was embarrassed about sharing so much last night. Had Mish been too nosy? She'd been curious, of course, but she'd tried so hard not to push. Floyd always said her nosiness would be the death of her.

That's not what he had always thought. When their son was little, Floyd had called her Georgie, after that cute little monkey whose mischievous curiosity always got him into trouble. At the time she had thought it was a compliment. It wasn't until later that she figured out it wasn't so nice. If she was George, then he was the man in the hat who knew everything and always had to fix all the problems the monkey caused. He got to be the grown-up, and she was the troublesome pet.

She knew she deserved some of the criticism. She'd caused more than her share of trouble over the years. And, yes, she was curious, but wasn't that a good thing sometimes? If she wasn't curious there's a mountain of things she never would have learned.

But there's a limit, a voice in her head said. *A limit you never seem to know. You were too nosy with Juliann and you pushed her away.*

No, that's not true, she argued with the voice. *I didn't push. She just opened up because we're friends.*

You are not friends! the voice insisted. *You're just a busybody old lady who is crazy enough to think God would choose her for some kind of mission!*

Mish couldn't stand it. She stood up and paced, trying to calm herself down and silence the critic. *I'm following the love,* Mish reminded herself. *That's all I'm doing—following the love. That don't mean I'm crazy.* Suddenly she stopped in her tracks. *I'm arguing with a voice in my head. Isn't that the very meaning of crazy?*

See? I told you! And now you think you're doing the world some big favor but you're really just being used by a teenage girl. You think she'd have brought you here if she didn't need you for money and a ride? She's probably laughing at you behind your back! You always were a fool!

When a hand touched her shoulder, Mish nearly jumped out of her skin. "Ma'am? Juliann asked me to give you this."

She took the folded piece of paper the nurse was holding out to her, barely mumbling her thanks as she unfolded it and read.

> Mish,
>
> I'm sorry I couldn't bring you into the office with me. I could tell it hurt your feelings. I can't explain it—I just felt like I needed to do this part of it on my own. You've been so wonderful and I didn't want you to have to carry any more of this than necessary.
>
> I don't know if I'll ever be able to find the words to thank you, and to tell you what you mean to me. You've not only protected my present but my future too.
>
> I still don't know for sure what you mean when you say you're "following the love," but I'm glad you do. Thank you for being my best-grand.
>
> See you in a little bit.
>
> Juliann

Mish didn't realize she was crying until a tear hit the page. She wasn't a pest. She hadn't pushed Juliann away. Juliann loved her, and the voice in her head—well, she knew who that voice belonged to. And the owner of that voice could go to hell…if he wasn't there already.

She fumbled through her canvas crochet bag for her notebook. She knew of only one way to deal with the emotions swirling inside her like a cyclone. Floyd had always made fun of her poems. If it was true that the dead could see the living, he was about to regret that.

Sometimes poetry took a good long time, but this one came out as if her hand had been waiting for years for her heart to be ready to speak. When she got finished, she read it through again.

> You told me that you loved me,
> when you asked me to be your bride.
> You told me that you loved me.
>
> The problem is: you lied.
> You told me that I was lucky
> to have you by my side.
> You told me that you loved me.
> The problem is: you lied.
>
> You said you was the expert.
> I wasn't qualified
> To argue with your logic.
> The problem is: you lied.
>
> You told me I was silly,
> something was wrong with me inside.
> You told me I was stupid.
> The problem is: you lied.
>
> You told me and I believed you.
> You yelled and terrified.
> But fear don't live beyond the grave,
> so now I'll tell: you lied.
>
> From here the story changes.
> I won't be brushed aside.

I'm a smart and best-grand woman,
and love will be my guide.

"Take your time getting dressed," the nurse said to her with a kind smile. "There's no need to rush. Once you're ready, open the door and I'll come back in with some last-minute instructions, all right?"

Juliann nodded, and the nurse closed the door. She didn't think she needed to take a moment, but for some reason she wasn't eager to move, either. So she just sat, checking in on how her body felt. Everything she had been told was correct. There had been pain, but it only lasted a few minutes. Now she just felt like she had a bad case of cramps.

She was less eager to take stock of her emotions. What was she supposed to be feeling? The pro-life people said she should be feeling guilt or shame for killing a defenseless baby. But others said she shouldn't feel anything at all. This was a legal medical procedure to terminate a pregnancy, nothing more or less. Was there any middle ground? Could she feel sad and glad at the same time? Could she feel bad for the life that would never be and still be relieved that it was over?

What about the future? Would this event stay with her always? When she finally chose to have a child, years from now, would it matter that she had terminated her first pregnancy? Would she ever tell her husband? Probably not. Hell, she couldn't even tell her boyfriend.

But Aiden was no longer her boyfriend, and he never would be again. She had ended it because she couldn't predict how he would respond to the pregnancy; she couldn't take the risk of telling him. But just for a moment she let herself imagine that he was with her, that he was another attentive boyfriend holding his girlfriend's hand as she did this difficult thing. Then she shook her head and dismissed the thought. It was over. She couldn't tell him then, and she sure as hell couldn't tell him now, after the fact.

She climbed off the gurney and dressed. She was glad she had Mish waiting for her. Mish wouldn't expect her to be any certain way or feel any certain thing. And if she didn't feel like talking, Mish was certainly capable of carrying on a conversation without her.

Juliann jumped when the phone in her backpack rang. She started to answer it and then remembered it wasn't her phone. She didn't recognize the number, so she let it go to voicemail. She'd have to remember to tell Mish later.

But remembering wasn't going to be a problem. By the time the nurse had finished giving her all the instructions—plus free condoms and a brochure on birth control—the phone had rung two more times. "Somebody is eager to reach you," the nurse said as she walked Juliann to the exit. Juliann was pretty sure this wasn't a good sign.

As soon as she stepped into the lobby and saw Mish sitting there, her eyes filled with tears. She tried to will them away but once they started, there was no going back. Mish walked toward her, looked into her eyes, and then wrapped her in a giant hug. Mish wasn't a big woman—she was several inches shorter than Juliann—but somehow, in her arms, Juliann felt safe. Protected. Loved. She just let Mish hug her for a little while before finally pulling away to blow her nose. Once she'd caught her breath, she said, "I still need to check out and pay."

"No, it's all taken care of," Mish assured her. "We're ready to go. I'll have you back home by bedtime."

"Oh, speaking of home, somebody has been calling you." She handed the phone over to Mish.

Mish looked at the number. "What in tarnation?"

"You don't recognize the number?"

"No, I do," Mish corrected. "It's my son's cell phone number. I just don't know how he got mine."

Juliann was confused. She knew Mish and her son weren't really close, but she didn't think they were estranged or anything. "You haven't given him your phone number?"

Mish shook her head. "Livie must've. She's the only one I gave it to. Well, he's waited this long. He'll wait a few more minutes." She put her arm through Juliann's. "If you don't need anything else, let's get going. Can you set my phone to talk through the car so I don't have to waste time talking to him? I'd rather hit the road."

"Sure, I can connect your phone via Bluetooth but then I'll hear the whole conversation. It won't be private."

"Oh, hon, I don't care about that. I can't imagine he wants to say anything you can't hear."

Juliann wasn't so sure about that, but when she got in the car, she did as Mish requested. Then she put her home address into the map app so she could navigate. She'd keep an eye on the map while Mish spoke with her son.

Mish pulled out of the parking lot, and Juliann guided her back to the interstate. "I guess I've put it off long enough. Go ahead and call my son."

Juliann tapped on his number and made sure it was going through the car's speakers. He answered on the first ring.

"Mother?"

"Well, hello there, Bobby. How are you today?"

"Where the hell are you?" he demanded.

His tone of voice made Juliann shiver.

"*Excuse* me?"

Juliann heard the reprimand in Mish's voice, but apparently her son had not.

"I said, where the hell are you? You leave town without telling a single soul, you get pulled over by the police—who you lied to, by the way—and now you call like nothing's wrong?"

"Well, there ain't nothing wrong. Except for you yelling at your mother, of course. There's something seriously wrong with that!" Mish's knuckles were starting to turn white on the steering wheel.

"Oh, but there's nothing wrong with you disappearing with God knows who, leaving your whole family worried sick. Don't you think you should have told us? You're eighty years old, for Christ's sake!"

"Actually, I am eighty-two years old. And the last I checked, that means I am a full grown adult. I can go where I want, when I want, with whoever I want. You don't get a say in that. You're not the boss of me, Bobby."

"Yeah, well, we'll see about that," he muttered. "So who are you with?"

"I ran off to Vegas with my new beau. Good-looking guy, still has all his own teeth. I like that in a man. We got married by Elvis in the all-night wedding chapel and now we're on our honeymoon. That's why I didn't answer the phone. We were busy having—"

"Mother, you were pulled over by the police in Maryland. You have a girl with you that you claimed was your granddaughter, but Olivia is still in school in Florida. Who the hell are you with? Is it this Ann person?"

They heard some rustling and suddenly a female voice came through the speakers. "Mom, are you safe? Did you get kidnapped? Just say 'yes' if you're in danger. Or—or—say something that will assure me that it's you and you're safe."

"Oh, bless your heart, Claudia honey, but sometimes you are crazy as bat shit."

"That's her," Bob said. "Now give me back the phone. Mother, I want to know where you are and who you're with and when you're coming home."

"Where am I? I'm in the state of 'none of your business,' and I'm with half a mind to knock you three ways from Sunday, and I'm coming home when I'm damn good and ready. In the meantime, you better change your tone because I will not be spoken to like a child. That's one lesson you learned from your daddy that you better unlearn mighty quick. Now hang up the phone."

It took Juliann a couple of seconds to realize what Mish had said. "Hang up?" she asked.

"Yes, hang up the phone. I'm done talking to my son."

"Mother, hold—"

The line went dead as Juliann pushed the button. She turned wide eyes to Mish. "Wow," was all she said.

"Wow," Mish repeated as she took a deep breath.

"I am so sorry. I got you into this mess and now you're in trouble with your son."

"I am not in trouble with my son," she corrected. "My son is in trouble with me. This ain't your fault so don't go blaming yourself for the fact that my son is being a jackass. Promise?"

Juliann nodded, but she didn't mean it. Mish could deny it all she wanted, but if it weren't for Juliann, Mish would be safe at home crocheting, not driving to DC to help a teenager get an abortion. If this incident caused a rift in Mish's family, it was another thing Juliann would have to try to forgive herself for. She would add it to the list.

13

Jeff stood at the large picture window in his living room, staring at the golden leaves against the bright blue afternoon sky. A Carolina blue sky was how he always thought of it, which probably wouldn't please all his West Virginia parishioners. Glorious fall weather always reminded him of his college days in the mountains of Western North Carolina.

Home. The word came to him out of nowhere and surprised him with its intensity. It was true that North Carolina was home to him, the place he'd longed for all his life. With his dad being a Methodist minister, they'd moved so often that he'd never had time to put down roots. Or maybe he had time, but after the first two, he didn't have the heart to try again. He knew it would all be ripped away with the next assignment, their family at the whim of the district supervisor who ordered the moves. But North Carolina was his. It had been his choice to go there for college, and his choice to stay until he went to seminary. Asheville was the closest to a hometown he'd ever known.

But last time he visited, it felt different. Favorite restaurants had disappeared and new ones had taken their place. Microbreweries were as plentiful as vegetarian restaurants had once been. Asheville had lost some of its funk. He left and the place had moved on without him. Just like the people. And now every time he thought of his once-beloved town, he couldn't help but hear in his mind the old Olivia Newton John song, "Home Ain't Home Anymore."

And West Virginia wasn't home either. He wondered if it ever would be. He didn't know how long he'd stay here or where he'd go next. Sometimes he envied people who were rooted in one place. Maybe he was bound to be rootless. He wasn't sure how he felt about that.

He heard movement behind him and then felt arms around his waist. "What are you thinking about?"

Jeff gave a noncommittal shrug. "Home."

"Geographically or metaphorically?" Stephen queried.

"Both, I guess." He turned in his partner's arms. "Do you ever miss it?"

Stephen tilted his head. "Home? Oh, you mean Connecticut. Sure, I miss my parents. I miss the familiar—driving by places where I have childhood memories. But that's just my hometown. It's not my home."

"Then where's home?" Jeff asked. "Is West Virginia home?"

"It is for now."

"How do you do that? After growing up in one place, how do you make some place you've only lived a few years 'home'?"

"Because home isn't a place. It's a state of being."

Jeff nodded. "You mean because we have each other."

"Yes and no," Stephen hedged. "I mean, yes, absolutely, home is with you. As long as we're together, in many ways I'm home. But that's not actually what I meant. I meant that if you're comfortable in your own spirit, if you're at home in your own body and soul, then you carry home within you. Then you can be at home wherever you go."

Jeff stepped out of the embrace and plopped down onto the sofa. He let out a long sigh and ran his fingers through his hair. "Do you think my parishioners know?"

"Know what?" Stephen asked as he sat down at the other end of the sofa.

"That you're more spiritual than I am. For all the talk about the 'spiritual but not religious' crowd outside the church, I'm afraid I represent the 'religious but not spiritual' contingent. I'm just the professional. You're the one with all the heart."

"I don't believe that's true. You have lots of heart. Your head just gets in the way sometimes. Take today, for example. What you did today was the perfect example of your heart. You dropped everything on your day off—when you're in a bit of a crisis your-self—because one of your people was in trouble."

Jeff waved away the comment. "Anybody would have done the same."

"I don't think that's true either, but I'll stop arguing with you. So do you want to talk about what happened today? You were pretty quiet on the ride home."

"I don't have much to say," Jeff said with a shrug. "I just have questions."

"Okay, then let's hear the questions." He nudged Jeff playfully with his foot. "If I'm not being too pushy."

"All right, here goes." Jeff began ticking them off on his fingers. "For starters, who is this Ann person? Is that who Mish is with? Why is Mish willing to give her twenty-five thousand dollars? Where did Mish even *get* twenty-five thousand dollars? How did some woman at a diner convince Mish that she was Jesus? How is she getting sent on these 'missions'? What's going to happen now that Mish's son knows about her delusion?"

"Delusion?" Stephen interrupted. "That's a bit harsh, don't you think?"

"Not at all. Thinking you're getting direct messages from God is pretty much the definition of delusional."

"Hmm."

"What is that supposed to mean?" Jeff asked.

"What is *what* supposed to mean?" Stephen replied. "All I said was 'hmm.'"

"Yeah, well, your 'hmm' always means something."

"I just thought that was an interesting statement coming from a minister."

"Just because I'm a minister, I'm supposed to believe that Jesus came back as a woman who frequents the Bluebird Diner and that my parishioner is getting text messages from God?"

"I didn't say that," Stephen said. "I just find it interesting that you don't believe in divine revelation. I thought that was kind of a job requirement."

"Well, when you put it like that, of course I believe in divine revelation. Of a sort. But that doesn't mean I have to believe Mish."

"So God wouldn't speak to Mish?"

"Oh, for Pete's sake, that's not what I meant. You're twisting my words all around."

"I'm just trying to understand how you can believe that God inspires your sermons but doesn't inspire Mish's actions."

"I never said God inspired my sermons." Jeff rubbed the back of his neck. He did not like the way this conversation was going. They weren't completely back to solid footing after their argument this morning, and now here was another one.

"Of course you have," Stephen said. "I've heard you say repeatedly, when someone thanked you for a sermon, that it wasn't from you, that it was from God."

"That's just something preachers say…"

"So you don't actually believe it? Why would you say it if you don't mean it?"

Jeff let out a loud huff. "I don't know, okay? I don't want to seem arrogant, so I just—I just say something to deflect the compliment."

"Do you seriously not believe God inspires your sermons?" Stephen asked.

"Well, they haven't been very inspired lately, so I can't say God is doing much of the work," he grumbled.

Stephen reached out and took his hand. "Oh, honey, do you honestly believe you are doing this job—that you *can* do this job—on your own? It's no wonder you're stressed."

Jeff pulled his hand out of Stephen's. "Thanks for the vote of confidence." He stood abruptly and grabbed his jacket from a nearby chair. "I'm going for a walk."

"Do you want—"

"No," Jeff answered and shut the door behind him, a little louder than he intended. He headed left and down the hill, away from the church. He just felt so amped up, on edge. Some space, even from his spouse, would do him good.

All right, maybe *especially* from his spouse. Stephen was just so damn sure of everything. He had this "everything happens for a reason" philosophy that drove Jeff absolutely crazy. He also believed that "the universe" gives you what you need to grow, and all kinds of other stuff Jeff used to dismiss as New Age nonsense. Because of Stephen he gave these ways of thinking more credence than he used to, but honestly, sometimes it just got annoying.

A short beep from a passing car interrupted his thoughts, and he automatically smiled and waved even though he had no idea who it was. Sometimes he hated living and working in the same neighborhood. The fishbowl existence was particularly tiresome on days like this.

It was just one of the things he disliked about the ministry. Some days he longed to have a normal job—the kind of job you could go to and leave at the end of the day, and not have to be nice to people in the grocery store because you never know if they know who you are and might judge your church because you got impatient with the incompetent cashier. Was this really how he wanted to spend his life?

People always ask ministers about their "call." When did you get your call? How did you know you were called? Blah blah blah. He usually gave the socially acceptable and not untruthful version of the answer: that it was a gradual dawning, a growing awareness rather than a mountaintop experience. But the whole truth was that he had simply followed the path of least resistance. He majored in comparative religion because it interested him, and then what do you do after that but fulfill everybody's expectations and go to seminary? Now he was thirty-two years old and stuck in a career he wasn't sure fit him. But there weren't a lot of career alternatives for someone with a Master of Divinity degree and a Certificate in Prophetic Preaching.

Can we stop with the existential questions for today? Between his parents and Mish, there were plenty of other topics for consideration. He let the thoughts of his dad go so that he could focus on Mish. He had shared some of his questions with Stephen, but there were so many more. Each one was rooted in the original mystery. Mish had received a text from someone she believed was Jesus, and who she claims she met at the diner. She mentioned one other encounter—his name was Ethan, Jeff remembered— and now it seemed clear that there was at least one more, this person who might or might not be named Ann. Who had lured Mish to the diner? What had they hoped to accomplish by doing so? This woman claiming to be Jesus—had she asked Mish for money? What angle was she playing?

It all came down to the phone. He just wished he could get his hands on that phone. If he searched through her text messages, he could figure out who was writing to her, maybe track them down. Clearly the police weren't interested, and so far he didn't have proof of any crime. He'd have to come up with some excuse to see Mish's phone. Maybe if he asked to borrow it…

And maybe I'm considering a huge invasion of privacy against a dear old woman I love! The thought brought him to a complete stop. What the hell was wrong with him? Being worried about her, being protective of her even, was one thing. But tricking her into sharing private information? To assume he was—what?—her rescuer or something? Why was he trying to micromanage her life? *Maybe because I can't manage my own?*

This second thought took his breath away, but before he could begin to process it, a car pulled up beside him—a big gold sedan with the window down. He tried to plaster a smile on his face and ducked his head so he could see the driver. "Good afternoon, Ruth," he called. "Lovely day, isn't it?"

"I need to talk with you about that sermon of yours yesterday," Ruth said. Her voice told him she wasn't pleased.

"I'll be happy to set an appointment to meet with you," he said, with his practiced pastor's smile. "Just call the office tomorrow and I'll find a time."

"I have time right now. You can get in the car and I'll drive us back to the church."

"Sorry, Ruth, but I *don't* have time right now. Please call the office tomorrow," he said in what he hoped was a polite but firm voice.

"Your walk is more important than my concerns about the future of this church?" Ruth demanded.

"No, but my day off takes priority over your desire to complain." He stood up straight and marched away. The car sped past him, swerving a little as it rounded the bend. He started jogging, then picked up his pace and broke into a run. He hadn't run for two years and he knew he would pay for it later. Then again, he was going to pay for that comment later, too, so what was the difference? Both rash decisions were going to leave him hurting.

Juliann's cover story had continued to work. Hailey had texted Juliann's mom for her, saying she was staying late to tutor, then would hitch a ride to dance lessons. Meanwhile, she had already told her dance instructor that she would be out today, so there would be no repeat of the mistake she'd made with the school secretary. All she had to do was send another text later to explain why she wasn't coming home from dance class on time, and that would cover her until they got home. Boy, she'd be glad when all this lying was over. Besides, these cramps were really kicking her ass.

Mish had been uncharacteristically quiet since the conversation with her son. Juliann had made a couple of feeble attempts at conversation, but for once Mish hadn't picked up on the cues. She turned on some mellow music and drifted off to sleep. She awoke with a start to the sensation of the car tires on the highway rumble strip.

"Sorry about that," Mish said. "You go on back to sleep. I'm sure you need it."

Juliann looked at Mish and realized how tired she was. She seemed to be blinking a lot and her face looked kind of pale. "No, I'm fine. I'll stay awake and keep you company." She straightened up in her seat as a thought occurred to her. "Are we in West Virginia yet?"

"Almost. Why?"

"Well, I have a learner's permit, so I can drive once we get into West Virginia if you want me to."

"Oh, bless your heart, that would be wonderful. We'll be crossing the state line real soon. As soon as we do, I'll let you take the wheel. I'm pretty tuckered out."

A few minutes later they crossed the state line into West Virginia and decided to stop for gas and a bite to eat. When they returned to the car, Mish tossed her the keys, and Juliann headed to the driver's side. "Hey, Mish, did you know you're missing a hubcap over here?"

"Yep, I've got some extras at home. I'll put one on tomorrow."

Juliann got in the car and began adjusting the seat and mirrors, like her driving instructor had taught her. "You keep extra hubcaps around?" she asked.

"I started doing that a year or two ago," Mish admitted. "I kept losing them, probably from hitting curbs. My son said it was a sign that I shouldn't be driving anymore. Well, there's no way I was going to let him take away my driving privileges, so I went to the store and bought a case of cheap hubcaps. Now whenever I lose one, I put a replacement right back on. That way nobody notices."

"That's actually pretty genius," Juliann said with a laugh. "A wee bit scary, but genius!"

Mish ducked her head. "Then I guess I shouldn't tell you about the spray paint."

Juliann slowed the car and looked over her shoulder to merge onto the interstate. This part always made her nervous. After she was safe in her lane, she asked, "What was that about the spray paint?"

"Well, my garage is a little bit tight. I've got too much stuff in there and sometimes my car doesn't fit right. A couple of times I've hit the edge of the garage door on my way in. Now I keep a can of white spray paint hidden in the garage so I can touch up the frame and he won't never see it."

Juliann glanced over at her with a grin. "Funny how you never mentioned any of this when you offered to drive me to DC!"

"Well, even if I had, I don't recall you having lots of options. I think you would have taken the ride anyway. You know, a bird in the hand is worth two in the bush."

Juliann laughed. "Yeah, something like that. And you're right, I would have accepted anyway."

"So keep your eyes on the road and quit giving me grief!" Mish teased.

Juliann gave a little salute. "Yes, ma'am!" Just then a beep interrupted their laughter. "Can you check my phone—I mean your phone?"

Mish looked closely at the screen. "It's your friend. She said your mom just texted to ask when you're coming home."

"Tell her to text my mom that I'm going back to Hailey's house, because she just broke up with her boyfriend and needs to talk."

Mish typed so slow that Juliann was tempted to pull over and do it herself. But Mish seemed so proud of herself for doing it, she didn't have the heart. At last she was done, and within a few seconds there was another ding.

"She said, 'My nonexistent boyfriend broke up with me? Gee thanks.'" Mish put the phone down on her lap but ten seconds later it rang. Mish answered it, and Hailey's voice came through the car speakers. "Juliann, I think we've got trouble. Your mom said she needs you to come home. I told her the boyfriend thing, but she still says you have to come home. I don't know what to say."

"Shit. I really need to call her, but I can't call her from Mish's phone. What should I do?"

Surprisingly, Mish was the one who answered. "It's too bad they don't have party lines anymore, like when I was a kid."

"Party lines?" Juliann repeated. "Wait, that's it! Three-way calling. Hailey, you're calling me from my phone, right?"

"Yeah, of course," Hailey answered.

"Okay, then just tap on 'add a call' and add my mom. I think it will show on her phone as coming from me. You'll have to stay on the line and be quiet."

"No kidding," she said sarcastically. "You're just lucky I don't have plans with my imaginary boyfriend."

"Hailey, just hurry," Juliann pleaded.

"Here goes."

A few seconds later a different voice came on the line. "I was just trying to text you back. Can you come home right away?"

Juliann heard the tense tone in her mother's voice, but she tried to ignore it. "I don't know, Mom. Hailey really needs me. She's very depressed about this break-up, and I don't think I should leave her alone."

"I understand, but, um, your dad is a bit upset. He says you can't skip out on family dinner two nights in a row."

Juliann let out a long, exasperated sigh. "How drunk *is* he?"

"Oh, I don't know. The usual I guess," she answered evasively.

"He's in the room, isn't he? He can hear you?"

"Yes, I would think so," her mom replied.

"Shit," she said again. "Well, Mom, I'm really sorry, but it's not possible for me to come home right now. It'll be a couple of hours."

"But..."

They heard some shuffling sounds and then a different voice spoke. "Juliann, get your ass home right now. I've had a bad day and I want dinner with my family. You've got fifteen minutes or you're grounded."

Juliann took a deep breath. The lies were unraveling, and there wasn't a damn thing she could do to stop it. "Well, then, I guess you'll have to ground me. I can't get there in fifteen minutes." She grimaced, preparing for the explosion. "It'll be more like two and a half hours."

"Two and a half hours?" he yelled. "Where the hell are you?"

She glanced over at Mish before answering. "Morgantown," she said at last.

"Morgantown? What the hell—oh, wait, you're at the university, aren't you? What are you doing, partying at some frat house or something? I should have known. I should have known you'd turn out just like your mother. My only question is: are you a whore or are you a slut?"

Juliann didn't know how to answer. She was so humiliated that Mish and Hailey were hearing all this. And having ended a pregnancy just hours ago, the simple fact that her father was making such accusations brought tears to her eyes. She blinked rapidly to clear her vision.

"I asked you a question," her father yelled. "Are you a whore or are you a slut?"

"What's the difference?" she finally choked out.

"A whore gets paid. A slut does it for free."

Juliann had barely been holding it together, but the absurdity of his accusation virtually forced a response out of her. "Oh, then I'm definitely a whore. That's how I get all my money for drugs. Did you want me to bring you some? Or have you crawled far enough into that bottle of scotch that it would be a waste of good cocaine?" Before he could respond, she said, "I will be home in two and a half hours. Do us all a favor and go sleep it off."

Then she grabbed the phone out of Mish's hands, pressed End, and let out a gasping sob as she handed it back.

"Pull over," Mish said softly.

"No, I can—"

"Pull over," Mish repeated firmly. "Now."

Juliann wrenched the wheel to the right, skidding slightly as she hit the gravel shoulder. She hit the brake hard and came to an abrupt stop. But she couldn't take her eyes off the road or her hands off the steering wheel. She was vaguely aware of Mish reaching over and putting the car in park. When Mish touched her hand, she looked down to see her knuckles, clinging to the steering wheel as if it were her lifeline to sanity. Mish slowly pried her fingers off the wheel and then pulled Juliann into her arms.

The breakdown came immediately. It washed over her in floods of grief, anger, and despair, each emotion like a wave threatening to drag her under. It reminded her of the riptide she'd experienced on vacation one time in Florida. The lifeguard had rescued her. Her father hadn't even noticed she was in danger. And now her mother was the one in danger, and Juliann was powerless to stop it, powerless to stop him.

Safe in Mish's arms, she cried for what felt like forever.

After the weeping she started gasping for air, and she sat up, her chest heaving with the effort. Mish kept holding her hand, patting it as Juliann stared out the front windshield, trying to catch her breath. Finally, she took the tissue Mish offered, dried her face and blew her nose. She ran a finger through her hair and realized with surprise that the top of her head was wet. Mish looked as if she'd been crying almost as much as she had. Juliann's head was covered with Mish's tears. Just the thought brought a renewed wave of sadness. She took a few more ragged breaths and finally found some words—just three, the only ones she had.

"I'm so sorry," she choked.

Mish shook her head. "There's not a thing for you to be sorry about."

"I'm sorry you had to hear all that," Juliann explained.

"And I'm sorry you were on the receiving end of that hatefulness. You didn't deserve that, hon. Not even if he'd known why we went away."

Juliann nodded. She believed what Mish said. She wasn't a slut or a whore. But to be called one—and by her own father—still made her feel dirty.

It took Juliann a few minutes to calm down and pull herself together. Mish offered to drive but Juliann said she was fine. Mish thought about insisting but then decided that maybe the girl needed to be behind the wheel. It would take her mind off things, and besides, maybe she needed to feel in control of *something* in her life.

Mish didn't think of herself as an angry person. And she certainly wasn't violent. But right now she was entertaining vivid fantasies of appropriate punishments for Juliann's father. She thought maybe a branding iron would be the right touch.

She and Juliann never had trouble talking, but the next two and half hours passed with neither one of them saying much. There was too much that needed to be said and nothing that could be said. So they rode mile after mile in silence. They were nearing Charleston when Mish finally spoke again.

"Juliann? Have you thought about—I mean, sure you've thought about it, but—well, I mean—what are you gonna tell your dad?"

"I haven't decided. And I know I'm running out of time. We'll be home soon."

"Do you want to say you went to Morgantown for a college tour? I know the kids do those these days, tour a college to see if they want to go there. Or I could tell him that you were doing me a favor, taking me to visit my sister or something."

"I appreciate the offer, but how would we explain how we met?"

"I dunno. Maybe a club at school connects you with lonely old women as a service project."

"That's actually not a bad idea," Juliann muttered. Then she shook her head. "No, he'd never believe it from me, and I'm not letting you come in the house. You've done more than enough."

Mish patted her leg again. "That's cute, hon, that you think you can stop me from doing something I want to do. This is my call. And I'm not letting you go in there to face him alone. If he's anything like Floyd, and I'm guessing he is, he will take it easier on you if there's a witness. So no more talk about whether I'm going in with you or not. Let's just agree on what we're gonna say."

By the time they reached Juliann's house, they had their story straight. When they pulled into the driveway, Mish couldn't help the "wow" that escaped her lips. The house was big and beautiful and looked like it belonged on the cover of the *Charleston Home and Garden*. Whatever kind of law her dad practiced, it must pay well.

Mish gave Juliann one last hug when they got out of the car, and Juliann threw her backpack over her shoulder and led Mish through the garage and into the kitchen. When the door opened, a small woman with dark brown hair jumped up from the stool at the counter and ran to hug Juliann, her bloodshot eyes filled with tears. "Oh, thank God," she began, but then she saw Mish. "What? Who…" she stammered.

Juliann dropped her backpack on the table. "Mom, I want you to meet my dear friend Mish. Mish, this is my mother, Nicole."

Mish moved forward to shake hands as quickly as her body, still stiff from the drive, would allow. "Nicole, it is so nice to meet you. I have to tell you—you have one amazing daughter. She dropped everything to help me out today."

Nicole looked confused. "She did?"

Mish heard heavy steps coming down the stairs and knew the real test was about to begin. Nicole heard them, too, and turned to stand beside Juliann and Mish as she called out to him. "Daniel, come meet Juliann's friend Mish."

"Mish? What the hell kind of name is Mish?" He entered the kitchen carrying a glass of amber liquid but stopped in the doorway when he saw the three women lined up on the other side.

"The name of an old woman," Mish said with a polite smile. "I was just telling your wife what a wonderful daughter you have here. She came to my rescue today, drove with me all the way to Morgantown to see my dying sister."

"We got connected through a program at school," Juliann rushed to explain. "It's a way of helping us meet our service hour requirements for graduation."

Daniel squinted at Mish. She couldn't tell if he was being skeptical or if he was so drunk he was trying to see only one of her. He turned his gaze to his daughter. "Service hours? I thought you were going to do your service hours in my office."

"I was going to," Juliann answered, "but the guidance counselor said that service done in your dad's law firm doesn't look that good to university admission boards. So I got matched up with Mish, and then when she called today I wanted to help her."

"Oh, isn't that nice, Daniel?" Juliann's mother gushed as her eyes darted between her daughter and her husband. "See, there was nothing to get upset about."

"Really?" he asked as he took a step toward them. "Nothing at all?"

He took another step. Mish grew more nervous with every step he took. Even though he swayed a little on his feet, he was still sober enough to be a serious threat.

"Then why did you lie to us?" He spoke so softly you might think he was calm, but there was nothing calm in the way he stared at his daughter. Mish suddenly remembered he was a lawyer; he must be a formidable opponent in the courtroom.

"Why did you say you were at dance class and then going to your friend's house, if you were not even in town?"

Juliann swallowed hard. "I didn't want you to worry," she explained. "I know how anxious Mom gets, and, Dad, you've had so much on your mind recently. I just didn't want to add another burden."

Mish thought Juliann was laying it on a bit thick, but maybe you have to go overboard with a drunk father.

"I see." He nodded, nonchalantly taking another step. "And what about your phone?"

Mish couldn't take her eyes off Juliann's father, but she heard the panic in the girl's voice. "My phone?" Juliann asked.

"Yes, your phone," he repeated. "I checked the family app, and it said you were at Hailey's house this evening. Clearly you were not at Hailey's house. So why would your phone be there?"

"That was an accident," she said in a rush. "I just forgot it there this morning, and—"

"Then how were you texting your mother from it all day?" He stepped closer.

"Well, no, I didn't leave it there in the morning. I had it with me at school until I left. And then, um, I forgot it. But Hailey saw it and took it home with her. And…"

"Liar," he whispered. And then Mish realized what he'd been walking toward. Without taking his eyes off Juliann, he reached for her backpack, which was right beside him on the counter.

The "no" that erupted from Juliann obviously confirmed her dad's suspicions. But she didn't move. Maybe couldn't move. She just stared at him as he unzipped it and opened it wide. He finally took his eyes off his daughter as he began pulling things out of the backpack. Notebooks. Yesterday's clothes. Hairbrush and toothbrush. Each was tossed onto the table without another look. And then he stopped. His eyes again sought his daughter's face as he pulled a handful of condoms from her backpack.

"Did they give you these at school? Or did Mish's dying sister give them to you?" He clearly thought his sarcasm was funny. He reached into the backpack, pulled out some loose papers, and began looking through them. "Lovely diagram on how to put on a condom." He tossed the page onto the table, then read the heading on the next. "Birth control options." It joined the other paper on the table. But Juliann's dad stared at the next page without moving. He stared so long that Mish risked taking her eyes off him in order to check on Juliann. She was shaking and so pale, Mish thought she might pass out.

He cleared his throat. "Post-abortion instructions," he read aloud.

Juliann seemed too terrified to speak. "It's not what it looks like," Mish rushed to explain.

He turned to glare at her. "Were you the one who got an illegal abortion today?"

"N-no, of course not," Mish said.

"Then shut the hell up!" he yelled.

His scream must've done what his whisper hadn't—woke Juliann from her trance. "Leave her alone," she whispered.

"What did you say?" her father demanded.

Juliann cleared her throat. "I said leave her alone. This isn't her fault. And it wasn't an illegal abortion."

"Of course it was!" he sneered. "It's illegal for a minor to get an abortion without parental consent in the state of West Virginia—even in a university town."

Juliann took a deep breath and squared her shoulders before speaking. "We weren't in West Virginia," she said at last. "We went to DC."

His face turned beet red. "So, I was right earlier. You're a slut. I always swore no daughter of mine would be a slut or a whore, but clearly you are your mother's daughter." He glared at his wife, who had backed up and was leaning against the wall, her shoulders slumped. He looked back at Juliann, his face filled with disgust. "Obviously I've been too easy on you all these years, too soft. I thought that just because you are smart, you are like me. Now I'm ashamed I ever gave you my name." He spat on the kitchen floor at Juliann's feet. "I swear, I should slap you into next week."

Before Mish knew it, she was standing between Juliann and her father. "But you won't," she commanded as she looked up at him. "You won't touch her. Not tonight. Not ever again. You've done enough damage here."

"Who the hell are you to tell me what I can and cannot do in my own house? Besides, I have never laid a hand on her. Ask her." When Mish didn't look away, he said it again. "Go on. Ask her. Ask her if I've ever hit her."

Mish was confused. She knew Juliann's father was abusive.

Juliann had said so. And he was clearly acting like an abuser at the moment. But she looked at Juliann anyway, to get confirmation that she was right, only to see a sick look on Juliann's face. "Juliann?"

Juliann lowered her eyes and shook her head. So he hadn't hit her. Well, that didn't matter. Hurting somebody's soul was just as bad as hurting their body. But then Juliann raised her eyes and looked again at her mother. Mish followed her gaze, saw Nicole cowering in the corner, and suddenly the whole thing was clear as day. *My father is a violent man,* Juliann had said at the clinic. *If he finds out, there will be hell to pay.* Mish had assumed Juliann meant for herself, but she hadn't. She meant for her mom. She hadn't been afraid to tell her dad for her own sake. She had known her mom would be the one to pay the price. This whole thing had been to protect her mother.

Mish looked back at Juliann's father and stared at him as she spoke to the girl. "Hon, go pack some clothes."

"Wh-what?" Juliann stammered.

"Go pack some clothes. You're coming to stay with me for a while. And, Nicole, I suggest you do the same." Mish looked at Juliann's mother, whose eyes had grown wide with terror. "I mean it, Nicole," she said again. "I'm doing for you what I never could do for myself. I'm handing you a lifeline. A way out. Take it." She spoke to Juliann again, without looking at her. "Go, Juliann. Get clothes for tomorrow." Juliann ran out of the room.

Daniel had closed the short distance between them and now towered over her. He crossed his right arm over his chest, and Mish knew what was coming. She'd been backhanded enough to know the pose, and her cheek stung in anticipation.

"You won't hit me," she said calmly, even while praying it to be true. "Your law partners at Schmidt, Johnson, and Stick-Up-Your-Ass may look the other way when you abuse your wife, but they will not look kindly on you getting arrested for hitting a defenseless old woman. So back off. Now!" she commanded.

He didn't move, but he did lower his hand. "You will pay for this," he whispered.

"Maybe so," she agreed. "But not today." She held his gaze for another few seconds before Juliann came running back in. But she wasn't holding clothes. Instead she held an expensive makeup case with an electric toothbrush sticking out the top.

"I've got your stuff, Mom. Come on, let's go." But Nicole just stared at her. "Mom, please!" Juliann begged. "Don't make me live with the knowledge that he killed you because I wasn't here."

To Mish's utter surprise and relief, Nicole reached for Juliann's hand. And without a backward glance, Juliann led them out of the house, Daniel's profanity-laced threats ringing in their ears.

14

Mish sat at her kitchen table drinking her third cup of coffee. She usually limited herself to two, but she figured she was entitled to indulge today. She'd gotten up at four-thirty to go to the bathroom and the whole time kept muttering to herself, "Don't think, don't think, don't think." But it didn't work. She thought anyway and couldn't get back to sleep.

Last night, when the three of them got to her house, she'd focused on getting Juliann and her mother calmed down and settled in their rooms. For the first time in a long time she was glad she'd given in to Floyd's Folly and built those big guest rooms with the nice bathroom between them. She gave them some old T-shirts of Floyd's to sleep in and then put their clothes in the wash for the next day. Mish was pretty sure a country club lady like Nicole wouldn't want to wear any of her old lady clothes.

They had talked a little bit about what had happened, but Juliann and Nicole seemed too shocked to have the heart-to-heart that they needed to have. And they probably needed more than one of those. It'd happen in time, Mish figured.

The girls, as Mish had started thinking of them, had both decided to call in sick today. They were dog-tired, for sure, but Mish was also pretty sure they were afraid of Daniel showing up at their work or school. She was worried too. Would he find out where they were? Would he show up at her house? Had her rash decision to invite them to come to her house put them all in danger?

Well, it was too late to worry about that now. She had other fish to catch, and that meant she needed to start a to-do list to keep it all straight. Now, if only she could find her notebook. Oh, right, she had dropped her knitting bag on the little table by the door when they came in last night. She'd dropped the bag on the answering machine, and when she picked it up, she was surprised to see the machine was blinking steadily. She pushed the play button.

Message received Monday, 9:05 a.m.: Good morning, Mish. It's Opal. Did you forget the Women's Society meeting this morning? Hope you'll be here soon.

Oh drats, she forgot to tell anybody she wouldn't be there. Oh well. She deleted the message and moved on to the next.

Message received Monday, 10:40 a.m.: Hi, it's Opal again. Mish, we're all really worried about you. Please call me as soon as you get this. We all love you. More than you know. Bye-bye.

Well, that was sweet, that everybody was worried about her. They were always so nice about including her in everything. But Opal sounded really worried. That was strange. Then again, so was Opal! She tried to think of the last time she'd missed a meeting, and she couldn't remember any time except the week Floyd died. Maybe that's why they were so worried. Oh well. She'd call Opal later.

Message received Monday, 3:07 p.m.: Mish, it's Opal again. I don't know where you've been, but the police say you're okay so I'm just going to trust that you are. Still, I need to tell you what happened, and why I got Pastor Jeff involved, and why the police have your money, and oh, it's a long story. Just call me as soon as you get back.

Mish stared at the answering machine, so shocked that she didn't know how to respond. Pastor Jeff? The police? And what money? And then she remembered the money she'd left for Juliann in case anything had happened to her. In all the upset, she hadn't even noticed it was gone. But what in the world was Opal talking about? She pushed the button to listen to the message again but still didn't understand. She moved on to the next message.

Message received Monday, 5:00 p.m.: Mother, I don't know where you are or when you plan to come home. You seem to be keeping quite a few secrets these days. But I want you to know that I'm ready to talk whenever you are ready to apologize and act like a mature adult. You know where to reach me.

Apologize? There was no way in h-e-double-toothpicks she

was going to apologize to her son. He was the one who owed her an apology, not the other way around. Well, he would just have to stew until she was good and ready to talk to him. Maybe sometime next month.

Opal, on the other hand, she needed to talk to right away. She checked the time, then dialed Opal's number and was glad when Opal answered on the first ring. "You worry too much, you know that?" Mish said by way of a greeting.

"Oh, Mish, I am so glad to hear from you! Where have you been? What happened? Are you okay?"

"Yes, I'm fine," Mish replied. "I just took a little overnight trip. I didn't realize that was a crime worth involving the law. So tell me about how y'all jumped to conclusions and got the police and my son involved."

Opal didn't need much encouragement to tell the story. It all came out in a rush, starting with all the ladies getting worried, then calling Pastor Jeff, and then him finding the money and calling the police. They knew about her getting pulled over in Maryland, but they didn't know where she'd gone or who she'd gone with. Just as well. Better to protect Juliann's privacy.

She knew they meant well, but it sure felt strange knowing that Pastor Jeff and even the police had been through her whole house. She was glad she'd washed her lunch dishes before leaving.

"So where did you go, Mish?" Opal asked at last.

"Sorry, but I can't tell you that. It's confidential. I was helping somebody. That's all you need to know." Opal was quiet for a minute, and Mish knew she was unhappy. "I'm sorry, Opal, it's not that I don't trust you. It's just not my story to tell."

Opal huffed. "Does this have anything to do with you meeting that woman claiming to be Jesus?"

Now it was Mish's turn to be silent. People questioning her mission was getting old. "She didn't claim to be Jesus," Mish said at last. "She just was. And, yes, I'm following the love. That means I'm helping people. Last I checked, that's kinda what Jesus was about."

"Of course Jesus was about helping people, Mish," Opal said

testily. "But that doesn't mean running all over the country with somebody you don't know, especially at your age. You can help people in other ways, you know."

"Like crocheting afghans and pot holders for the harvest bazaar?" Mish scoffed. "If that's what you have in mind, you can count me out from now on. And if you ever want to do something real, you let me know."

She hung up the phone and buried her face in her hands. She felt the tears pricking her eyelids. She had just yelled at and hung up on her best friend. What was wrong with her? She picked up the phone and called Opal back to apologize, but Opal didn't answer. "Dag nab it!" she said out loud.

"I'm sorry—am I interrupting?"

Mish jerked her head around to see Nicole standing in the doorway, looking rather young and small in an oversized T-shirt. Mish forced a smile. "No, just frustrated with myself. Would you like some coffee? It's not fancy but it gets the job done."

"I'd love some. Thank you," she said politely.

"Mugs are in the cupboard above the coffee maker. Help yourself. I was thinking of making bacon and eggs for breakfast. Or maybe pancakes. What suits your fancy?"

Nicole poured herself a cup of coffee and took a sip. "I don't usually eat much breakfast, but I'm sure Juliann would love pancakes when she wakes up. If it's not too much bother."

Mish chuckled to herself. After all she'd done for the girl, she didn't figure that making pancakes would be too much trouble. She and Nicole sat in silence for a few minutes while Mish snuck looks at her, trying to figure out how old she was. Her skin was smooth and young-looking, so maybe mid-thirties? That would make her a pretty young mom. But those worry lines on her forehead and the creases between her eyebrows suggested a decade more. Of course, living with an abusive husband left its own kind of mark on a woman's face.

But they had more important things to discuss this morning. "So what's your plan?" Mish asked pointedly.

"Plan?" Nicole echoed.

"Your plan for getting through this mess. Do you have your own money or is it all together? That husband of yours will probably put a freeze on your joint accounts as soon as the banks open, if not before. But you could try and beat him to it. You'll be needing some cash. You also probably better start thinking about an attorney. If your husband is well-known, it might be difficult getting another attorney to take your case. On the other hand, if he's a jerk to everyone, some lawyers might be eager to face him in divorce court."

"Divorce court?" Nicole repeated.

Mish was starting to wonder if the lady had a hearing problem, the way she kept repeating everything. Then she realized that Nicole was just overwhelmed. "I'm going too fast, aren't I? I do that sometimes. My husband used to say I talk fast and think slow, which is a dangerous combination. But I'm rambling so I'll shut up now and let you think."

Nicole just stared at her and blinked. Mish searched for the term to describe her—something from the army, she thought. *Shell-shocked.* Yeah, that was it. So she reached out and tried to pat Nicole's arm, but the woman flinched. Nicole tried to hide it by reaching for her coffee, but Mish knew what she had seen. It must've been a long time since anyone touched her nicely. So she tried to talk gently, like she would if she was talking to a hurt animal. "Let's talk about what you've done to survive," she murmured. "One thing you did to keep from making him mad. And I'll go first, okay?" Nicole nodded.

"Floyd used to fall asleep while I was cooking dinner. If I called to him to tell him it was ready, he would get mad at me for yelling. If I went closer and touched him to wake him up, he would grab me by the arm. So I found a way to wake him up without him knowing it was me." She paused and allowed a grin to cross her face. "Squirt guns."

Nicole gave a tentative smile. "Squirt guns?"

"Squirt guns," Mish confirmed. "I would stand in the kitchen and send a shot in his direction, then hide behind the wall before he could see me. He never did figure out why he woke up with his shirt all wet." She giggled. "He even called a roofer once. Paid two hundred and fifty dollars for the guy to tell him there was nothing wrong with the roof and maybe he just drooled!"

Nicole actually laughed in response. "That's brilliant!"

"We all do things to get through," Mish replied. "So tell me one of your tricks."

"I don't know if this is exactly what you mean, but I did something whenever we went out for ice cream," she admitted. "If I ate my ice cream too quickly, I was a pig. If I ate it too slowly, he would either take it and eat it, or throw it away. So I watched him closely and always finished at the exact same time as him. That way I got to eat my own ice cream."

"That's brilliant," Mish said, repeating the word Nicole had used. "Now think of your money as your ice cream. How are you going to get what's yours?"

Nicole took a big breath. "You're right. Daniel will block the account. I think maybe I should try to get to the bank first thing, just to get some cash. Can you drive me?"

Mish jumped up. "Of course! Want to go now?" she asked eagerly.

Nicole looked down at herself, at her T-shirt and bare legs. "I think maybe after laundry."

"Be back in a jiffy," Mish called over her shoulder as she left the room. She was back in a few seconds with Nicole and Juliann's laundry, the small stack folded neatly. "My granddaughter also left some clothes a while back—mostly stuff she'd wear horseback riding, but they might fit you or Juliann if you need them. They're in the dresser in Juliann's room."

Nicole thanked her and left to change. Mish picked up the phone again and called Opal, but it went to the answering machine. This time she waited for the beep. "Opal, I'm really sorry. I don't know what got into me. I was rude, and you didn't deserve what I dished out. I hope you can forgive me. Call me. Please."

She hung up, still not satisfied, but at least she'd tried. She knew she would need to apologize again before Opal would forgive her, but in the end, her friend would come around. True friends don't walk away because one person said a stupid thing. If they did, the way her mouth worked, Mish wouldn't have any friends at all. She would have to call Pastor Jeff later, too, and she figured she'd better go to the police station this morning, if only to get her money back. She also needed to call the alarm company. Floyd had insisted on an alarm when they built the place, but he got tired of accidentally setting it off so he'd disconnected it. With Nicole and Juliann moving in, she thought an alarm wasn't a bad idea.

Nicole came back into the kitchen half an hour later wearing yesterday's clothes and a full face of makeup, with Juliann trailing behind her. Mish fixed them all breakfast before they headed to the bank. They got there five minutes before the place opened so Nicole tried the ATM, but she got an "Insufficient Funds" message when she tried to take two hundred dollars from their checking account. Juliann went with her into the bank, and when they returned twenty minutes later they were both in tears. Daniel had, indeed, been one step ahead of them. Apparently, he couldn't close their accounts without her permission, so instead he transferred almost all the money out of them, moving it into accounts that didn't have her name on them.

"It was humiliating," Nicole said through tears. "As soon as the teller realized what was happening, she called the manager who took me into her office to explain. I've banked there for years, even consulted on the interior design when they redecorated the place. Now everybody there knows what my husband has done to me. And in this town, word will be out by the end of the week."

Mish thought Nicole was underestimating the town. More likely the word would be out before the end of the day, but she decided to keep her mouth shut for once.

"The manager did see that I have direct deposit from my employer, and she advised me to change that immediately and have it put into a separate account. I'll do that tomorrow, but I don't want to use the same bank. Do you have a bank you trust, Mish?"

"I use the credit union. Good people there, and they don't seem the gossipy type."

"Sounds good. Can you take me there so I can open an account? No, wait. How much do you think I need for an opening balance? I don't carry much cash."

"I have forty bucks, Mom," Juliann said from the back seat. "And we didn't check my savings account. He might have left that one alone. I'm not sure if his name is on it."

Nicole put her head in her hands. "This is so embarrassing. Needing a loan from my teenage daughter."

"You don't need a loan from her. You can get one from me," Mish said. "I just need to stop by the police station first to get my money."

Nicole looked up. "I don't know which to do first. Decline your generous offer, or ask why you keep your money at the police station."

Mish laughed. "My friends got worried about me yesterday, and long story short, they ended up calling the police to check on me. The police took some money I had left out for—for an emergency, and I have to go pick it up. I'm told I'm supposed to see a Lieutenant Samson. Would y'all mind going in with me? I've never been in a police station before and it makes me a little nervous."

That wasn't true, strictly speaking. It was true she hadn't been in a police station before, at least not in years, but she wasn't nervous. She just thought that this lieutenant person might be able to give Nicole some advice.

She had been right. Mish left them in the lobby while she went with the officer. Once she got her money back, along with a lecture about keeping too much cash lying around, she told him about Nicole and Juliann's situation. He not only had good advice, but he also offered to send a police officer with them to get their clothes and stuff. He offered a female officer, but they all agreed that in case they ran into Daniel, a male officer might be better.

Ninety minutes later, they were leaving their house with suitcases, computers, and even a couple bags of groceries Nicole insisted on giving to Mish. She'd also found some cash she'd set aside for a trip, so she at least had a few hundred dollars to last until payday. Mish was pretty sure this was the smallest budget Nicole had lived on for years, but it was better than nothing.

"I'd like to take you girls to lunch," Mish said as they pulled out of the drive. "My treat and no arguments. Where do you like to eat?"

Nicole hesitated. "Thanks, Mish, but you've done enough. We can just go home and make a sandwich."

"Who in their right mind would choose a cold sandwich over a hot meal? So come on, tell me—what do you like to eat?" When Nicole didn't answer, Mish looked in the rearview mirror and caught Juliann's eye.

"She doesn't want to go to any of her usual places," Juliann explained, "because she doesn't want to risk running into any of her friends."

"I see," Mish said. "Then how 'bout I pick the restaurant? I'm in the mood for comfort food, and no offense, but those kind of places don't really seem your usual style."

After lunch at the Bluebird Diner, Mish dropped the girls back at her house, then drove to the church. There was no point putting off this conversation with Pastor Jeff any longer. Waiting wasn't going to make it easier. She entertained the hope that he wouldn't be there, but she knew he would be. Monday was his day off, Tuesday was his catching-up day, and Friday was the day he wrote his sermons. She didn't know what he did on Wednesday and Thursday, but since this was Tuesday, he'd be there.

She turned in the parking lot and immediately saw his little car. It was one of those hybrids, and he said he drove it because it got such good gas mileage. She knew that was smart, but around here there were so many pickup trucks and SUVs that his little car always looked like it had shrunk in the wash. She parked next to him and was barely at the sidewalk when the door burst open and Pastor Jeff came striding out. Assuming she had caught him as he was fixing to leave, she tried to step out of his way. But he stopped a few feet in front of her, his arms stretched out. She understood the invitation and walked into the hug.

She held on for a minute and he let her. It had been a long time since she'd been in a man's arms, and even longer since a man's arms had felt completely safe. She felt tears but willed herself not to cry. He already thought she was a little bit crazy. She didn't want to go convincing him he was right by crying on his tie.

Mish pulled away, suddenly feeling awkward, but Pastor Jeff didn't seem to notice.

"I am so glad to see you," he said. "I wanted to call today but figured I'd intruded enough. Please, come inside so we can sit and talk." He motioned for her to go in front of him, so she did. They didn't speak again until they got settled in his office. "I know you've talked to Opal," he began, "but I don't know if you got the whole story of what happened here yesterday. Do you need me to fill in any gaps?"

Mish hesitated. She did wonder about quite a few things, but she wasn't sure what to ask. Finally, she settled on the question that had bothered her the most. "Opal said at first they thought I forgot the meeting, and then they got worried that I had fallen or taken ill. But there was more to it than that, and she didn't say why. They seemed to think I was depressed or something, or even that I was thinking of hurting myself. Why would they think that?"

Pastor Jeff seemed to chew on his words before he spoke. "It was the way you acted on Sunday. Apparently, you went around giving compliments, telling people things you admired about them. Remember? You told me what a good job you thought I was doing."

"Well, it's the truth," she argued. "I always try to leave people feeling better than when I found them. Why would that worry anybody?"

"Those compliments and everything—that's the kind of thing people do when they aren't sure they're going to see someone again." She just stared at him so he continued. "Sometimes when a person has decided to—to end their life—well, they want to say goodbye. But they don't want their friends and family to know they're saying goodbye. When you didn't show up for the meeting, people started talking and it seemed like that's what you were doing. You were saying goodbye."

"Well, I guess I kinda was, but not the way you thought. I knew I was leaving town that afternoon, and nobody else knew where I was going. I'm usually not one to keep secrets so I guess it made me a little nervous." She shrugged. "I've been wondering, though—when you came to my house, did you think you were going to find me with a broken hip or…" She couldn't bring herself to finish the sentence.

Pastor Jeff shook his head. "I didn't know. I just knew I had to find you. And then when I read your note, well, it sounded like you were saying goodbye there too. Then I saw all that money, and so it seemed like calling the police was the best thing I could do, the only thing I could do, to make sure you were safe."

Mish tried to take it all in. The whole situation felt weird—that all these people had been talking about her, searching her house, all that stuff. But the weirdest part was realizing that some of them thought she had actually taken her own life. "I guess I still don't understand. I've known people to jump to conclusions, but this seemed like an Olympic-sized jump. Had I seemed depressed? Sad, even? Or confused?"

"Well, no, not depressed." His voice trailed off and he cleared his throat. "But sometimes people get confused about…about life."

She studied him for a minute, then suddenly realized what he was suggesting. "You're saying 'confused,' but I don't think you mean confused. I think you mean crazy."

"No!" he rushed to say. "Not crazy. Nobody thinks you're crazy. You've just been, well, different lately. Since you met the lady at the diner. First you started meeting people you didn't even know, and now you're leaving town without telling anybody, and you're ready to give somebody you don't even know your life savings."

"My life savings?" she said with a laugh. "I think your Stephen must be wearing off on you because that's a bit dramatic, don't you think?"

Pastor Jeff looked overly serious. "Mish, you left twenty-five thousand dollars for someone whose name you don't even know. Of course I don't know your finances, but—"

"Oh, Pastor Jeff, are the deacons still not letting the pastor see the giving records at church?"

"Well, no, but what does that—"

"Do you know the Mountain View Estates on the edge of town?"

Jeff was looking at her strangely again. "Of course, but—"

"Do you know what the old-timers used to call that property, before it was split up into lots?"

When Jeff shook his head, Mish said, "Atkinson Mountain." She paused to let that sink in. "We owned a few other sections, where the highway went through and the gas lines went through. When we were young, I convinced Floyd to buy every piece of land we could get our hands on. I figured land was the best investment because they ain't making no more of it." She shrugged again. "Of course, I had to make him believe it was his idea, but in the end, I was right."

Pastor Jeff was sitting there with his mouth hanging open. "So you're—"

"I'm in a position where I can help somebody who needs it," she said firmly. "And if something happened to me on that trip, I wanted a particular young woman to get some help. There's no crime in that," she reminded him.

"Of course not, Mish, but don't you see? That makes you even more of a target. Whoever lured you to the diner and told you they were Jesus was probably after your money."

Mish grabbed the arms of her chair and sat up straighter. "Nobody lured me to the diner, and nobody is after my money," she said sternly. "Nobody has even asked me for a dime."

Pastor Jeff shook his head again. "But that's how they work, Mish. They don't come right out and ask—they let you think it was your idea so you won't get suspicious. How many different people have been calling you? How are they getting your number? If you let me look at your phone, I could check out the people who've called you and—"

Mish stood up. "I think you've done quite enough nosing into my private life, Pastor Jeff. I appreciate your concern, but this ain't none of your business."

He jumped to his feet too. "Mish, I'm sorry. I didn't mean to push. I'm just worried about you. I want to help you."

"You want to help me?" Mish asked. "Then back off. You have your calling, and I have mine, and—"

"Yes, of course, but—"

"I believe in your calling, but you don't believe in mine. Why is that?"

"It's not that I don't believe in your calling. It's just that—"

"Is it because I'm not as smart as you?" Mish interrupted, her voice rising with her temper.

"No, of course not. It's just that—"

"Is it because I'm just an uneducated farmer's wife?"

"No! If you'd let me finish—"

"Is it because I'm a woman?"

"No! I just don't believe in—"

"What's your problem, Pastor Jeff? Spit it out!"

"I don't believe in God!" he shouted. Suddenly his eyes widened. "*That* God," he whispered. "I meant to say I don't believe *that* God...that God works that way."

Mish didn't know whether to be angry or feel sorry for the man. She took a deep breath to calm her nerves. "Maybe your tongue tells more truth than you realize," she said at last. "And maybe I shouldn't feel bad that you don't believe in my calling— because you don't seem to believe in yours neither."

Juliann thought Mish had been unusually quiet during dinner, and she had gone to her room while Juliann and her mom cleaned up the kitchen. But when she came out an hour later, she seemed better.

"Girls, I need your help," Mish announced as she walked into the family room.

Juliann and her mom both looked up from their phones. "Of course. What can we do?" Nicole asked.

"Help me drag that god-awful chair out of here."

Juliann looked at her mom and saw her glance around as if trying to determine which of the awful chairs was the god-awful one.

As if she understood, Mish pointed. "That one. The green-plaid monster recliner."

"You know, I'm an interior decorator," Nicole began, and Juliann stifled a groan. "If you're thinking about redoing the room, I would be glad to give you my expert opinion—free of charge, of course!"

Juliann was so embarrassed. Honestly, her mother was such a snob sometimes. Why couldn't she just accept people as they were, instead of always trying to improve them?

Mish nodded thoughtfully. "Well, that is a mighty fine offer, Nicole, and I will keep that in mind. But for now I just want to get rid of the one chair. Will you help me?"

Juliann stood up. "Of course. Where do you want it?"

"Outside," Mish answered without explanation.

Juliann shrugged. "Lead the way, and Mom and I will carry it." A couple minutes later they had the ugly green chair outside.

"Bring it over here," Mish said, pointing at her feet. She was standing on the far side of the house, in the middle of the dirt lane that led through the gate to the pasture and out to the barn.

Juliann stared at her. "Are you sure? We can carry it down to the road and put a Free sign on it. Or carry it out to the barn. Or—"

"Nah, we don't need to take it that far. Just bring it right here."

Juliann looked at her mom and they both shrugged, then did as they were told. When they had it where Mish wanted it, they stepped back as if to examine the effect. Nobody said anything for a few seconds. Juliann thought they'd look odd if somebody drove by and saw the three of them standing around staring at an empty chair.

Mish finally broke the silence. "This was my husband Floyd's chair. He watched *Jeopardy* and *Wheel of Fortune* from this chair. He watched the news from this chair. He yelled at the football games from this chair. Most of the last ten years of his life were spent in this chair."

"Then why—" Nicole began, but Juliann hushed her.

"Floyd also threw things from this chair. He barked orders from this chair. He told me I was stupid from this chair. Now he haunts me from this chair. And I'm done with it. I'm done with taking orders. I'm done with being made to feel stupid. I'm done with living in fear. So I am done with this chair." She reached into the pocket of her apron and pulled out a box of matches. "So we're gonna have us a little bonfire."

"Mish, I don't think that's a good idea," Nicole said softly.

Mish put her hands on her hips. "Why the blazes not?"

"Because that fabric is fire resistant." Nicole began to smile. "You're going to need an accelerant."

Mish grinned. "Juliann, run back to the garage and get me a can of gas."

Juliann found the little red can without a problem and hurried back. She handed it to Mish, who took it, pulled off the stopper, and tilted it over the chair. Gasoline began splashing out. Without looking at her, Mish handed the can to Nicole. "Want a turn?"

Nicole's smile was almost wicked. "Oh, I definitely need to add some fuel to this fire."

Juliann noticed how her mother's expensive manicure looked strange against the gas can. But she thought she understood why her mom needed to participate. Maybe when your life is falling apart, watching something else go up in flames is therapeutic. When her mother handed the can to her, Juliann took it and added another splash, then moved the can twenty yards away for safety.

They all stood staring at the chair again. "I don't want the gas to burn off too fast," Mish whispered. "We need to let it sink in for a minute."

As they waited, Juliann let the weight of what they were doing sink in. She stared at the chair and thought of all it stood for. She thought about how Mish's husband had treated her, how Juliann's father treated her mother, how her father treated Juliann herself. She thought about other people in her life who belittled her, male teachers who said girls weren't smart enough to major in science, the guys who catcalled her and her friends on the street and made them feel dirty and afraid. She thought of the silence she'd had to keep because of fear. She thought of the decision she'd made about the abortion and her fear of her father's reaction. And she placed it all in that chair. The ugly green-plaid chair was full of all the ugliness of her life. And it all needed to burn.

When Mish tossed the match onto the chair, the response was instantaneous. Flames leapt to the sky like dancers on the edge of ecstasy. And then she heard it. It started like a rumble, like a car engine trying to start, but as it grew Juliann recognized the sound. The laughter was starting from a place so deep inside Mish that she vibrated with it. Mish threw back her head and opened her mouth, and the sound came out like a prisoner set free. It was rage and relief, protest and praise, the sound of liberty long denied and finally claimed.

The vibration multiplied as first Juliann and then Nicole joined in. The laughter was their story, and it was theirs to tell. Together.

15

The next day the girls decided to return to school and work, and Mish was glad. She had something she wanted to do, and she'd been waiting a long time.

Mish was a little nervous when she opened the door to the dog shelter. She'd never tried to get a dog before and didn't know what would be involved. But she had made up her mind. She wanted a friendly little white dog.

The woman at the desk was feeding a tiny puppy with an eye dropper.

"He's so small!" Mish exclaimed. "What happened to his mama?"

"We don't know," the woman answered, barely giving Mish a glance. "Some jerk abandoned the puppies here before we opened this morning."

"There's more of them?"

"Two brothers and a sister to this little guy. They'll make it, but if it had been any colder, it might be a different story." She finally looked up at Mish. "So can I help you?"

"Do you have any dogs?" Mish asked feebly.

The woman laughed. "Why, yes, we do. What kind were you looking for? Big? Small? Young? Old? For protection or—"

"For cuddling," Mish said, then immediately regretted it. She probably sounded stupid. "Is that a dumb reason to want a dog?"

The woman stopped and looked up at her. "That's a perfectly wonderful reason to want a dog," she said with a smile. "Let's go take a look."

The woman introduced herself as Katie, then led Mish through a steel door, still carrying the tiny puppy. They were immediately greeted by a wall of sound as every dog in the place began barking and vying for attention. As Mish looked around, it seemed like every one of them was saying, *Pick me! Pick me!* She saw it right away. A little white bundle of fur that was just as excited as it could be—jumping and running in circles and yapping enthusiastically. "Tell me about this one," she said to Katie.

"He's a cutie, isn't he? Our best guess is he's part Westie and part Maltese. He's very food motivated so if you have treats, he's your best friend. Here, try for yourself," she said as she handed Mish a tin of tiny dog treats shaped like bones.

Mish spent a couple of minutes giving the cute little thing some treats, and the woman was right—as long as she was feeding him, she had his full attention. But once she stopped, he quickly lost interest. It made her sad. The dog looked exactly like the dog in her mind—but she didn't really want a dog who was only interested in what she gave him. "If I wanted that, I'd get a man," she muttered under her breath.

She walked on down the row, pausing at each dog's crate. They were all different sizes and colors and temperaments. One of them leapt so furiously at the gate of his kennel that she backed up in fear. "Oh, don't let him scare you," Katie said. "He's all bark. He wouldn't hurt a flea."

Yeah, I've heard that before. She kept walking. She reached the last kennel and at first thought it was empty. But then she realized there was a brown bundle in the corner. It looked up at her with the saddest eyes she'd ever seen. "Tell me about this one," she asked.

Katie sighed. "I'm afraid this old gal is not what you're looking for either." When Mish didn't turn away, she continued. "She came in about a month ago. None of us have been able to get her interested in anything. She eats, but she won't come to us when we call her. She won't play. She doesn't interact with the other dogs. And there's not a thing wrong with her physically."

Mish looked at the dog more closely, then raised an eyebrow at Katie.

"Okay," Katie conceded, "she's got some problems. She was covered in sores when she came in. Her hair was so matted she couldn't even squat to do her business. She definitely got attacked by another dog at some point—you can tell by the shape of her ear. But she's not sick or seriously injured. It seems to be more emotional than physical. None of us have been able to draw her out. I don't know if we'll ever find a home for her."

Mish studied the dog. There was something about those eyes that just grabbed at her heart. She wished she could sit down on the floor, but she knew that if she did, she'd never get back up. "Would it be too much trouble to get me a chair?" she asked.

Apparently not, because Katie was back in less than a minute. It was a short chair, like a kid's size, but it was better than nothing. She lowered herself with a grunt and then studied the sign on the door of the kennel.

Gender: Female
Breed: Pekinese and Shih Tzu mix
Weight: 8 pounds
Age: 8-9 years
Name: Unknown; we call her Sadie
History: Found on the streets; had been cared for in the past but on her own for a long time

Mish looked around to make sure Katie was busy elsewhere, then leaned toward the crate. "Hi." She cleared her throat. "I'm Mish, and I've never had a dog before." She didn't know why she was telling the dog this. It just seemed only fair she admit it up front. "I've always wanted one but, well, it didn't work out. So I'm looking for a dog that I can love, who might love me back. What do you think?"

The dog stared at her for a minute, then stood, stretched, and walked to the door. Mish stuck her fingers through the holes and the dog immediately licked them. Mish giggled. She put her other hand through the door and scratched the top of the dog's head. "Is it okay if I let her out?" she called to Katie.

Katie glanced over. "The door probably isn't even latched. She never leaves unless we make her, so we don't always bother."

Mish gave it a little tug, and sure enough, the door was un-locked. As soon as the door was open a few inches, the dog pushed her way through and then put her feet up on Mish's lap. "You wanna come up?" she asked, patting her lap. With one little leap the dog was up in Mish's lap—licking her face and wagging her tail. Suddenly she noticed that Katie was at her side.

"How did you do that?"

"Do what?"

"Get her to come out to you. Get her to interact. She hasn't done this for any of us, and I give you two minutes alone with her and she's all Miss Personality?" Katie shook her head in disbelief.

"You were just waiting for the right person, weren't you, Honeybear?" Mish scratched between the dog's ears, and the dog responded with what she swore was a contented sigh.

"Honeybear?" Katie repeated.

"Yep. I think that's her name. What do you think, Honeybear?" The dog let out a little yip and wagged her tail harder.

"Well, I'll be damned," Katie said under her breath. "I think you found yourself a dog."

Mish beamed. "Yes, I have. Can I take her home today?"

Katie thought a minute. "Well, technically, you're supposed to fill out some paperwork, including references, and then we're supposed to run background checks on you before we let you take her. But she's been here so long, and you're so obviously the right fit, that yeah, what the hell, you can take her today."

Mish let out a little cheer, and Katie rushed on. "I still need you to fill out an application for our files, and of course there is an adoption fee to cover our costs."

"Oh, of course. What's your fee?" Mish asked as she rubbed noses with the little dog.

"Our usual fee is a hundred and fifty dollars, but for Sadie I'm sure we can—"

"Her name isn't Sadie," Mish interrupted. "It's Honeybear." She was rewarded with another lick on the chin. "And will five hundred cover it?"

"Oh, yes, ma'am. I was going to say you didn't have to—"

"Honeybear doesn't need to hear what you were going to say. If I give you five hundred dollars, then you'll get more money for her than all the other dogs in here, right?"

The lady grinned. "That's right. She's a high-priced dog."

"And worth every penny," Mish said with a nod.

Half an hour later, Honeybear was curled up on the passenger seat while Mish drove to the grocery store. Mish carried on a full conversation while she was driving, and every time she glanced over at the dog, Honeybear was staring at her as if hanging on Mish's every word. Mish parked the car in the shade, put the windows down a few inches, and then turned back to the dog. "It's not hot, and I'll only be a few minutes so I think you're okay here in the car." The dog's ears drooped and she reached out a paw and put it on Mish's leg. "I can't take you into the grocery store, and I'll be right back. I promise!" Mish climbed out of the car, quickly closed the door so the dog couldn't escape, and then opened the back door to retrieve her reusable grocery bags. But somehow while she had her back turned, Honeybear had jumped into the back seat and was lying on the bags. She tilted her head and wagged her tail hopefully. Mish couldn't help but laugh. "All right, but you have to hide in the bag and you better be quiet!" The dog's tail wagged even faster. So Mish pulled the strongest of the bags from underneath the dog, then scooped up Honeybear and put her in it. The dog looked up at her and grinned. Or at least that's what it looked like to Mish.

Mish got a cart, put the bag in the front section, and then stuck her nose inside. "You be quiet now, you hear?" She reached in and scratched the top of the dog's head, then pulled the edges of the bag back together to hide her from sight. The last thing Mish needed today was to be kicked out of Foodland.

Mish rushed through the produce section, trying to figure out what kind of fruit to buy. She usually just bought the basics this time of year—bananas, grapes, and apples—but Nicole was such a fancy lady. What kind of fruit would she want to have in the house? Kiwis? Pomegranates? Something Mish never even heard of? She didn't know what kind of vegetables to get either. And she used to think picking coffee was easy, but there were so many options in that fancy brand they liked. Life was simpler when your choices were Folgers, Maxwell House, and Sanka.

The meat counter was easier. She got a pot roast and a pork roast and some chicken breasts, then added a few other basics she knew she was running low on. Juliann had liked the yogurt at the hotel so Mish got some of that too. She was just about finished when she heard the tone telling her she'd gotten a text. She fished the phone out of her jacket pocket.

Hi.

Mish looked at the brief text and frowned. Who texted just to say "hi?" *Hi yourself* she texted back.

How r u?

There was way too much going on in her life to put in a text. And besides, she didn't even know who this was. *Who is this?* she asked.

Don't you recognize my number?

She looked at the number again and it didn't look familiar. *Should I?*

I thought our interaction was memorable.

"Excuse me," a voice said from behind her. Mish turned and realized she was blocking the aisle. She apologized to the other customer and moved her cart.

You had a lot to say to me the night we met.

Mish racked her brain, trying to think through everybody she'd met since getting her phone. They'd met at night, apparently, and the only person she could remember meeting at night was the young man at the diner. *Ethan? How you been?*

She waited about ten seconds before the reply came.

Great. Can we meet?

She smiled. She would love to see Ethan again and find out if he had taken her advice and followed the love. *Sure. When and where?*

Where are u now?

Supermarket.

Which one?

She wondered why he needed to know, but she told him anyway. She'd gone to the one on the edge of town. She hadn't felt like running into church folks.

I'm nearby, can u meet at the park down the street in 15 min? By the fountain in the center.

Mish wasn't crazy about the plan. She knew the park—it was the same one where she'd met Juliann that first time. She just wanted to go home, put her groceries away, get Honeybear settled, and then grab a nap before dinner. There had been so much emotion in the last few days that she was feeling extra tired. But Ethan was a good boy, and she really did want to know if he'd found love yet so she agreed.

The checkout line was extra long. Mish had one too many items to use the express lane, and the woman in front of her seemed to be buying for a small country. She kept reaching into the bag to pet the dog, but nobody seemed to notice her. Twenty minutes later, she was at the park, proudly walking Honeybear on her new leash. She spotted a guy with his back to her, and she called out to him.

"Ethan?" When he turned around, she immediately saw her mistake. He was bigger than the young man she'd met at the diner and not nearly as friendly looking. His arms were folded across his broad chest, his flannel shirt rolled up to his elbows. "Oh, I'm sorry. You're not Ethan."

"And you're not Marsha," he replied.

"Is that who you're waiting on?"

"I thought I was, but I guess I was wrong. You are who I texted, right? You were in the grocery store?"

Mish was confused. "Well, I guess so. But I thought you were somebody else."

He crossed his arms over his chest. "And I thought the girl I met in the bar had given me her real number."

"That's how you got my number? From a girl in a bar?"

His lip curled. "Obviously she was a lying bitch."

Mish was getting really sick of hearing men talk about women like that. "Watch your mouth, son," she said with a sigh.

He dropped his hands to his side and took a step closer. "Who do you think you are?" he demanded. "You're not my boss and you sure as hell ain't my mama."

Not another one. Not another man who thinks he can scare a woman into shutting up. "I'm just giving you a little free advice. Because if that's how you came across to this Marsha girl, it's no wonder she gave you the wrong number."

In one giant stride he was smack dab in front of her, staring down at her with hatred on his face. "And you are a nosy bitch so just shut the hell up!"

As she took a couple steps back from him, she heard a low growl come from her dog. "You're the one who called me out here. I'm sorry this Marsha girl lied to you, but that ain't my fault." She was starting to get nervous and looked around to see if anybody was watching. They were alone.

She didn't see his arm reach out until it had clasped around her left wrist.

"Since you're not Marsha, I guess my problem isn't with her. It's with you."

As Honeybear's growl grew louder, Mish tried to size up the situation. Her best bet was to keep the guy talking until he calmed down or somebody else came along. "How could you have a problem with me? We just met." She tried to smile. "Usually people have to get to know me before they have a problem with me."

"But we have met before—at least by text. And you disrespected me."

The man's breath was hot on her face, smelling of smoke and beer. She was having trouble concentrating. "What text? I didn't—"

"I sent you a photo and you made fun of me. I won't allow a nosy old bitch to disrespect me like that."

"Your photo? What—?" She suddenly realized what he was saying. "That was you? The dick pic?" Her fear collided with the memory of the altered photo, and the absurdity of the whole situation made her laugh.

She knew immediately she'd made a mistake, but it was too late. One push. That's all it took. One push, and her leg crumpled beneath her and she was falling, arms flailing, hands grabbing the air, and then pain, massive pain, as her head hit the ground. And the world went dark.

16

She heard the voices on the shore. People talking. A dog barking. They were calling for her, but they were so far away and she was so warm here under water. Maybe she'd swim a little more, go deeper. The deeper she swam the warmer she got. It would be so easy to keep going down, down, where she knew it would be peaceful. Quiet. But the voices were growing louder, insistent. Why wouldn't they let her be, let her swim? The voices weren't on shore anymore. They seemed to be right above her, and as the voices grew louder, she got colder. She started to shiver. She had to tell them to hush, let her swim, let her sleep. She tried to open her mouth but no sound came out. She tried to open her eyes but they felt so heavy. It was much easier to just float. But she was getting colder every second and there was another noise. So annoying. Stop. Make it stop.

Then somebody was opening her eyes, one at a time, and the sun was too bright. She tried to swat their hand away but wasn't sure if she'd even moved. The voices started coming into focus.

"Ma'am? Can you hear me?"

She tried again to speak but was only able to groan.

"Ma'am, can you tell me your name?"

"Mish," she said. Or maybe she just thought it. She tried again. "Mish."

"I'm sorry. I didn't get that. One more time?"

This time she was sure she said it, loud and clear.

"Mish, my name is Amanda. I'm an EMT. I need to ask you a few questions, okay?"

Mish nodded, then wished she hadn't. Her head hurt. So bad.

"Can you tell me what happened? What caused your fall?"

Her brain was fuzzy. She couldn't think clearly. She knew she hadn't fallen but couldn't remember for sure what had happened.

When she didn't answer, the woman said, "Mish, can you tell me how old you are?"

"Eighty-two."

"Excellent. And can you tell me what day it is?"

Mish tried to figure it out, but it was too much work. She frowned. She knew that wasn't a good sign.

"Okay, what about your last name?"

"Atkinson," she murmured.

"Mish Atkinson," the woman repeated. "Excellent."

Was it excellent? Mish wondered. Was it excellent to be Mish Atkinson? Or just to remember she was Mish Atkinson? She wasn't sure.

"And can you tell me who the president is?"

Mish grimaced. She knew who it was, of course. She just preferred to think of him as he-who-must-not-be-named. And that took too much energy to explain.

The woman asked her a few more questions as other EMTs checked to make sure she could move her fingers and toes. She wasn't sure she could. Something felt weird on her left side. As they worked on her, her mind cleared a little. She could answer their questions but she still felt a little hazy, slow, like her brain was underwater. She also remembered what had caused her fall. "Didn't fall," she suddenly announced. The EMT stopped and looked at her. "I didn't fall," she repeated. "I was pushed."

"All right, Mrs. Atkinson," the EMT responded. "The police will want to talk to you when you get to the hospital. And is this your dog?"

Mish smiled. She had a dog. "Honeybear," she whispered.

"You can thank her for helping you. She may have saved your life."

"Honeybear?" she repeated.

"She kept barking until someone found you. Other people in the park said she never left your side."

"Can she come—" Mish began.

"I'm sorry, she can't come in the ambulance. The police will take her for now."

"Mrs. Atkinson." A new voice spoke somewhere above her

head. "I'll take her with me back to the station. We'll be in touch with you so you can get her back."

"So scared," Mish whispered. She just knew the little dog would be terrified without her.

"I know you're scared," the EMT began, "but we'll take good care of you. Don't worry."

Mish didn't have the energy to argue and was quiet as they moved her onto a board and finally put her up on a stretcher. When they set her purse on the stretcher, she suddenly remembered. "My phone," she said as she tried to sit up.

The EMT put a hand on her shoulder. "Lie still, ma'am. We've got your belongings right here. They're fine."

"Gotta call."

"The hospital will take care of calling your family. But if you tell me who you want them to call, I can relay that message."

"Juliann," she said at once. "Number's in my…"

"Yes, ma'am, I'll tell them. Now lie back and rest. We'll be at the hospital in no time."

๛

Let her be okay, Juliann prayed silently as her mother drove to the hospital. *Please, God, let her be okay.*

She couldn't remember the last time she'd prayed. Oh, wait— yes, she could. When she waited for the pregnancy test results. God hadn't answered that one, but then again, she wasn't sure she'd deserved a miracle, especially since she was pretty sure she didn't believe in God.

But Mish does, Juliann pleaded. *She's such a good person. Please. Let her be okay.*

Juliann and her mom didn't know much. The call from the hospital just said there had been an accident, and Mish had asked for them to come. They wouldn't tell her any more than that. But if Mish was speaking, that was a good sign, right? She was conscious. Juliann told herself she was over-reacting. It could be just a sprained ankle or something. But then Mish would have made the call herself. Maybe a broken hip? Old people got those, and they were bad but not life-threatening. Should she hope for a broken hip?

Her mother reached over and squeezed her hand. "She's going to be fine," Nicole said. "Everything will be fine."

Juliann started to argue with her mom, to remind her that there's no way she could know that. But she didn't have any fight left in her. She just squeezed her mother's hand and hoped she was right.

They found a parking space and hurried into the emergency room. Juliann reached the desk first but suddenly felt uncertain. She had never been to the hospital before and wasn't sure how the process worked. She turned to look back at her mom, who immediately stepped up. "We're here to see Mish Atkinson," she told the receptionist.

The woman studied her computer screen, her brows furrowed. "Mish?"

"Artemisia," Juliann supplied. "Artemisia Atkinson."

"Got it," the receptionist said. "Are you family?"

"Yes," Juliann said quickly before her mother could respond. "I'm her granddaughter." She saw her mother look sideways at her, and Juliann hoped her surprise wasn't a giveaway, but the receptionist didn't seem to notice.

"I'll buzz you through these doors, then turn to your left. She's in bay 112."

They heard the lock mechanism as they approached, then the door opened with a whoosh. Once again Juliann took the lead, her mother trailing behind. But when she reached the glassed-off partition with 112 above it, she stopped, suddenly nervous. The curtain was pulled on the other side of the glass. What if Mish was in really bad shape? What if she had tubes coming out all over? What if she was already... No! That was not going to happen. Mish was not going to leave her like her grandmother had. She'd just had an accident. It was no big deal. *Just open the door*, she told herself. But her hand didn't move. *It's just a sliding glass door. Just open the damn door.*

Suddenly the door opened without her help. The doctor leaving the room almost bumped into her, muttered, "Sorry," and rushed away. She exchanged another look with her mom, then walked through the door the doctor had left ajar.

"Hey, hon. Thanks for coming."

Juliann let out the breath she'd been holding. It came out sounding like a laugh. She was at Mish's side in three steps. "Of course I came. I've been so worried. What happened? All they told us was that there'd been an accident. Was it a car accident? Are you okay? Where did you—"

"Ssshhh," Mish whispered, and Juliann stopped at once. "Gotta give me time…"

Juliann laughed and took Mish's hand. "Okay, go!"

Mish took a deep breath but didn't speak right away. She put a hand up to the bandage on her head. "I fell." Juliann nodded. "They ran some…some tests. Waiting."

"We're waiting for the results?" Juliann supplied helpfully. Mish nodded. Juliann started to speak, but Mish raised her hand and Juliann fell silent again.

"Might be just a…a…" Her voice trailed off.

"A concussion?" Nicole suggested.

"Right," Mish said. "If it's more…well?" She shrugged. "We wait and see."

"But how did you hit your head? Did you fall?" Juliann stroked Mish's hand absently as she tried to figure out what had happened.

"No," Mish answered.

"I don't understand—" Juliann began.

"Hon, please…my brain and my mouth…not working together."

Juliann swallowed hard and nodded. She didn't know what was going on, but she was starting to get scared again. And now that she looked closer, something about Mish's face didn't look quite right.

"I was pushed," Mish said at last. "Police will be coming. I have to give a… I have to tell them. But I wanted you to know…" Her voice trailed away

Mish looked up at Juliann's mom, and a horrible thought suddenly occurred to Juliann. "Oh, God! It wasn't Dad, was it?"

"No, no," Mish assured her. She took another deep breath. "It was the dick pic guy."

"What? But how did—?"

Mish shook her head again, then winced. "Long story. Don't want to tell it twice." She paused again. "I need you here. Help me fill in…fill in…blanks. All right?"

Juliann nodded. Her throat was so tight she wasn't sure she could speak if she tried.

"Nicole, I need your help too."

"Of course, Mish. Anything!" her mother said quickly, stepping forward.

Mish smiled her thanks. "Get my dog."

The surprise made Juliann find her voice again. "You have a dog?"

"Got her today. Police took her to station. Name is Honey… Honey…"

"Don't worry, Mish. I'll go get Honey."

Mish shook her head, and the frustration on her face told Juliann they'd gotten something wrong. But Mish apparently decided it wasn't worth correcting at that moment.

"Call my son," she continued. "Bobby. Tell him I'm in the hospital with a possible…concussion." Juliann noticed that she seemed pleased she had remembered the word this time. "Number in my phone." She waved absently to her phone, which was on the table next to her gurney.

"Juliann, I also need…" Her voice trailed away, and Juliann had to prompt her to continue. "Call Pastor Jeff. Same message. Then come back and sit with me?"

Tears filled Juliann's eyes as she remembered how much it had meant to see Mish waiting for her after her procedure. "Of course," Juliann choked out. "Where else would I be? You're my best-grand." She leaned down, placed a kiss on Mish's cheek, then took Mish's phone and stepped out of the cubicle. Cell reception was terrible, and she had to get back near the entrance to get enough bars to place a call.

She found Bobby's number and sent it to her mom, who gave her a quick hug, then left to do as Mish requested. She found the number for Mish's pastor too—there weren't very many in Mish's contact list—but hesitated before placing the call. She didn't actually talk on the phone very often, and especially not to adults. Texting was so much easier. But she figured this wasn't the kind of news an adult would want to get by text. She took a deep breath and placed the call.

"Hello?"

Juliann paused, realizing she should have rehearsed this beforehand.

"Hello?" the voice repeated.

"Um, hi, is this Pastor Jeff?" Juliann asked.

"Yes, and who is calling?"

"My name is Juliann. I'm a friend of Mish Atkinson." She heard a sharp intake of breath. "She asked me to call you."

"What happened? Is she okay?"

"Yes, she's… I mean, no, she's not fine. She's in the hospital. She had a fall and—well, not really a fall. She was pushed, actually, and she hit her head. We're waiting on test results."

"She was pushed," the pastor repeated.

"Yes, sir," Juliann responded.

"By whom?"

Juliann wasn't sure how to answer or how much to say. "Well, by a guy in the park. It's a long story. But she wanted me to call and tell you she's in the hospital."

"I'll get there as soon as I can," the man promised. "Wait—what did you say your name was? Juliann?"

"Yes."

"And did you recently go away with Mish?"

Juliann winced. She wasn't about to tell a minister about their trip. "Yeah, but I don't think that's really—"

"I'm sorry, Juliann," the man said kindly. "I'm really not just being nosy. I've been trying to solve a mystery and to keep Mish safe. I'll be there in about thirty minutes. Will you still be there then? I'd really like to talk with you."

Juliann assured the pastor she would be here, and they said their goodbyes. She would talk to Mish before she talked to the pastor. She wasn't about to talk to the man without Mish saying it was okay.

When Juliann walked back to Mish's cubicle, she found that a police officer had just arrived. Juliann helped Mish tell the story of the guy who'd sent the picture and what they had sent back in return. The officer was disappointed that Juliann had deleted the original message but was thrilled Mish still had his most recent text. After taking down all the details, he assured Mish that catching the guy would be easy. They'd probably have him in custody within twenty-four hours.

After the officer left, Mish looked up at Juliann. "Hon, I'm awful tired. Is it okay with you if I nap?"

"Of course," Juliann said as she patted her arm. "I'll just sit here with you."

Mish gave a smile and a slight nod as she closed her eyes. Juliann went back to her seat, disappointed that she would have to wait to ask about the pastor. She wasn't sure why talking to him made her so nervous. It was probably just the abortion thing.

More out of habit than anything else, Juliann pulled her phone out of her back pocket and scrolled through her social media accounts. But her friends' pictures were silly and their complaints were petty, and it all seemed so irrelevant and meaningless compared to Juliann's situation. She remembered it had been like this when her grandmother died. It had felt so weird that everybody else's life went on the same, while her heart had a hole in it. Some of her friends had lost grandparents, but they weren't close like Juliann and her grandmother had been, so they didn't really understand. They all said they were sorry and everything, but the next minute acted like nothing had happened. She had never felt so invisible.

The worst had been the funeral procession from the church to the cemetery. Most people had recognized the funeral procession for what it was and showed respect, but some of the people had been assholes. They honked and yelled when the procession turned left in front of them, blocking their path. Now she thinks that when the guy in the big SUV gave them the finger, she should've given it right back. But the thought had never occurred to her in the moment. All she'd been thinking was that if her grief didn't stop the world, it should at least stop traffic.

Now there was Mish to worry about. *This is different. Mish just has a concussion. She isn't going to die.* Juliann repeated the words, hoping that if she said them enough, they would be true. But something nagged at her, warning her that this was wishful thinking. It was partly Mish's speech. She kept pausing, like she was losing her train of thought. Plus, she had trouble finding words. Juliann thought she'd seen an episode of *Grey's Anatomy* where that had happened, and it wasn't good.

When the sliding door to their cubicle opened, Juliann looked up, expecting to see her mother or another hospital employee. Instead a middle-aged couple came rushing in and went straight to Mish's bedside.

"Mom?" the man asked nervously. Mish stirred but didn't answer.

The woman looked at Juliann. "Is she okay?" The man turned and seemed to notice her for the first time.

"She's just asleep," Juliann assured them both. "We're waiting on the test results."

The man looked at her with narrowed eyes. "Who are you?"

"I'm—" She paused. She had started to say she was Mish's granddaughter, but obviously she couldn't say that to Mish's own son. "I'm Juliann. I'm just—"

"My friend," the soft voice from the bed explained. They all turned to look at Mish. "Juliann, this is my son Bobby and…and Claudia."

Juliann tried to smile. She thought maybe she was supposed to shake their hands, but since they didn't reach out, she didn't either. She put her hands in her pockets as they both turned their attention back to Mish.

"What happened, Mom?" Bobby asked. "We got a call from some woman who told us there'd been an accident and you were in the hospital with a possible concussion. That's all we know."

Mish reached up and Bobby took her hand. "I was talking to a young man, and…" She paused. "He pushed me and I fell."

"He pushed you?" Bobby repeated. "That's assault! Have you notified the police?"

Mish nodded, then winced again. "They'll catch him."

The door slid open again, and another man entered the room. Juliann thought it was the same doctor who'd almost ran her over when they arrived. He introduced himself as Dr. Campbell, then got straight to business. "Mrs. Atkinson, I got the results of your MRI. Do you want me to share the news with you privately or—" His voice trailed off as he motioned to those gathered around. Claudia and Bobby both looked at Juliann.

Juliann dropped her gaze and nodded. "I'll wait outside."

Claudia started to thank her but Mish interrupted. "Stay. Please. You are family too."

"I'm afraid the news isn't good," Dr. Campbell began, addressing Mish's son. "When she arrived, she was conscious and responsive, which are very good signs. But her speech aphasia and numbness in her extremities caused us to do the MRI. The scan showed a subdural hematoma. A brain bleed."

"How bad is it?" Bobby asked.

"It's pretty severe. If she were younger, I would recommend a craniotomy, which creates a large opening in the skull so that the clot can be evacuated. But at her age, I don't know if she is strong enough for the surgery. So I recommend we take a more conservative approach, inserting a catheter through a small hole drilled into the skull."

"Will that be as effective?" Bobby asked.

The doctor kept talking, but Juliann had stopped paying attention. *Cranial* this and *hematoma* that, and although she would normally be interested in learning about the brain, this was not science class. This was real life. This was Mish. She couldn't believe this was happening. It wasn't fair. Not so soon after she lost her grandmother.

"Excuse me," Mish said.

Juliann looked at Mish. Clearly the doctor hadn't heard her because he kept talking to Mish's son.

"Excuse me," Mish repeated, louder. This time they fell silent. "This sub—sub—"

"Subdural hematoma," the doctor supplied.

"Yes, that," Mish agreed. "Does my son have one?"

They all looked at each other, confused by the question. Finally the doctor said, "No, ma'am, you're the one with the brain bleed."

"So why are you talking to *him* about *my* brain?"

Bob reached out and patted her arm. "Now, Mother, don't get too excited. The doctor is only trying to—"

But Mish pulled her hand away, put her first finger and thumb together, then ran them over her own mouth. The message was clear: *Zip it!* To Juliann's shock, her son suddenly looked like a ten-year-old—well, a ten-year-old with a receding hairline—and Juliann had to fight the urge to laugh.

"So, Doctor Campbell," Mish began again. "You can't decide whether to…" she paused again. "Whether to cut my head open or drill into it?"

"Yes, ma'am." The doctor's attention was completely on Mish now. "We can drill and insert a catheter and evacuate as much blood as possible, then hope your body will absorb the rest."

"Or?" Mish asked.

"Or we do a craniotomy and open the skull."

"I want that," Mish said immediately.

"But the risks at your age—" the doctor began.

"Life is full of risks," Mish said, with a wave of her hand. "I'd rather die…"

She paused, searching for the word, and Claudia panicked. "Mom, no!" she said, lunging forward.

But Juliann surprised herself by putting a hand on the woman's arm. "Let her finish."

Mish smiled. "I'd rather die trying to live than live afraid of dying."

Juliann wasn't sure if that made sense, but she liked the way it sounded.

"Legally, we will have to discuss the risks of surgery with you. You may not survive the surgery. And if you survive, you may still have permanent limitations. You will have to sign saying you understand these risks."

"Yes," Mish agreed. "There's one other thing you need to know." She paused again, searching. "I'm a—a—bacon and eggs gal. I don't have time for sugarcoating."

He looked her in the eyes for a moment before answering. "I understand. So I will say this: the odds are not in your favor. I can't promise anything."

"Life ain't the shopping channel," Mish said.

The doctor exchanged looks with Bobby and Claudia, but it was Juliann who interpreted for them. "It doesn't come with a money-back guarantee."

❧

Mish felt jittery. Nervous. Not about the surgery. What would be, would be. She wanted to live but wasn't afraid to die. She was anxious because she had some things she needed to communicate and didn't know if she'd have time. Or the words.

For someone who'd lived her life speaking her mind, it was incredibly frustrating to have to think so hard to find the words. Her brain was moving in slow motion, and sometimes the words just wouldn't come out. But this was important. It couldn't wait. She took a breath to begin, but the door slid open again. Pastor Jeff.

Mish smiled and reached out a hand. He moved to get close to her, and Juliann flattened herself against the wall to let him through. After leaning down and kissing her on the cheek, Jeff said, "They told me only three visitors are allowed at a time, so I won't be able to stay long."

Juliann ducked her head. "I'll wait outside."

"No!" Mish corrected. "Claudia—sorry, hon. Can you—?"

Claudia clearly looked hurt, but Mish couldn't worry about that now. Claudia clutched her big purse to her chest and walked out.

"Can somebody fill me in on what's happening?" Jeff asked.

Mish looked first at her son, then at Juliann. Better to let her communicate. She didn't trust Bobby where Pastor Jeff was concerned. She nodded her permission at Juliann. The girl gave Jeff a quick summary of the situation, and when Jeff turned back to look at Mish, his eyes were full of tears.

"We need to talk," Mish said. "In case I don't make it."

"Now, Mother, I don't think that's necessary," Bobby began, but Mish interrupted.

"You heard the doc. Not much time." She closed her eyes and swallowed hard. This was not the way she wanted to do this, but she didn't have a choice. When she opened them again, she got straight to business. "For funeral, no psalm…psalm…" *Why can't I remember the blasted number?* "The shepherd one."

"No 23rd Psalm," Jeff finished. "Got it. What else? Any special readings?"

"Poems."

"Fine. Do you have a favorite poet?"

"Juliann."

The girl's eyes widened. "You can't be serious! You've never even heard any of my poetry!"

"One of yours. One of mine. Promise?"

Juliann stared at her for a few seconds, then shook her head. "This is ridiculous. You're not going to die. The surgery will fix everything, and you'll stay around to help me for a long time. You can beat this." Her voice broke on the last word. "Promise me you'll try," she begged.

"I promise I'll try. You promise you'll write me a poem if—if—" Mish reached out her hand. Juliann took it and nodded. "There's coconut in the fridge."

Juliann looked confused.

"There's coconut in the fridge," she repeated. "Use it."

Juliann and Jeff exchange confused looks. She'd have to let Juliann figure that one out on her own. She looked back at Bobby. "Now. Let's talk about will."

"Who is Will?" Bobby asked.

"Will Jorgens? From church?" Jeff supplied.

She rolled her eyes. "My will. Don't have time for lawyer. I have to trust you."

"Of course you can trust me, Mother. Why would you even say something like that?"

She knew she'd offended her son, but she didn't have time for that either. There was a time for worrying about feelings and a time for getting things done. "I left some for Livie and some for the church."

"I know," Bobby said. "I'm the executor of your estate, remember? Those two bequests come off the top, and the rest goes to me as your only child."

Mish held up a finger. "One change." Bobby looked sideways at Jeff and Juliann. Clearly he did not want to be having this conversation in front of the others. She didn't care. "My house."

"What about it?"

"Trust," she said.

Bobby let out a heavy sigh. "You can trust me, Mother."

She covered her eyes so she could think clearly. Words were getting harder to come by. "House. Trust!"

"Excuse me," Jeff said carefully, casting a leery glance at Bobby. "Mish, do you mean you want the house put into a trust?"

She let out a deep breath. "Yes. Trust."

"Okay," Bobby said. "That's easy. But I need to know your end goal. Who is the trustee? What is your long-term plan for the property?"

"Juliann and her mom."

Bobby let out a huff of disgust, just as she knew he would. "You want to leave the house to complete strangers? I mean, it's your house, and you can do what you want with it. And your estate is plenty big so I'm not complaining about the money. I just don't understand why the hell you would you do that for people you barely know."

Mish looked at Juliann, who looked terrified. She tried to communicate with her eyes, but it wasn't working. "No, Mish, you can't do that. We don't need your house. We'll figure out a way."

"Trusty!" Mish insisted. "Trusty!"

It was Jeff who again figured out what she meant. "I think she's saying she wants Juliann and her mother to be trustees, not owners of the house."

"Yes!" Mish was so relieved someone was finally understanding her.

"For how long?" Bobby asked.

Mish thought for a moment. "Ten years. No rent."

"And then what?" Bobby demanded.

"Give the house to…to…"

"To whom, Mother?" Bobby prompted.

"The shelter."

"What kind of shelter? Animal shelter?"

Mish shook her head, but the pain was so bad when she did that. She had to remember not to move her head. But there was so much to remember. Too much. She had to go on. She looked at Juliann, knowing that the girl was the only one who could explain. Mish couldn't. She didn't want these to be her last words. So she mimed the event that symbolized it all. She pretended to light a match and then threw her hands up and let out a "whoosh."

The girl began to cry. "A women's shelter. Because of Floyd," she whispered. Mish gave her a small nod.

Bobby was staring at Juliann now. "Why would she want to give money to a women's shelter for my dad?"

Juliann looked to Mish again, clearly looking for permission. Mish closed her eyes and gave her one more nod. Juliann took a deep breath, straightened her shoulders, and looked Bobby straight in the eye. "Not *for* your dad. *Because* of your dad. Your mother wants her house to go to the women's center for domestic violence because of your dad."

Mish saw the deep furrow between her son's eyebrows. She was sorry he was finding out this way. But he needed to know the truth. About his father. About his mother. About himself. Before it was too late.

"I don't understand. My dad yelled and, okay, he got pretty angry sometimes. But he was never violent."

Juliann swallowed hard. "Yes, he was. Floyd was emotionally and physically abusive to Mish. You can try to deny it if you want, but I know the signs." Her voice started shaking, but she kept talking. "I know because I have grown up in an abusive household. I have seen my father terrorize my mother. I have seen how she covers for him. That's why Mish took us in—to save us—because she knows how it feels."

Jeff moved closer to Juliann, then turned to face Bobby. The message was clear. It was two against one. "I have seen the bruises," he began. "I didn't recognize them for what they were. And Mish lied to me about them, tried to cover for your father. I'm ashamed to say I believed her story when I should have known better. What Juliann is saying is true." He looked at Mish, and she gave him a sad smile. He turned back to Bobby. "Please. Honor your mother by honoring her wishes. She needs to do this. It's like…" It was his turn to search for words, and Mish's turn to supply one.

"Redemption." She looked at Bobby, tried to tell him with her eyes how much she loved him. He still looked shocked. "Don't become him," she whispered. "Please. My sweet boy. Please." And finally he broke. The sob that escaped him reminded Mish of when he was a young boy and his 4-H calf died. He had cried so hard she thought the ground would shake. And suddenly her son was at her side, his tears falling on her arm, and he cried, "Don't leave me, Mama! Please!"

She patted his head. Her sweet son, smelling like hay and sunshine and little boy. She kissed his head and tousled his hair. *He'll grow up to be a fine man.*

It was her last thought as the darkness closed in again.

17

Juliann pushed the orange mac 'n' cheese around her plate. God, she hated this stuff. For some reason her mom thought that anything Juliann had liked as a child was "comfort food." She couldn't remember ever liking the flavor. As a young girl she had only liked the straight little lines of pasta because she could stack them or use them to perform math equations.

She hadn't wanted to leave the hospital, but her mom had insisted. They needed to get the dog home, and there really wasn't anything they could do at the hospital while Mish was in surgery.

Bobby stayed to sign paperwork, leaving Juliann to walk back out to the waiting room with Mish's pastor. Juliann was not at all in the mood to have an uncomfortable conversation with Jeff, but she didn't know how to get out of it. After they talked, she wished she'd found a way, because their talk just confused her more.

He told her about the woman Mish met in the diner, and how Mish believed she was on a mission to "follow the love." He thought that somehow people were getting Mish's phone number to take advantage of her, and he wanted to know how Juliann met her. She explained that she had just written a phone number down wrong, but she did acknowledge that, yes, Mish had come out to meet her without even knowing who she was. And how many others had been texting Mish? As far as Juliann knew, there was the girl who wrote to Mish for fashion advice, and the dick pic guy. Pastor Jeff also knew of somebody named Ethan. But nobody seemed to be taking advantage of her, so what was all this about?

The day they first met, Mish had mentioned Jesus sending her, and of course she had talked about following the love several times, so what Pastor Jeff said made sense. But what did all this mean for their relationship? Did Mish really care about her, or was Juliann just some kind of mission project or something? She wasn't exactly sure why, but it made her really sad to think Mish did all that for her just because she thought Jesus wanted her to. She wanted Mish to have done it because Mish wanted to, not because she was following some misguided sense of responsibility.

And as if that weren't enough, Mish had gone and taken care of Juliann and her mom, even though she was in crisis herself. Juliann still couldn't believe what Mish had done. If Mish died, they would have a free place to live—for ten years!

If Mish died. Just thinking that phrase made her want to puke. It was all too much to take in.

She gave up on the mac 'n' cheese and went looking for the dog to see if she could coax her into eating. The dog was curled up on the end of the sofa, which she seemed to have claimed as her own. "You can have that seat for now, but you'll have to move when Mish gets home. That's where she always sits." The dog looked at her with sad eyes. She set the plate on the floor but the dog didn't move.

The phone in her pocket buzzed, and she automatically pulled it out to check it. But it wasn't her phone. Her phone was in the other pocket. This was Mish's phone. She had forgotten to return it after calling Jeff.

She wasn't sure if she should look at it. When they were on their trip, she had permission. Now it felt more like an invasion of privacy. But it was clearly a text from that girl who always asked for Mish's opinion. And suddenly she had an idea.

> *Hi I'm a friend of Mish. Can you tell me how you got her number?*
>
> Who's Mish?
>
> *The owner of this phone. How did you get her number?*
>
> She gave it to me at a party but her name isn't Mish.
>
> *What did she look like?*
>
> Pretty with brown hair and blonde highlights, great fashion sense. That's who I've been texting.

Juliann almost laughed.

Actually, you've been texting an 82yo woman named Mish with no fashion sense.

WTF??

Trying to figure this out. How old was the girl?

IDK maybe 20 or 21.

And she just gave you this number?

Juliann waited while the girl typed a long response.

> Yeah, she was really cool and I was asking her where she shopped and advice on clothes and stuff. I kind of thought I was bugging her and was ready to stop but then she said she had to run but I could text her when I needed advice. And she gave me this number. Why would she do that?

Juliann wasn't sure what to say. It seemed obvious to her that the pretty girl was trying to get rid of the other girl and gave her a fake number. But she thought it would be rude to say so directly.

IDK. Do you think it was on purpose?

There was a long pause and Juliann wondered if she said the wrong thing. Finally, the response came:

> Yeah, probably.

Juliann could imagine how she felt. The girl obviously thought she had been friends with somebody much higher up on the social food chain, only to discover that she had been ditched. Juliann knew how it felt to be on the outside, looking in.

For what it's worth, I agree with Mish. You have good taste.

Thanks but how old are you? Am I texting another 80yo?

LOL I'm 16.

I'm 18. So have you seen everything I sent her?

Just this time and the time with the royal blue jacket, black leggings, and boots. Loved the boots.

Those are my new favs from a consignment shop.

Srsly? I've never been to one.

OMG they're the best. Maybe we could go together some-time.

Juliann smiled. It was weird, but she felt kind of connected to this girl. Maybe it was because they both accidentally found Mish. They exchanged names and numbers, and Juliann explained that Mish was sick so Juliann was busy and might not answer right away.

But I'm not ghosting you, K?

K, thanks. I guess I'm kind of glad that girl gave me the wrong number.

The statement reminded Juliann of what she needed to be doing. She said bye and clicked out of that conversation, then looked through the text history on Mish's phone. She was about to solve a mystery.

Jeff took a detour on his way home, stopping at his favorite scenic overlook for a few minutes. It wasn't the highest spot around or the most dramatic—it was just green pasture, rolling hills, and a hint of mountain behind—but somehow it soothed him.

He got out of the car and sat on the large rock he thought of as his resting rock. He recited the psalm he had learned as a boy. "I will lift up my eyes unto the hills, from whence cometh my help. My help cometh from the Lord, who made heaven and earth." But neither the verse nor the view was going to do anything for him. There was no help coming from the hills, regardless of what the psalm said. There was no help for what ailed him.

He was tired. Tired of the relentless pressure of weekly sermon preparation. Tired of questioning if he even believed what he was preaching. Tired of petty grievances. Tired of knowing he was on call 24/7. But mostly he was tired of the loss. He was tired of burying people he had grown to love.

Grown to love. It was a strange phrase. His love for his people had grown, certainly, but he had grown too. His heart had grown to make room for so many. He had grown in order to be able to love that many, that much.

And it sucked. Loving was highly overrated. He was still reeling from the news about Carl, and now he might lose Mish. He wasn't ready. He wasn't ready for any of it. But death would come, of course, if not soon then soon enough. Death would call, "Ready or not, here I come!" and he would once again find himself sitting beside a grieving family as they chose the casket for their mother, and he would agree that, yes, she always looked good in blue.

The sound of tires on gravel startled him, then he swore under his breath because his quiet spot was about to be invaded. He started to wipe his tears but stopped. Maybe whoever it was would decide to leave the crying crazy man alone. He felt the presence of the man behind him, as the wind brought the soft scent of aftershave. "How did you know I would be here?" he asked without turning.

"You didn't call after your trip to the hospital," Stephen explained. "And when you didn't answer your phone, I thought you might be sitting out here. I assume this means the news isn't good."

Jeff shook his head. "She's undergoing a risky surgery, and I don't know if…" His voice trailed off. It was weird how the closer he was to someone, the harder it was to give voice to reality.

Jeff shifted on the rock as Stephen slid behind him and wrapped his arms around Jeff's waist. Stephen didn't say anything. He didn't need to. Jeff leaned back into him and Stephen held him steady. Together they sat in silence, staring at the hills and the pasture, watching the clouds cast shadows on the hillside. They sat there until the cold from the rock seeped into their bones.

But when they stood, Jeff's heart was a little lighter. He felt stronger, more ready to face whatever would happen.

His help hadn't come from the hills. His help had come from his beloved's arms.

Juliann was rifling through the kitchen drawers when her mother walked in. "Looking for anything in particular?" Nicole asked.

Juliann slammed the drawer shut. "I found two squirt guns and a roll of Santa wrapping paper, but I can't find a single recipe box or cookbook."

"You want to bake? Now?"

"I've got to do something! I can't just sit around waiting for a call or text that may never come."

"Somebody will think to call you," Nicole assured her.

"But what if—"

Nicole put her hands on Juliann's shoulders. "And if they don't, you have the pastor's number. You can just text and ask if he's heard how the surgery went. Okay?" Juliann nodded reluctantly. "All right. So cookbooks. Did you check the small cabinet above the stove?"

Juliann abandoned the drawer she'd opened and went to look. Sure enough there was a wooden recipe box and a few old, well-worn cookbooks. "How'd you know?" she asked.

"It's a common place—those small cabinets don't hold a lot. And Mish is short so she wouldn't put anything up there that she needs very often. I'm guessing that, at her age, she doesn't use recipes much anymore."

"Well, I'm hoping she has a recipe for coconut pie."

Her mom reached for one of the cookbooks. "Coconut custard or coconut cream? I have a simple recipe for coconut custard pie if you want it."

"I don't know. Mish made a point of telling me there was coconut in the fridge. Thought I should make something with it."

"Is it all right if I help?"

"Actually, I was thinking about making Grandma's piecrust and Mish's pie filling. But your recipe box is at the old house."

Her mom smiled. "I know it by heart."

They sat and looked through recipes for a while and finally decided on one in Mish's box for coconut pecan chocolate pie. The card was frayed on the edges and had a few stains, so they thought it must have been one of Mish's favorites.

After rolling out the pie crust and placing it in the pan, Juliann let her mother crimp the edges—she never did that part well—and started gathering the ingredients for the filling. She had trouble finding the coconut because she was looking for the familiar blue bag she'd always seen in their own fridge. But she finally found it in the back—an old can with a plastic top.

"Mom, do you think this is still good? Does coconut expire?"

Her mom glanced over at the can. "Open it up and see if it's dried out."

Juliann pulled off the lid and stared at the contents. She couldn't believe what she was seeing.

"Is it okay?" her mom asked.

Juliann swallowed hard to find her voice. "Well, if we want to make this pie, we better go to the store because there's no coconut in here."

"That's no problem," her mom said as she finished crimping the edges. "The crust will wait. Do you want to go now?" She grabbed a tea towel to wipe her hands, then caught sight of what Juliann was holding. A wad of cash. "What the—"

"They're hundreds," Juliann said. "All of them. They're all hundred dollar bills."

Nicole stepped closer to see for herself. "Why would Mish leave this kind of money in her refrigerator?"

Juliann laughed. "I don't try to understand Mish. I just love her!"

"Well, it doesn't belong to us. Put it back where you found it."

"Fine," Juliann muttered, then grinned sheepishly. "Can I at least count it?"

Her mom chuckled. "Knock yourself out."

She was up to $20,400 when her phone dinged. Pastor Jeff had remembered her.

> Mish had a stroke during the surgery. She made it through but next 24 hours are crucial. She's in ICU so visits are very limited. I'll keep you posted.

A flash of relief was quickly followed by renewed fear. Mish was still in danger. She still might die. She pushed away from the table, away from the money. It didn't matter. Nothing mattered. Nothing except Mish. Her best-grand. The wisest woman she'd ever known. Juliann had the book smarts, but what Mish had was much more important.

And suddenly she had an idea for a poem. A poem she hoped never to deliver but needed to write.

18

Jeff sat in the corner booth, fiddling with his placemat. It was the cheap paper kind with ads running around the edges. Bob's Auto Body. Loveitt Insurance. Outdoor Video Projection. He shifted the placemat, trying to get it to line up evenly with the edge of the table. The scalloped edge always made that harder than a straight edge. He took his hands away to make sure he had accomplished his goal and noticed that the same ad appeared on both the right and left corners. "Do you have extra love to give? Consider becoming a foster parent! Children and teens need YOU! *Right*, he thought. *Because I need more stress in my life!*

He turned his attention to the employees of the small diner. There seemed to be just two at the moment—a cook, who occasionally called out from the kitchen, and a waitress. He guessed a midmorning weekday shift didn't require extra help. Still, the woman was definitely keeping busy. She seemed to handle it smoothly and with good humor. He could tell by the way she multitasked that she'd been doing this for a while. He was so intent on watching her that when she turned suddenly and approached his table, he hadn't even looked at the menu.

"Coffee?" she asked as she raised the pot.

"Please." He pushed the cup to the edge of the table. He'd already stopped by his favorite independent coffee shop and enjoyed his usual roast, but he figured he should buy a cup of coffee here too.

"Cream and sugar are on the table," she said with a nod. "What else can I get you?"

"Do you have any muffins?" he asked.

She rattled off a whole list of flavors, and he was about to ask her to repeat them when he noticed the chalkboard sign over her shoulder. Today's Muffins: blueberry, chocolate chip, cinnamon-apple, corn, cranberry, and pumpkin. She had said them in the exact same order.

"Alphabetical," he said with a smile. "Just the way I like my menu."

She smiled in return. "They're all homemade, and they're all delicious. But if you're looking for a recommendation, you can't go wrong with the cinnamon-apple."

"Sounds great," Jeff replied.

"Grilled?"

"Yes, please."

She gave him a sharp nod, then turned and headed toward the kitchen. Jeff took a calming breath. This was exactly the kind of waitress he was hoping to find. If she was on duty that day, she would be able to tell Jeff what he needed to know. He doubted she missed much that happened in her restaurant.

Of course, the place was busy enough that he didn't want to try to monopolize her time. She wouldn't respond well if he kept her from providing good service to other customers. Best to wait it out and hope for the best.

He couldn't really say why this was important to him, or why he had not told Stephen where he was going. Obviously his instincts had been right, that Mish was in danger. But he was still so curious about how all this started. And he couldn't figure out what angle they were playing, which was driving him crazy. If he could just find that woman, maybe he could interest the police in the case. And maybe that would loosen the vise of guilt that had been plaguing him. If only he had sounded the alarm louder or been more pointed in his warnings to Mish. Maybe he could have prevented this. Even as he thought it, he knew better. He had already, in Mish's words, nosed into her business more than she wanted. He was her pastor, not her savior.

He needed answers. He just didn't know if they were for Mish or for himself.

After several customers left, the waitress moved at a slower pace. When she offered him a refill, he decided the time had come.

"Ma'am, I was wondering if you could help me with something."

"I can try."

He handed her his phone, where he had pulled up the church directory app. It was open to Mish's picture. "Do you know this woman? She was in here a few weeks ago."

The waitress looked at the phone, then back at Jeff. "Mind if I ask why you want to know?"

"I'm sorry. I should have introduced myself. I'm Jeff Cooper. I'm her pastor, and she's in the hospital and—

"Mish is in the hospital? Is she gonna be all right?"

The knot in Jeff's chest eased. If the waitress knew Mish, this was going to be much easier. "We don't know," he said truthfully. "It's a wait-and-see kind of situation. So you obviously know her. Do you know her well?"

The waitress shook her head. "Not really. She comes in here occasionally, and she's so friendly that of course I know her name. I'm sure sad to hear she's not doing well. She's an awful sweet lady."

"Yes, she is," Jeff agreed. "Maybe too sweet." The waitress raised an eyebrow at him so he hurried to explain. "I've worried for some time that someone was trying to take advantage of her. And now she's been hurt by somebody she tried to help."

Her hand flew to her mouth. "Somebody hurt her? What happened?"

"Well, the whole situation started a few weeks ago, here in your restaurant."

She slid into the seat across from Jeff, clearly concerned. "What do you mean?"

"She was here a few weeks ago," he repeated, "and she met someone—"

"No, she didn't," the woman corrected. "She *came* here to meet someone—said somebody had texted her and asked her to meet them for breakfast. But she didn't know who it was, and she left without meeting anybody. I guess they didn't show."

Jeff frowned, then tried a different tactic. "Maybe the person

she met isn't who she planned to meet, but she did talk to someone that day. It was an African American woman who might have
been mentally ill, or maybe someone who would target senior
citizens."

The waitress looked puzzled, then started laughing. "Oh, I
know the woman she talked to, but I assure you she is not mentally ill, and she certainly wouldn't target senior citizens."

"But she told Mish that she was Jesus! What kind of person
would do that?"

"Told her she was Jesus? No, that's not right. I don't know
what Mish heard—or thought she heard—but Liza is no threat.
And she's a good lady but I'm pretty sure she's not divine!"

"Do you have any idea what Mish might have heard that day?
Anything she might have misinterpreted?"

The waitress gazed off into space before she spoke. "I don't
know what Mish and Liza talked about when I was helping other
customers, but when Liza and I talked…hmm. I think she was
telling me she'd been put in charge of the police department's
Facebook page. She was complaining about how they had just
a handful of followers, and she was supposed to perform some
kind of miracle and get as many followers as that police department up in Maine."

"Police department?" Jeff echoed.

She nodded. "The woman you're looking for is Detective Liza
Hughes."

Jeff shook his head, trying to get the pieces of the puzzle to
shift into place. "The woman's a detective? Mish said the woman
told her she was Jesus Christ! This still doesn't make sense."

The waitress got back to her feet and looked down at Jeff with
what he could only describe as pity. "Well, you know, Pastor, not
everyone who says the name Jesus is praying."

Juliann sat in the ICU family waiting room. She didn't think she
would be allowed to go in, but she couldn't stand just waiting at
home. At least she'd be close enough to hear news. If there was
any.

She'd been there half an hour when Bob and Claudia came out and saw her. Bob headed for the elevator, but Claudia stopped and put a hand on Juliann's arm. "I added your name to the list of approved visitors. You can go sit with her if you want. They removed the breathing tube, but she's still in and out of consciousness. She probably won't know that you're there, but I'll be glad to know somebody is with her in case she wakes up before we get back."

Juliann smiled and nodded her thanks, then went in and sat in the chair at the foot of Mish's bed. Juliann watched her chest rising and falling, afraid that Mish might die right before her eyes. When her breathing didn't weaken or slow, Juliann relaxed and sat back in her chair. She leaned her head back and closed her eyes. She must've drifted off too because when she heard footsteps, she nearly jumped out of her skin. Pastor Jeff had arrived.

"Okay if I sit with you for a few minutes?" he whispered.

"Of course," she whispered back. "In fact, I wanted to tell you what I learned. I solved a bit of the mystery."

Jeff's eyes widened. "Really? So did I. What do you know?"

"A girl, maybe twenty or twenty-one years old, has been giving out Mish's number."

Jeff's look of interest turned to confusion. "On purpose? Why?"

"Well, she gave it to one girl who was apparently getting on her nerves. And she gave it to at least two guys. One of them—Ethan—told me about how they met at a club, and he asked for her number and she gave it to him—or he thought she did, only it was a fake number. I'm guessing that's what happened with the other guy, the one who—"

He nodded. "The one who hurt Mish."

Juliann noticed his fist clench in his lap. "Right. So I think maybe this girl, instead of making up a number on the spot to give to people she wants to dis, actually gives the same number all the time. And it happens to belong to Mish."

Jeff nodded as he stared off into space. "I guess that makes sense."

"Yeah, it's a coincidence, I know," Juliann admitted, "but I think I know why the girl chose Mish's number. See, I like to play around with numbers and patterns. The last four digits of Mish's number—5375—I liked them because they made a diagonal pattern on the keypad. But if you look at the letters associated with those numbers on the phone, you can spell the word 'jerk.' I think the girl giving out the number thought she was being funny."

"That is the piece of the puzzle I was missing—how these people were reaching her. What *I* learned is the identity of the woman she thought was Jesus."

Juliann glanced at the bed to make sure Mish was still asleep. "Who is she?" she whispered.

"Her name is Liza Hughes, and she's a police detective, of all things. Mish must've misheard something the detective said. That's the only explanation I can come up with for why she thought the woman was Jesus."

Juliann tucked her hair behind her ear. "Let me make sure I have all the pieces. She got a text from someone she didn't know, and when she went to meet whoever it was, she met a woman who she thought was Jesus. The woman told her to follow the love, and then when she got more texts from people asking for help or advice, she thought they were part of this same project or mission or whatever. Then she got herself into these different situations, some of them dangerous, because a woman told her to follow the love and because a girl gave out her number."

"That about sums it up," Jeff agreed through gritted teeth. "What kills me is that none of this—" he gestured angrily toward her bed— "was necessary. She could die because she had this crazy idea that God was sending her on these missions." His voice began rising. "It wasn't God. It was never God. It was a woman, who"—he lifted his hands in exasperation—"for some unfathomable reason, Mish believed was Jesus. She could die because she had faith!"

Juliann stared at the pastor as his words hung in the air between them. They both turned when a sound came from Mish. She was agitated, muttering. Juliann got close and called, "Mish? Did you say something?"

"Doesn't matter," Mish mumbled. "Doesn't matter."

Juliann and Jeff exchanged looks again. "What doesn't matter?" Jeff asked, but Mish didn't answer. They turned in unison when Bob and Claudia entered the room, accompanied by a girl who looked a few years older than Juliann. She was crying as she ran to Mish's side. So this was Mish's granddaughter, up from Florida. She had come to see her grandmother. She had come just in case. Just in case this was goodbye.

Juliann lifted Mish's hand to her lips and kissed it, then stepped away. It was time for family only, and she wasn't Mish's family. She wasn't blood. She only felt like she was. She only wished she was.

She took one last look at her best-grand, then turned and walked out the door.

Jeff stared at the blank page on his screen, struggling to get started on his sermon for Sunday. But the words wouldn't come. All he could think about was Mish.

She was still in ICU, still in critical condition. He caught himself trying to figure out what he would say at her memorial service, and he had no words for that sermon either.

He had officiated at more difficult funerals, strictly speaking—the sudden deaths of younger people, for example—but few that had been as difficult emotionally as this one would be. *Might be*, he corrected himself. There was still time. There was still hope. But what was hope? And what good was it?

He loved Mish—and not just in that vague way that some pastors talked about loving their parishioners. She was so endearing. Yes, she was quirky, eccentric even, but in such a loveable way.

He had buried plenty of people he cared about, but this was different for him because the whole situation had been so preventable. If Mish hadn't believed this whole "follow the love" business, she never would have gone to that park. It was her delusion that had put her life in jeopardy. Stephen didn't like for him to use that word for Mish, but it was better than saying her faith had caused it, like he'd accidentally done with Juliann. He still felt a flush of shame every time he remembered that Mish may have heard him say that. She had mumbled, "It doesn't matter," but he wasn't sure what she'd meant by that. Did it not matter that she'd heard him? Did it not matter that the woman wasn't Jesus? What didn't matter?

Jeff was left with only one conclusion for himself: none of it mattered. What he did for a living—it didn't matter. He tried to keep his small church alive in spite of the statistics that said the church in America was dying. Sometimes he felt like his efforts were worthwhile, but inevitably he would come back to the realization that he was rearranging deck chairs on the *Titanic*. No matter what he did, it didn't make a difference. He tried to help people, but most of the time he failed. He tried to help people believe in God, but he wasn't even sure why. He wasn't sure *he* believed, so why should they? He wasn't sure it mattered.

And then there was his dad. His shining example. His mentor. His symbol of everything a minister was supposed to be and do. If even he couldn't do this job with integrity, how in the hell was Jeff supposed to?

"Pastor Jeff?"

Jeff looked up to see Carl standing in the doorway. He tried to smile, but Carl was the last person he wanted to see at the moment. The reminder that he was about to lose another person he cared about was just too much.

"I won't take much of your time," Carl began. "I just came from my doctor's office and wanted to give you an update. Is that okay?"

"Of course," Jeff lied. "Come on in."

They took their usual seats, but this time, instead of staring at his pants leg, Carl looked him straight in the eye. "I'm afraid you won't be getting rid of me quite so soon."

"Does that mean…" Jeff fumbled for the right words. "What does that mean?"

Carl smiled. "I told my doc I wasn't going to do the aggressive treatment he suggested, and he gave me another option—a low dose of chemo that won't cure me, but it will probably buy me a little time, without bad side effects."

Jeff grinned, but Carl held up his hand. "It's no guarantee, but

I think it's worth a try. And I think I owe it to my family to try. After all, my first grandbaby is on the way!"

"Oh, Carl, that's wonderful! Congratulations—on the baby, I mean. And I'm so glad you changed your mind about the treatment."

"Well, that's the other reason I came by. I wanted to thank you for our talk. I expected you to argue with me, which you did a little, but then you understood and accepted my decision. I had been so busy thinking about how I could defend my decision—to you and to my daughter—that I forgot to make sure it was really what I wanted to do. And then you asked me if I had no reason to live. I've been thinking about it, and I do. I have lots of reasons to live. Oh, I'll still say no to drastic treatment or what they call extreme measures. But if I have a chance of even one more year with quality of life, I should take it. Life is a gift. I don't want to throw away the gift just because I don't like the whole package."

Jeff, already on the verge of tears before Carl had come in, was having even more trouble holding them back now. "Thank you," he began and then stopped and cleared his throat. "Thank you for telling me, Carl. I'm glad something I said was helpful."

Carl stood up and grabbed Jeff in a big hug, patting him on the back before he let go. "I don't know if it was you or God, but I guess it doesn't matter. Either way, I'll take it."

19

Several Weeks Later

Mom, I don't have anything to wear," Juliann called over her shoulder as she stared at the closet. When she and her mom had gone back to their house to pack up their clothes, she had taken almost everything, not sure when she'd be back. But she hadn't thought to pack her dress clothes. She had a black dress that would be fine, but it was at her house. Her old house. Her dad's house.

She turned around when she heard her mother enter the room. "Can we go back to the house and get my black dress?"

"No, we can't," her mother said softly.

"Come on, Mom. We can do it when Dad's at work," Juliann argued. "It'll take, like, two minutes."

"No, we can't," she repeated. "He changed the locks."

"Shit," Juliann announced as she plopped down on the bed.

"Indeed," her mother replied, sitting next to her.

"What does he want?" She knew her father, and she knew he did everything for a reason—usually for some personal gain. He wanted something.

Her mom played with a loose string on the floral bedspread, not meeting Juliann's eyes. "He wants a meeting."

"With me," Juliann said. It wasn't a question.

"Actually, with both of us."

Juliann thought about that for a minute. She could see several ways this could go. Her dad could play nice, try to convince them he had changed, promise Juliann a new car, *blah, blah, blah*. Or he could go into one of his rants and try to intimidate her mom into giving in. Most likely he would try the nice route and get mean when it didn't work. *If* it didn't work. But what if it did? Would her mom cave and go back? Maybe it was time to have that hard talk. She took a deep breath. "Mom? Why did you stay?"

Her mom stood up and turned toward the door. "I don't really think this is the time for that conversation. We have lots of other things to deal with and—"

"Mom! Sit down!" Juliann was shocked that she had actually given her mother an order, then shocked even more when her mother actually obeyed it. She took her mom's hand. "I'm not being judgey. I just need to understand."

Her mom let out a heavy sigh. "I've always known this day would come. But I'm going to need some chocolate for this conversation. You with me?"

Juliann tried to smile as her mom pulled her to her feet. They went to the kitchen, and Nicole opened the pantry door. "Cookies or candy?"

"Yes!" Juliann answered. "And chips." She couldn't help but smile as she pulled them out of the sparkling clean trash compactor where Mish kept them.

They gathered their stash and went to the family room. Juliann found the remote and turned on the gas fire, then they took their places on the sofa beside the dog. They sat for a few moments without speaking, Juliann waiting for her mother to take the lead.

"I was going through a difficult time when I met him," her mother began.

"Difficult how?" Juliann asked, but her mother hushed her.

"I need to tell this my way. You need to be patient."

Juliann bit her tongue.

"I was going through a difficult time," she repeated, "and Daniel was so thoughtful, caring. He promised he would take care of everything, and I believed him. He was almost done with law school and—since he was smart and charming—he showed every sign of being headed for a successful career. I did not have resources—you know your grandparents were never wealthy—and his promise of a house at the country club sounded so inviting. It's not that I married him for his money. It just added to his appeal and to the idea that he was rescuing me. I truly loved him.

I couldn't believe he had chosen me, and I felt so lucky that he would marry me, especially given the circumstances."

"What—" Juliann started to ask, then stopped herself. "Sorry," she muttered.

"He was okay at first. Moodier than I expected, but we'd had such a whirlwind romance, there was a lot I didn't know. The problems really started after you were born. Not that it was your fault," she rushed to explain. "It was mine. I had postpartum depression. Bad. I got overwhelmed by…well, by everything. I took care of you, but that's all I did. I stopped taking care of myself. He would come home from work wanting dinner on the table, and I'd still be in the clothes I'd worn the previous day, last night's dirty dishes still in the sink."

Juliann couldn't keep quiet. "He expected you to cook and clean when you'd just had a baby? What an ass!"

Her mom gave her a sad smile. "I know. But I didn't know that then. He had already started isolating me, so I didn't have friends I could talk to. One day he lost his temper, and he said he never should have married me and that I was useless and that I better snap out of it. And when I didn't respond, he grabbed me and pushed me against a wall. That was the first time. He told me he could kill me if he wanted to, and I said he should go ahead, put me out of my misery." She paused, rubbing her neck. "He used that as an excuse to have me committed. Said I was suicidal."

"Committed?" Juliann burst out. "Like in a mental institution?"

"The psychiatric floor of the hospital where you were born, actually. They transferred me to a lovely inpatient mental health facility. I was there for a month. Daniel never came to see me. When I got out, he was nice again—as long as I kept the house clean and had his meals ready when he wanted and kept you from crying too much. But you know your dad. The quiet never lasts. The next time he got abusive, I threatened to take you and leave. That's when I found out his plan. If I ever left, he would sue for full custody because I had a history of mental illness. If I ever left him, he would take you away from me." She took Juliann's hand in hers. "I couldn't stand the thought of losing you. And I couldn't stand the thought of abandoning you to him. So I stayed in order to be a buffer. I made a deal with the devil and that's the price I had to pay."

She let go of Juliann's hand to reach for a cookie. But she didn't eat it—just stared at it. "All that time I had one way out; one piece of information that could have saved us both. I was just too scared to use it."

Juliann took a deep breath. She had a feeling that whatever was coming next was going to be big. She put a hand out to the dog, who licked it, as if puppy kisses could protect her from what was to come.

"That 'whirlwind romance' I mentioned? We got married so fast because I was pregnant."

Juliann was surprised. They had never told her, but it wasn't as if that really mattered in the end. She felt a little let down, actually, having expected something much bigger.

"The baby wasn't his."

Juliann's mind swirled as she tried to figure out what that meant. "But...the...the baby," she stuttered. "That was me?"

Her mom nodded. "That's the circumstance I was talking about. I found out I was pregnant shortly after we started dating. I expected him to dump me when I told him, but he didn't. He said he didn't care if he was my first—he would be my last—and he assured me he would love my child as his own." She looked pleadingly at Juliann. "I thought I was doing the right thing for you, for us. My boyfriend had broken up with me and gone off to join the military, and I didn't know how to reach him to tell him I was pregnant. And I didn't want him to marry me out of guilt or responsibility when he had already said he didn't want to be with me. That's why, when Daniel wanted to marry me, I thought I had hit the jackpot. I didn't realize he would hold it against me for the rest of my life."

The pieces were starting to fall into place inside Juliann's head. "That's why he always called you a slut, wasn't it? I thought that was just his standard insult to women. But he was reminding you that he took you in when you were pregnant, and in return you should be, like, eternally grateful or something."

"Yes," her mother said simply. "And that's why he was so furious when he found out you had gotten pregnant. To him, it proved that you were like me. He had tried so hard to make you like him, to make you really his."

Finally, Juliann said, "But I'm not." She had been waiting to say the words, saving them until they would have her full attention. "I'm not his," she repeated. "He's not my dad." She looked to her mom for confirmation.

"No, he isn't," her mom answered, looking at her warily, clearly not sure what to expect in response.

Juliann grabbed a throw pillow from the sofa and tossed it up into the air with a loud whoop. "He's not my dad!" she shouted. "The jackass is not my dad!" She grabbed the pillow as it fell. "Wait! Then who is?"

Her mom didn't speak right away. When she finally did, it was with a misty kind of voice that Juliann hadn't heard before. "He was a very kind and gentle young man who would have married me, even though he'd already broken up with me. He would have been a good father to you." Her voice hardened. "And I will never forgive myself for being too proud to track him down and tell him."

Juliann didn't know how to respond. She wished her mom had chosen differently, too, but it seemed rude to say so. She had tried to protect her mom from getting hit. But she couldn't protect her from her own guilt.

Her mom stood suddenly, smoothing her dress over her hips. "But that's another conversation for another day. Now we have to figure out what you're going to wear. We have a Celebration of Life to attend."

❧

Jeff stood in his office, staring at what he planned to say. He wasn't sure it was right. He wasn't sure it was enough. Mish deserved better. But it was all he had to give.

The phrase reminded him of his favorite professor in seminary. One day in class she was talking about class participation, trying to encourage everyone to participate whether what they had to say was brilliant or not. She said, "Sometimes it's like a potluck dinner. You go, and there's all this good food, and you feel bad because all you have to give is a peanut butter and jelly sandwich that got squished at the bottom of your backpack. But you give it anyway because it's all you have. And you just never know—a squished peanut butter and jelly sandwich might be exactly what someone else needs."

Thank you, Dr. Newsom, he thought to himself as he put his tablet under his arm and headed to the door. As he turned the lock he paused to look at the photos on his bookshelf. The first was one of his favorite pictures of Stephen, taken at a scenic overlook on the Blue Ridge Parkway. Beside that was a candid photo from their wedding day, both of them laughing with their heads thrown back and their arms around one another. Last was a picture taken at his seminary graduation, his parents on either side of him. His mother was looking at the camera, but he and his dad had been looking at each other. Jeff could still remember the joy he'd felt when his dad had looked at him with such pride. The relationship brought no joy now, only confusion. He'd finally spoken to his father, but when his dad began to offer excuses, Jeff had cut him off. He wasn't ready to hear them. It would take time. But he would try. He had witnessed the corrosive power of regret—in Mish's son, Bob, and in so many before him.

On his way to the sanctuary, he stuck his head into the reception hall to do one last check.

"Everything is fine here, Pastor Jeff. Stop hovering!" Opal said with a smile. He smiled back at her. She really was a dear. Bossy, but a dear.

He went to check on the family, but they had already entered the sanctuary. It was time.

He walked onto the platform and nodded at the organist, who brought the prelude music to an end. He cleared his throat and stepped into the pulpit, then took a deep breath before speaking. Their little church was packed to the rafters.

"Friends, we are gathered here today to celebrate the life of Artemisia Louise Atkinson." He looked down at the front row and saw Mish in her wheelchair, wearing a fuzzy purple hat to cover her scar and bald head. On her lap was an ugly little dog. Technically speaking, only service and therapy dogs were allowed in the church, but there wasn't a soul who would tell Mish that today. Not even Ruth.

He smiled at her, and she grinned back, her smile as wide as the sky and about as bright. "As you all know, we were afraid we would be gathering here for Mish's funeral. Things did not look good right before or after her surgery, and many of us were preparing for the worst. When Mish beat the odds, she found out all the wonderful things we had planned for her service, and—true to form—she decided she didn't want to miss the fun. So we agreed to throw a Celebration of Life now, while she is here to enjoy it. Now, while we have time to tell her—" He swallowed hard over the lump in his throat. "While we have time to tell her how much we love her. And to celebrate her life—past, present, and future. So let's begin by singing one of her favorite hymns, 'Amazing Grace.'" He started to sit down, then remembered. "Oh, with one word change. Instead of 'saved a wretch like me,' we will sing 'saved a soul like me.'"

"There ain't no wretches in this house!" Mish called out, and the congregation laughed.

Jeff studied Mish as they sang. She wasn't back to her normal self yet. The doctor at the rehab facility had been reluctant to let her attend today because she was still so weak. Jeff had a suspicion he had agreed only because he knew she would do it anyway, and this way he had a say in her transportation. Nobody knew how long she would need to stay there before returning home. If she ever returned home.

Mish caught him staring at her and winked. He smiled back. She looked awfully pale, but her eyes were twinkling and she looked like she'd never been happier. Perhaps she hadn't. Bobby was sitting beside her, solicitous and caring as he held the hymnal for her, then whispering something to her that made her smile.

After the hymn, he read the scripture she had chosen—nothing shall separate us from the love of God—and then he delivered his homily. He spoke of faith and doubt, of purpose and calling, of love and where it leads. He tried to be truthful, preaching only what he could honestly say he believed. There wasn't much God talk. He didn't know what he believed. But he knew he believed in love. And he believed in Mish.

Juliann's hands were sweaty. She was clinging so tightly to the red spiral-bound notebook that she had little curved lines on the palm of her hand. She let go of the notebook and wiped her hands on her thighs. The fabric of her borrowed dress was a little slick and not very absorbent, but it was better than nothing.

Pastor Jeff was talking, but she wasn't listening. She just let his words wash over her, the rhythm and pitch of his voice soothing her. She was up next. She didn't know how she was going to do it, how she was going to keep from crying. She was so relieved, so grateful, that she cried every time she thought about what might have happened.

She had spent hours reading Mish's poetry, looking for the right one for the service. After reading through the red notebook that she knew was in Mish's crochet bag, she saw a bookshelf full of similar notebooks. They were all filled with poems. Most of them—she had to be honest—were not good by poetry standards. They were full of inconsistent rhythms and forced rhymes and occasionally a metaphor so bad it would have been laughable. But they were also filled with Mish's unique view of the world. There were poems about little things, like the daisies next to the manure pile, and big things, like her concerns about the future of the country. There was sweetness and laughter, worry and fear. In other words, there was life. There was Mish.

The right poem had been in the first book, though. In fact, it was the last poem Mish had written before she ended up in the hospital.

Juliann was really nervous about speaking—her public speaking experience was limited to class presentations and oral reports. She'd never read anybody's poem out loud, and especially not her own. She also wondered about how people would react to her being asked to speak. They had all known Mish so much longer, so much better. But it was Mish's request so there was no way she could refuse.

An elbow in her side drew her back to the present, and she suddenly realized Pastor Jeff had stopped talking. Her mother gave her a smile of encouragement, and Juliann stood from the second row, climbed the steps to the platform, and took her place at the podium.

"My name is Juliann," she said softly as she opened the note-book where she'd written down her speech. Suddenly Pastor Jeff was at her side. He pulled the microphone closer to her mouth. She nodded and tried again. "My name is Juliann," she repeated, and this time she heard her voice magnified through the sound system. "In just two weeks Mish Atkinson changed my life. We met each other by accident. I made a mistake when I wrote down a telephone number, and even though she had no idea who I was, she came to my rescue. I almost ran at first. I didn't think this crazy old lady in her flowered blouse would be able to help me with my teenage problems." When she heard a few chuckles in response to her words, she looked up from her notes. Mish was smiling at her, and so was everyone else. She felt her shoulders relax just a bit.

"But before I knew it, I was spilling my guts, and she was making me feel like she had known me my whole life. There is something about her that just makes you feel safe. She says it's because she is strange. An odd duck, she calls herself. She says she is glad she's odd because it makes people feel like they can be themselves with her. I don't know if it works for others, but it sure worked for me. I told her one day that she had become like a cross between a best friend and a grandma. So I call her my best-grand.

"When she was in the hospital, she asked me to read two po-ems at her service—one of hers and one of mine. I'll read hers first." She cleared her throat again before beginning to read.

> I might've been wrong. It's hard to tell.
> I don't always hear right, can't always tell
> when someone is kidding or has something to sell.

I might've been wrong. It's hard to tell.

I might've been wrong. It's hard to say
to jump right in, to go away.
I might've been wrong to simply obey
but I'd rather be wrong than walk away.

I followed the love, and I have no doubt
that following love is what life's about.
So maybe I'm crazy or on my way out,
but I followed the love, and I won't back out.

I followed the love and it leads me still
when the road is easy or all uphill,
though others may question, I never will.
I followed the love and it leads me still.

Juliann looked out at the audience to see a mix of tears and smiles. Some of them, like Mish's daughter-in-law, cried openly. Mish's son used a white handkerchief to wipe his eyes. Mish didn't even bother to wipe hers.

But Juliann was only halfway done. She still had to read her poem, and it was hard to read it in front of so many people. It had rough edges and fast rhythms and could only be spoken with fierce passion.

"This is the poem I wrote for Mish when I was afraid she was...when I didn't know if she was going to make it. Mish, I hope you like it." She took a deep breath. It was now or never. She began to read.

I am smart.
They've been telling me that my whole life
as if whole were the sum of the parts of my soul
and integers gave absolute value to my existence
and alpha particles could explain my amorphous matter.
I am smart.
They've been telling me that my whole life.

I know things.
I can explain capacitive reactance and anti-matter
and discuss the anti-climax of *The Grapes of Wrath*
and what it means to breastfeed a starving stranger.
I know things.

But I don't know how to give without fear.
I don't know how to welcome without motive.
I don't know how to love without reason or rhyme.
I've had little time for freedom
and little room for faith
and little cause for hope
and I have little hands for holding on.
You taught me how.

I am smart,
but you are wise
and in your eyes I saw the reflection
of a me I didn't dare to believe.
I am smart enough to decide what matters,
brave enough to determine my own absolute value,
bold enough to drink the wine of vision and vice
and pay my own price for pleasure.
I will not give in to the pressure on my spine
to bend
to another's will,
to bow
to another's wish,
to hang my head
for someone else's shame.
I am not to blame.
I will not lower
my gaze,
my expectations,
my flag to half of what I can be.
I can be

smart and silly,
scared and still brave,
the second-oddest duck on my lake of dreams.
You taught me how.

So I will not let death take you,
remake you,
or erase you from my heart.
You were my greatest teacher,
my best-grand,
the best hand I ever held.
It holds me
still.

The silence was so thick that Juliann thought they must have hated it. But then she realized why everyone was silent. Mish had handed her dog to her son and was slowly, painstakingly, pushing herself up out of her wheelchair. Once she got to her feet, she began to clap, and the whole audience joined in. Mish was smiling from ear to ear, even as tears poured down her face.

They were an odd pair, she and Mish. But it worked. *They* worked. And to whomever or whatever started Mish on this strange journey, Juliann was thankful.

Mish looked around the crowded room. She still couldn't believe so many people showed up for her celebration. It took forever and a day to get through the line of folks waiting to greet her, and now everybody was mingling and chatting. Except one. Ethan had been standing against the wall sipping a glass of punch, but now he was edging toward the door. She waggled her fingers at Juliann, who immediately bent down beside her wheelchair.

"Go stop that young man by the door," she whispered. "Tell him I want to speak with him." Juliann returned a minute later with Ethan in tow. "Now go find Emma," she instructed Juliann.

"The girl who texts for advice about clothes?"

"That's the one," Mish confirmed with a smile. She'd been

planning this introduction for some time. She took Ethan by the hand. "So have you found your Miss Right yet?"

He ducked his head as he blushed. "Not yet. But you told me to follow the love so I haven't given up."

"Good. Because here's your chance." She saw Juliann returning with Emma. "And compliment her clothes," she whispered before the girls arrived.

"Mish, you wanted to see me?" Emma asked, her eyes darting from Mish to Ethan and back again.

"I surely do. My friend Ethan here was about to leave our little gathering because he doesn't know anybody here, and I want him to stick around for a while. I was wondering if you'd be willing to keep him company."

"Um, yeah, I guess," she stammered. Then she looked at Ethan. "I mean, sure, I'd love to," she said with a smile.

Ethan smiled back. "That's a really nice jacket."

"Thanks! So how do you know Mish?"

"Oh, don't talk about me," Mish interrupted. "That's boring. I'm sure you two young people have more interesting things than me to talk about. Go on," she urged, waving her hands. They laughed and turned away, still talking.

Mish motioned to Juliann again. "I'm getting tired but—"

"Are you okay?" Juliann interrupted. "Do you need anything? Should we take you back to the nursing home?"

"It's a rehab center," Mish corrected her kindly, "and I'm all right for now. But I am running out of gas and need to talk to Pastor Jeff before I leave. Can you take me to him?"

"Of course! Let's go find him." Juliann pushed the chair through the crowd, which parted easily for them, everyone smiling at Mish as she passed.

"On second thought, just take me back to the sanctuary. Then bring Pastor Jeff to me there."

When Juliann left her, Mish took the opportunity to enjoy the calm away from the bustle of the reception. She wasn't sure why she was so tired after just sitting in a chair for a few hours. She'd had similar conversations with Sheila, the nurse back at the rehab center. Every time she complained about being tired, Sheila reminded her that she'd just had brain surgery, for crying out loud. To which Mish always replied, "Sure, but I slept through the whole thing!"

She reached up to scratch behind her ear, then pulled off the purple hat and rubbed her hand across her head. Her hair was starting to grow back. She wouldn't have worn the hat at all except for the scar. It still looked kind of Frankensteiny and she didn't want to make people uncomfortable. She was putting the hat back on when Pastor Jeff came in and sat down on the front pew, facing her. "Thank you for the beautiful service."

His smile was warm and full of love. "I'm just so glad you were here to enjoy it."

"So how are you?" Mish asked.

He brushed away her question. "Oh, I'm fine. The real question is how are you?"

"No, the real question," Mish corrected, "is the one I just asked. And, Jeff?" He didn't meet her eyes. "I want the truth this time. You've visited several times since my surgery, but we've never named the bull in the room."

Jeff chuckled. "I think the expression you're looking for is the elephant in the room."

"I've lived on a farm all my life," Mish replied. "There's a much bigger chance of a bull being in my living room than an elephant. Plus, I'm pretty good at recognizing bullshit when I see it. So don't tell me you're fine. You've been in a spiritual crisis for months now."

Jeff let out a heavy sigh. "You heard me in the hospital, didn't you?"

"When you said I could die as a result of having faith? Or when you professed your love for me and said the age difference didn't matter?"

His hand flew to his mouth. "No, Mish, I didn't—" His hand dropped to his heart and he leaned toward her. "I mean, I don't know what you heard…and I love you but not in *that* way and… and Stephen—"

Mish burst out laughing. "Take a breath, Jeff! I know you never said that!" He flopped back against the pew, his hand still at his heart and his head thrown back. "But notice which one of those statements you argued with."

Jeff was silent for a long time, eyes closed. If he was her age, she would think he'd fallen asleep. But he finally whispered, "I'm so ashamed."

"Whatever for?"

He opened his eyes and stared at the ceiling. "I'm supposed to be your pastor. I'm supposed to be the one with all the faith, and with at least some of the answers. Instead you have seen me at my worst. You'd already heard me say I wasn't sure I believed in God, and then when I said that in the hospital—well, I don't know if I'll ever be able to become your pastor again."

"When you said that, in the hospital, did you hear my response?"

"You said it didn't matter," he replied, still not meeting her eyes.

"Good. I wasn't sure if I had said that out loud." She paused, trying to find the right words. It was important that Jeff understand this. "It's like with that Jesus woman. The woman I met in the diner?"

He finally looked her in the eyes. "Yes?"

"I have a confession to make." Mish took a deep breath. "I don't know if she's real."

Jeff's brow furrowed. "Of course she's real. She's—"

"I know she's a real person," Mish corrected, "but I don't know for sure that she is Jesus. That's what I meant in my poem. Don't you see? It doesn't matter."

"How can you say that? Of course it matters. Why else would you have risked everything—"

"Because she was real *to me*. She told me to follow the love. How can that be bad? I got to go on a grand adventure. I got to meet interesting people. I got to help some of them. I even got me a dog. Why does it matter whether she was Jesus or not?"

"Because you almost died!" Jeff argued.

"Oh, so you want someone to blame? If the woman was Jesus, then you get to blame God? And if she wasn't, then you get to blame me, for believing? Or you get to blame fate or Juliann or some guy in a park who—"

"Yes! I blame him! You never would have met him if you hadn't—"

"No!" Mish said with all the strength she possessed. "I will forgive you for just about anything, Jeff. I will forgive you for doubting me. I will forgive you for doubting God. I will forgive you for far more than you'll ever forgive yourself. But I will not forgive you if you steal my miracle. It's mine, and I will not let you make it small and grubby. It saved me. It saved Juliann. Hell, it saved Honeybear. It doesn't matter if you believe. It doesn't matter if she was Jesus. You judge a tree by its fruit. And it's damn good fruit."

When she finished her speech, she felt all the energy leave her. She hardly noticed the tears as they fell. Then she felt the hands around hers.

"You're right," he whispered. "It is damn good fruit."

She looked up at him, the tears in his eyes matching her own. "I just wanted to follow the love," she whispered.

"I know, and you did."

"And I ain't done yet so don't be thinking we're through," she said, regaining her fire. "I still got me some living to do, and I'm gonna keep following the love until the day I die," she promised. "And maybe a few days more."

"I'm counting on it," he assured her.

"Thank you, Pastor Jeff," she said, squeezing his hand. "But you better hold on tight." She grinned. "It's gonna be a helluva ride."

ACKNOWLEDGMENTS

I would like to thank Jackie for forcing me to go to a writers' meetup, which prompted me to get off my butt and finally start writing beyond the third chapter of this book. The meetup dissolved but a small writing group formed, adding Joan and Alice to my team of supporters and cheerleaders. Their kind critiques were invaluable in my writing and editing process. Thanks also to Salt and Sage Books for the excellent developmental edit, and to Nancy for the title idea.

I also want to thank all the wonderful "church ladies" I have been privileged to know over the years. Thank you for inviting me into your lives.

Big thanks to everyone at Regal Publishing, especially Jaynie Royal, who shared my vision for the work, and Pam Van Dyk for helping my writing to shine.

And finally, I thank my family. Jackie, you may call me your angel, but you keep me from flying in circles. And to my darling children, Amelia and Joshua: although your demands on my time may have slowed the writing, you have always been my greatest teachers. I am a better person for your presence in my life.